WHEN DARKNESS MEETS DAWN

Cover Illustration: Ryn Katryn Book Cover Designs

Profession Editing: Jenny Sliger, Owl Eyes Proofs and Edits

The editing and beta reading team: Martha Collins and Lauren Meghoo

Feel free to contact me with questions, requests, or comments: Author@RK-Munin.com

And, as with many writers, your reviews on Amazon, Goodreads, and/or Kindle help immeasurably, even if it's just clicking on the stars.

Thank you to all my readers!

-There are several scenes of fighting and violence

-Talk of previous sexual assaults, nothing on page.

-Several characters speak about previous torture and threaten torture in the future, nothing on page.

-This book contains graphic sex scenes between two men and a woman. This book is **MMF** which means there will be crossed swords (in other words the two male main characters will enjoy each other as much as they enjoy the female partner).

Thank you to Dori, my sensitivity reader. You can't know how much appreciate your help!

Imani

Laying on a filthy floor, Imani worked on keeping her breathing even and remaining as still as possible. Her long braids were trapped under her back, but she was too scared to pull them free and potentially make a sound.

In the alley below, she could hear two sets of footsteps moving loudly as they searched. If they found her, she was probably dead. Everyone liked killing vampires, and she wasn't powerful enough to defend herself yet.

Her mother had taught her how to be a strong, independent Black woman, but never gave her any lessons on being a vampire. Not that either of them knew vampires existed, so her mother could be forgiven for not preparing her to deal with her current intersectionality.

"Where did she go?" one of them asked, clearly upset. She could hear him pacing the alley like a dog along a fence line.

"Vanished," the other one answered, his tone frustrated. His low voice would've been hard for a human to hear at this distance. Her vampire enhanced hearing made the words quiet but still audible.

"But why did she run from us?" He sounded hurt, making her want to snort.

Was the guy kidding? Might as well ask why the rabbit ran from the wolf. No one wants to get eaten!

As a young vampire turned less than two years ago, Imani was easy prey for many preternatural predators. First and most dangerous were the tooth-pullers who'd love nothing more than to sell her body parts off—probably harvested while she was still alive—to be used in spells. Tooth-pullers were followed closely by the majority of non-humans who wouldn't think twice about killing a vampire given the chance! Her kind had a reputation for brutality and mercilessness that led many to revel in destroying weak, recently turned vampires.

In another five decades, she would be strong enough to be the apex predator all others feared, but that would only happen if she survived.

"We scared her," the guy with the deeper voice answered.

No, duh, these two large shifters had scared her.

She'd come back in from a break to find two large, muscular men horsing around and embracing inside Pounders, the dive bar where she worked. When the owner, Phill, yelled at them for being gay, she'd come to their defense.

What she hadn't expected was for the guys to turn their attention to her. They'd rushed to where she was standing behind the bar, then started aggressively flirting with her. She'd been amused until the moment each of them was holding one of her hands. A shock of power had hit all three of them, making her gasp.

Her fangs had descended, and an intense, almost mindless bloodlust had taken hold. If the men's auras hadn't screamed powerful shifters, she might have jumped on one of them and tried to sink her fangs into his neck, or maybe do something else. Something she didn't want to examine too closely—like lick him all over.

What was wrong with her? Her instincts were all jumbled, like a scene in a movie shot shaky-cam style where you couldn't focus on any one thing to figure out what was going on. She was a chaos of impulses and desires.

It was all she could do to remain still and not act on any of her inappropriate and confusing urges.

"Mine," the smaller of the two large men had said. He gripped her hand tightly and his unnaturally bright gold eyes were intensely focused on her. Then his gaze bounced between her and the other man. "You're both meant to be mine."

Mine.

That word echoed around in her head. It implied ownership—control and possession.

Self-preservation had her ripping herself free from them and moving away.

"Stay the fuck back," she'd hissed and fled. Using all the preternatural speed she possessed, she'd vaulted over the pass-through and sprinted across the sparsely crowded bar. As she ran, one of the guys yelled to the other.

"I'll follow her. You go out the front and circle the building. Meet me in the alley so we can box her in."

She didn't have time to grab her things as she barreled out the back door. The building housing Pounders and the building across the side-by-side alleys formed a kind of U at one end and led to a wide-open street at the other end. If one of the guys was following her out the back door and the other was circling the building, that left only one direction to go—up.

Without breaking stride, she flung herself across the wide, trash strewn alley, and over the short wall that separated the bar's back alley from the next alley over. A hard launch allowed her to grab the second-floor window of the building across the two alleys from the Pounders.

The small back window she aimed for had been broken for as long as she'd worked at Pounders. She discovered why they'd never bothered fixing it when she heaved herself over the sill and into the room. When the old brick building had been renovated, they'd left a lopsided and tiny triangular room in the spot where she'd landed. There weren't any regular doors leading out of the room, only a small, locked access door that she'd have to crawl through to get out.

Now she lay perfectly still, hoping like hell they'd give up and she'd be able to leave before the night was over. The though of being trapped in this room for the day was terrifying. She didn't know if this place was sheltered enough from the sun and being burned to a crisp while she succumbed to her daylight sleep wasn't how she wanted to die.

She listened to the sounds of the men walking the alley and even pushing the dumpster aside while they searched. There wasn't much real estate to the alley. Soon they'd either find her hiding spot or leave. The window was partially hidden by the angle of the roofline. The only reason she knew it was there was because she'd spent many of her breaks in the alley, staring up at the building as she contemplated her life.

From her brief interaction with them, she knew both men were shifters. One was a chimera; she'd seen that type of aura before on her friend's mate. Chimera shifters were even more rare than vampires. Out of all the dive bars in San Diego, how was she unlucky enough to have one stop by Pounders while she was on shift?

This was not turning out to be her decade.

"She didn't smell like a shifter, but no human is that fast," the one who'd declared *mine* said, his voice puzzled and upset. "And I could only smell her when we were touching. Then it was like I couldn't pick out what she was, only that she was mine."

Feeling a little hysterical, she decided to name them Big and Bigger. The chimera shifter's human form had been above six feet and the other one was probably around seven feet tall. Damn shifters were almost always large in human form. To add to the inequity, they were also far stronger than she was, even when wearing their skin instead of fur. The only reason she was still alive was her speed.

"It was the same for me," Big agreed. "Once I was holding her hand, I could smell her and feel this strong connection. How is that possible?"

Imani fingered the wooden disk hanging from a cord around her neck. Her new friend Briar had given her several of the expensive charms and up until now, they'd done a great job of keeping her hidden. Even when preternatural beings had happened into the bar, none had thought she was anything but human. It was only luck that she'd never made skin to skin contact with any of them until now.

Now that she knew these charms didn't work if someone touched her, she'd make damn sure everyone kept their distance.

"It has to be a charm," Big guessed accurately. "Whatever she is, she's probably using it to hide from powerful predators."

Safe in her hiding spot, Imani rolled her eyes at his words. Way to work out the obvious. At least they didn't know she was a vampire yet. They were only looking for her themselves, not calling in a tooth-puller for some quick cash. Everyone knew tooth-pullers paid good money for information on young, vulnerable vampires.

"We'll find her," Bigger declared. He sounded confident, almost making her scoff out loud at his arrogance. She was superb at hiding. Even Briar had commented on how well she'd stayed off the grid, and that woman would know. She was a notorious hacker who liked to work her way into government computer systems for fun.

If she was careful, it was unlikely they'd ever find her. That thought should have made her feel relieved, but sadness welled up instead.

Damn it, what was going on with her? She hadn't been this emotional since she was sixteen.

The two started talking too quietly for her to hear as their footsteps moved away. She didn't trust that they'd left, so she fished her cheap disposable phone out of her back pocket. Setting the timer for twenty minutes, she let the counter run down before she called the bar phone.

"Pounders," Phill answered, sounding pissed as hell.

"Hey Phill, are those two guys still there?" she asked.

"Who the fuck were they?" Phill barked. "They came in here and demanded I tell them where you live and your phone number and all that shit."

Imani wasn't concerned. Even when Phill had inevitably folded and gave them access to her employee paperwork, it wouldn't do them any good. It was all fake. The only thing Phill had that was real was the number to this burner phone. Good luck tracing that without the help of the FBI. She was sure not even Briar could do it.

"Are they gone?" she asked again, ignoring Phill's blustering.

"Yeah, they left ten minutes ago. You comin' back to work or what?"

She hung up on him without responding and stood up. Tucking her phone into her back pocket, she poked her head out the window to survey the alley. No one was in sight so she dropped to the ground from the high spot.

Entering through the back door she grabbed her backpack, helmet, and jacket from Phill's miserable excuse for an employee breakroom. Gear in hand she strode to the cash register. Phill started complaining the moment he saw her.

"I don't know what kind of drugs you're dealing, but I don't want that shit around here," Phill said, following her to the cash register. "I'm not going to let you get away with anything, you hear me? The cops are only one phone call away. I got a friend working there, that means I can get them here in minutes."

He kept up this threatening monologue even as she opened the register and started emptying it into her backpack. She was almost done when he finally realized what she was doing.

"That's my money!" he cried out and tried to take the backpack from her. She put a hand on his chest and pushed. It wasn't even a hard push, but he went flying back. Falling to the floor with a cry of surprise, he stared up at her with equal parts anger and fear.

"Hey! What the hell do you think you're doing?" one of the customers yelled. She looked over to see Jeff striding across the bar. Jeff was a regular who enjoyed walking the fine line of being insulting without being too overt about it. Of course it would be him trying to play the hero.

Casually, she waited until he was leaning over the bar to grab her before she took a handful of his shirt, pulled him all the way over the bar top, and tossed him on top of Phill.

"Today is not the day to test me," she warned him. "Phill ain't worth your concern. He waters down the piss beer he buys and double charges you when you're too drunk to notice. He's not your friend."

Holding up the backpack, she met the eyes of the half dozen other men in the bar. "I've turned in my notice and this is my back pay. Anyone want to object?"

Not a single one of them stepped forward. Satisfied with their response, she looked down at Phill. Jeff had rolled off him and crawled as far away from her as he could. Phill was looking up at her with pure loathing.

"I'll send the cops after your Black ass, you goddamn bitch," he threatened. "You'll never get out of prison after assaulting an innocent business owner."

"And I'll send them all the pictures I've got," she countered. "And I'll give them names, times, and dates. Want to be prison pen pals?"

It was a bluff. She didn't have any pictures, but it was enough to make Phill pale. The Phills of this world were always doing shady deals, and this one was no different.

"You're lying," Phill blustered.

"Do you really want to risk it?" she taunted. "I'm leaving now and never coming back. If anyone comes looking for me, you've never even heard my name. Yeah?"

Mulishly, he didn't answer right away, so she took a threatening step forward. "Do I need to repeat myself?"

He flinched and held his arms over his head. "I don't know you. Never did."

"That's right," she agreed and left. This time, no one tried to stop her.

Lex

Lex stared at his phone as Mac drove, debating about calling the number Phill had given them. When Mac had demanded the keys to his truck, Lex hadn't hesitated. He was agitated and ready to rage against anyone so it was probably best he didn't dive. Thankfully, Mac had originally gotten a ride share to the bar, always planning to grab a ride with Lex after drinks.

Now they had a number and nothing else for a mate who was so scared she'd run from them. This was one of his worst nightmares. The urge to call her and demand, plead, promise, or beg was strong. To make any connection to her.

"Don't," Mac said.

He looked over to see Mac staring intently at the road ahead. "Don't?"

"Don't call."

"What, you reading minds now?" Lex tried to joke, but it felt flat.

"I know you, Lexington," Mac rumbled. "We need to have a plan before we call because if she ditches that phone, we're out of leads."

"Don't call me Lexington. Only Mama calls me that," Lex muttered, going back to staring at his phone.

When Phill had turned over Imani's paperwork, both he and Mac had realized right away it was all fake. This number was the only thing they had on Imani because Phill had admitted it was how he told her when to come in for extra shifts.

Imani. He hoped that was her real name because it was beautiful. The sound of it slid around in his head like a soft touch.

Sighing, he dropped the phone in his lap and looked at Mac. He never expected to have two mates. Hell, he'd thought he was destined to die alone, sure that he was one of the rare chimeras that didn't have a mate. Even though his brother Memphis had ended up with two mates, Lex assumed Memphis's situation was an absolute anomaly. And yet here he was, another chimera who had two mates.

Dejection hit him. No sooner did he find them both than he lost one.

Suddenly being in the same car as Mac wasn't enough. He needed to touch him too. Hoping the shifter wouldn't get upset, Lex eased his hand onto the other man's thick thigh, ready to pull back at any hint Mac didn't want to be touched. The moment his hand was resting on Mac's jean-covered leg, he felt better.

"You can touch me as much as you need to," Mac assured him, his deep voice a gentle rumble. Without taking his eyes off the road, Mac wrapped a broad hand around the back of Lex's neck and drew his upper body close. With a sigh of happiness, Lex let Mac guide him. Soon he was snuggling his face against Mac's massive pec.

It was almost perfect.

"I lost her," he whispered.

"*We* lost her," Mac answered. "It wasn't your fault."

"I think I'm the one that spooked her," Lex confessed.

"We don't know that. Let it go for now," Mac ordered. "We're going to find her. Between the two of us and all the resources we have, she won't disappear again."

"Anything it takes," Lex whispered.

"I'll call in all my favors," Mac promised, but that wasn't exactly what Lex meant.

Lex agreed with Mac; there was no question they'd find Imani. The hard part would be convincing her to give them a chance. Why she ran from them after feeling the same magic they did was a mystery, but something about the situation had spooked her. Most preternaturals were overjoyed to find their mate, but Imani might be from a group where being mated was scary or even dangerous. He didn't agree with them, but there were some preternatural societies that didn't treat their mates well.

That wasn't him or Mac. Chimera shifters were well known for the way they adored their mates. Mac was a sloth bear shifter and while his kind had a reputation for quick tempers and ferocious fighting, it didn't extend to their friends and family. Lex had never felt anything but safe and happy while hanging out with Mac over the years. Once Imani got to know them, she'd realize they'd never do anything to hurt her.

The flip side of the situation was his absolute need to be with her. His chimera would never let him simply walk away if she asked them to leave her alone. If he had to, he would resort to kidnapping. It was morally questionable but potentially necessary. His mate wouldn't be happy, but she'd be safe and that was more important.

As a professional mercenary, he'd developed a malleable sense of morality. His moral compass was more of a mood ring.

Mac wouldn't agree to kidnapping, but Lex was positive his massive mate wouldn't try very hard to stop him. Standing at almost seven feet tall, covered in tattoos with thin lips and a severe, square face, Mac might look scary, but he was really a marshmallow inside.

What had that gaggle of giggling wolf shifter pre-teens in Mikey's pack called Mac? Oh, that's right. Mac was a cinnamon roll.

He'd met Mac a few years ago when they'd both been hired to work the same mission. Lex found himself drawn to the calm, easy-going shifter. Even after their assignment was over, he'd sought Mac out and they'd developed a strong friendship. Over the years Lex ended up spending as much time down in San Diego crashing on Mac's couch as he did up in Bend, Oregon, where his house was.

He'd worked in a lot of inhospitable places on earth, spending his fair share of time dodging bullets. Sometimes he was more successful than others at the dodging part. Luckily, being a chimera shifter meant he was hard as fuck to kill. He'd never felt much about any of the men he worked with but having Mac as part of his team had spoiled him. Mac showed Lex what it meant to be with someone you could truly lean on during missions or downtime.

How could they have been friends for all these years and not realize they were mates? It boggled his mind.

"Why?" Lex whispered to himself. "Why now?"

"Maybe we needed a third to make a true connection," Mac answered. His voice rumbled through the side of Lex's head where it rested on Mac's chest. It didn't surprise Lex that Mac understood exactly what he meant. The bear shifter knew him better than his own siblings.

"I guess," Lex agreed. "They say some shifters have an affinity for triads."

"What do you mean?" Mac asked.

"I've told you about the Alpha of the Anawal pack, right?"

Mac shook his head. "Refresh my memory."

"She and her mate were together for years before they became the flock of a vampire named Soren back home in Bend," Lex explained. "And now my brother Memphis is in a flock with a vampire and a human."

"You're thinking triads run in your family," Mac murmured, moving his hand up from Lex's neck to rest on the back of his head.

Lex didn't even let his siblings touch him like this, but it was different with Mac. Instead of making him feel trapped, Mac's touch calmed something deep inside. For the first time since he was a kid and could curl up in his dad's lap, Lex felt safe.

"Something like that," Lex agreed. Mac was so tall that even while resting his head against Mac's chest, Lex could clearly see out the windshield. He watched as Mac steered the truck onto a freeway and realized that he didn't know where they were going.

"I thought I'd take you home," Mac said, as if reading his mind. "We can talk, and I can call in those favors to help us find Imani."

The thought of waiting killed him. Without them, their mate was in danger. They needed to do more than call in favors. They needed to—

A thought made him sit up. Mac's arm fell away, but Lex snatched it up and held Mac's massive hand in his. "I've got a better idea."

"Oh yeah?" Mac asked, obviously intrigued. "What is it? Just remember, this isn't some remote area out in a jungle or in the desert. We can't run around in our shifted forms."

"Briar," Lex said. "She's helped Memphis find people in the past. I bet there's a lot she can do with a simple phone number."

"Oh, that's right. Your brother's human mate is a hacker," Mac said, then made a negative sound.

"What? What's wrong?" He could clearly hear the building panic in his own voice.

"Easy," Mac said, reaching out to cup the back of Lex's head again and guide him down to rest against Mac's chest. The contact helped soothe his fears. Lex had never felt so out of control of his emotions before and was eager for the stability Mac's touch offered.

"Sorry," he mumbled.

Mac chuckled. "You're fine, love."

Lex stilled. "Love?"

"You don't like it?" Mac asked.

"No, I do," Lex rushed to assure him. He goddamn adored the way Mac had called him love. He wanted to hear it again. "I really do."

"My mom was British, and she used the term all the time. It's funny, I never felt like using it before. Not with anyone but you," Mac confessed.

"Good," Lex declared.

"But back to this hacker. I'm all for getting her help, but didn't she, your brother, and that vampire get married today? Or have their, what's the vampire term, Alighting Ceremony?"

"Oh, yeah, that." Lex made a dismissive sound. "Briar won't care. She said she went along with the ceremony so they could have the party afterwards."

Mac laughed. "She told you that?"

"No, she told her friend Maddy that. I overheard," Lex explained.

"Because they probably didn't see you standing nearby," Mac commented. "I've never known anyone who could blend into a dark corner faster than you. If I didn't know for a fact that you were a chimera shifter, I'd think you were a shadow jumper."

Now it was Lex's turn to laugh. "Shadow jumper? Hardly."

"Yeah, you don't fit the typical willowy body type for one of them," Mac agreed. "But back on topic, I'm not so sure about crashing your brother's Alighting Ceremony."

"Once we tell him we're trying to find our mate, he'll understand," Lex promised. "They're over at the Dapper Dog."

"Is that the place the wolf shifter pack Lobos Gris just opened?" Mac asked as he steered the truck off the freeway.

"Yeah, that's the one."

"Okay, we'll be there in about twenty," Mac predicted as he easily maneuvered through traffic with only one hand on the steering wheel. "Want to call and give them a heads up?"

"No," Lex said. "It's better I don't."

Mac

"What?" The roar was loud enough to shake a few windows and cause some people on the sidewalk outside the bar to startle and jump. There was no malice in the word, only utter shock.

This was only the second time Mac had met Lex's brother Memphis. While he might be taller than the bearded, tattooed chimera shifter, he was still mildly intimidated by the sheer volume of Memphis's one word question. Who knew anyone outside of a banshee could shake buildings with their voices?

Lex wasn't fazed by his brother's volume. He was perfectly composed as he repeated his words. "I have two mates like you. Mac and a woman. But we scared her, and she ran away. Briar needs to help me find her."

Mac winced. Lex's short version of their encounter with Imani made the two of them look bad.

"Did you grab her, get all intense, and say *mine* in that gravelly voice?" Briar asked with a grin. "Because it's both a turn-on and a threat, you know? Sometimes it's hard for a girl to figure out which one. Especially if she's human."

To Mac's surprise, Lex's face went bright red. "I might have said that." he mumbled.

"Oh shit, no wonder she ran off," Briar cackled. "But don't worry, my man. Give me what you got, and I'll see what kind of magic I can perform. We'll find her so you can explain you don't mean her any harm."

"Can't all of this wait?" Tobias asked, eyeing him and Lex with a scowl. He looked at Briar, his expression turning gentle. "You've been looking forward to this party all week. You even let Maddy drag you to the manicurist."

This was Mac's first time meeting the vampire of this triad and, so far, Mac wasn't a fan. The vampire's expression had turned sour the moment Lex requested to speak to Memphis and Briar alone. Now that Tobias knew they needed Briar's help, he was downright hostile.

Briar turned to look at her vampire mate. "The party has been fun, but this'll be fun too." Wrapping her arms around him, she smiled up at Tobias. "And I might get to use the new access I got to the DMV. You know I've been wanting an excuse to dive into their database!"

Tobias's expression went from disapproving to indulgent in a flash. "If this makes you happy, I'll fetch your laptop from the Land Rover."

"That would be great, thanks," Briar agreed as she let go of him.

Before he left the room, he caught Mac's gaze. "Mine," he snarled. "My human. My chimera. My flock."

Huh, okay, maybe this guy wasn't so bad. One thing Mac could understand was being protective and possessive of the people you love.

"Got it," Mac said, holding his hands up with the palms out. "I know better than to mess with a vampire's flock. They're safe."

With a nod, Tobias left the room. When Mac looked over, Lex was still red in the face and staring a hole in the floor. He hated seeing the chimera so uncomfortable. Reaching out, he pulled the chimera against him until Lex's back was flush against his front. With a soft sigh, Lex relaxed into the embrace.

"Wow, that's not something I thought I'd ever see," Memphis said. "Lex doesn't like to be touched."

Mac didn't bother commenting on that because the truth was right there. Lex loved being touched, but only by him.

"Aww, you guys are cute," Briar said. "You're both so big you make me think of bulls cuddling or something."

Mac blinked, not sure how to respond to Briar's comment. Memphis groaned and drew her into his arms, mirroring how Mac was holding Lex.

"You say the weirdest shit sometimes," he murmured, making Briar laugh.

"Ah, you love it," she retorted, then turned her attention back to the two of them. "What details can you give me about your runaway?"

"We have a phone number," Mac told her. "But the rest of the information we got from her boss was fake."

"Yeah, that's going to make it harder," Briar agreed. "But not impossible. Between me and Memphis, we can track her down. Did Lex tell you Memphis can find anyone?"

Mac met Memphis's gaze and saw the chimera blushing under his thick beard. "Not always," Memphis argued. "But mostly."

Looking back, Briar went on her toes to nuzzle her mate's neck. "Don't be so modest." Then she focused back on him and Lex. "Let's start with what we know. Give me the name of the place where she worked, her boss, and all the fake stuff she put on her employee paperwork. Sometimes people unconsciously put true stuff down they don't realize is important. Like a birthday that's only off by one year. Even something small can help."

"She worked at Pounders," Mac explained. "It's a dive bar out by—"

"Are you talking about the gorgeous Black chick with magenta hair?" Briar asked, interrupting him.

Lex jerked in his arms at the same time Mac felt a jolt of surprise go through him too. "How did you know that?"

"Shit, you're talking about Imani," Briar said easily. "Why didn't you start with that?"

Mac felt his jaw drop. "You know her?"

"Sure," Briar said with a grin. "She's a friend too, even though Tobias doesn't approve. I know vampires don't like other vampires around their flock, but she's totally in control. It's not like she's going to accidently attack me or anything."

Mac was stunned into silence by Briar's revelation. It was Lex who spoke. "She's a vampire?"

"You didn't know?" Briar asked. "Can't you guys sense that stuff?"

"She was probably wearing a charm," Memphis said. "Remember, you bought her a whole bunch of charms as a gift."

Briar nodded. "Oh, yeah, those were expensive as fuck, but I wanted her to be safe. I guess they worked if these two couldn't figure out what she was."

As Briar and Memphis talked, Mac looked down to find Lex's eyes trained on Briar with an intensity he didn't like. It was the same kind of look Lex got when honing in on a target during a mission.

"Easy, love," he whispered into Lex's ear. "Upsetting Briar won't get us closer to Imani."

Lex didn't acknowledge Mac's words. "Call her," Lex demanded. Mac could tell Lex was trying hard to keep his voice normal, but it had slipped into an animalistic tone.

"I will but—"

"Call her!" Lex growled and tried to pull out of Mac's embrace to get to Briar. Mac held on.

While they were both in their human skin, his strength could match Lex. Thankfully, he didn't have to worry about Lex shifting and mauling him. He knew deep down that Lex would never do anything to deliberately hurt him.

Recognizing his brother's instability, Memphis pushed Briar behind him and bared teeth at his sibling. "Don't threaten her. Mama doesn't need eight sons. She could be perfectly happy with only seven."

"She sure will miss you," Lex shot back, struggling against Mac's hold. "But I'll put your picture in a nice frame."

"Damn it Lex, chill!" Briar said from behind Memphis. "I'm going to call her, but we need to come up with a game plan. Do you want her to meet you or run off into the night because she thinks you might try to kill her?"

Briar's words had an immediate effect on Lex. He stilled and started taking in large lungfuls of air. Mac's hold on Lex turned into an embrace and he murmured soothing words as Lex pulled himself together.

When Lex spoke, it was a plea. "Please, Briar. She's not safe out there without us."

Mac tightened his arms into a hug. "She'll survive until we find her. She's got the charms and she's smart."

"But right now, we're stronger," Lex argued. "She needs her *Somnum Custos*."

"What's a *Somnum Custos*?" Briar asked, stepping around Memphis despite his growl of disapproval.

"It's Latin for Sleep Guard," Tobias said as he stepped into the room with Briar's laptop tucked under his arm and a battered backpack slung over one shoulder. Mac had never seen a laptop so big.

"I wasn't sure if you wanted the small laptop, the big one, or the tablet," Tobias explained as he set his burdens down on a small table in the employee's break room. "So I brought all of them."

Once everything was on the table, he moved to Briar's other side. Now she was bracketed by a vampire and a chimera. Mac knew that wasn't by accident. These two men made a conscious effort to protect the most vulnerable of them, and Briar probably didn't even realize it.

"Thanks," Briar said and went up on her toes to kiss him. "You're the best. But what's a Sleep Guard?"

"We are," Memphis murmured. "You and I guard our home while Tobias is vulnerable during the day. Now that he's fully recovered, Tobias is old enough to be able to move around even if the sun is up. If attacked, he could defend himself unless exposed to direct sunlight. When vamps are young, they actually sleep when the sun is up, they can't fight it. They're totally defenseless."

"*Somnum Custos* sounds so cool. I want patches made to go on our leather jackets," Briar enthused.

Mac could feel Lex getting tense as this conversation moved away from Imani. Before he could say anything soothing, Lex growled loud enough to turn everyone's attention to him.

"Words buddy, we've got to use our words. 'Kay?" Mac teased, despite feeling tense and on edge himself.

Predictably, Tobias scowled at him and Lex. "Why are we talking about *Somnum Custos*?"

"The woman Lex and Mac met tonight is Imani," Memphis explained.

To Mac's surprise, the vampire's expression turned sympathetic. "Oh, I understand now. You're her flock."

"If we're her flock, why did she run?" Mac muttered. "Shouldn't she want to be with us, even if we're big, scary shifters?"

"She's young," Tobias reminded them. "Within six months of being turned, she was successfully living on her own without giving into her blood lust, that's unheard of. Every waking moment must be a challenge for her. She's been fighting her hunger for so long that she probably doesn't trust her instincts."

"On top of that, she doesn't know you guys wouldn't sell her to a tooth-puller," Memphis commented.

"The bottom line here is that you guys are going to need to approach her carefully, right?" Briar stated.

"Do you have a suggestion?" Mac asked. He had far more confidence now that they had a direct line to Imani, but he also understood that they'd need to tread carefully. That last thing he wanted was to make Imani feel hunted or trapped.

Briar pulled out her phone with a pensive expression. "I've got an idea. It's not totally kosher, but I think the situation calls for it."

Imani

Imani stared down at the bag of blood she was holding. Her hand shook as she fought the impulse to sink her aching fangs through the plastic and drain the bag. Vicious hunger cramped her belly, making her hiss with pain and hunch over slightly. It took all her willpower, but she stayed strong and didn't drink.

She'd gotten home a few minutes ago, starving for blood after expending so much energy running from the two shifters. Still, it was important to wait. She couldn't consume the precious and expensive liquid until she was fully in control of her impulses. Drinking the entire bag would be a risk she might not survive. This scant pint of blood was all she could get for the next forty-eight hours. She needed to drink half now and save the other half for tomorrow, or she might be tempted to attack a human.

If she was a wealthier vampire, she could buy a dozen units of blood any time she wanted. With her current lack of resources, she couldn't afford more than a unit or two at a time, and the couriers knew that. They weren't willing to make a delivery more than a few times a week to her area. When she'd offered to go to them, she'd gotten the brush off. Young vampires didn't get to know where the blood was stored. Whether the delivery was three blocks or fifty miles, the price was the same.

It left her with the problem of getting deliveries even when she had the money to buy more frequently, not that buying extra was a luxury she could afford often.

Sweat broke out on her skin as she waited for the cramping in her stomach to diminish. Even if she gave into the impulse to consume the entire unit, it wouldn't satiate her bloodlust. Nothing did. That was the single worst aspect of her life as a vampire, the constant gnawing hunger.

"Deep breaths," she reminded herself. "I finished that crazy hike my college roommate talked me into. If I could survive on nothing but a single nutrition bar for ten hours, I can handle this now."

It was a poor analogy to compare her human self to this vampire body and the instincts she now possessed. It could take decades before newly turned vampires no longer suffered from a constant, driving need to feed. The vampires of legend who wiped out entire villages weren't ancient creatures of myth. They were inevitably the young ones who managed to slip out of their maker's control and feast on any nearby humans.

"As much as some humans deserve it, I can't go around eating them," she muttered, her voice rough, a reflection of her inner battle.

To the vampire part of her, all the humans she interacted with were nothing but walking, talking feasts. Every time one of them got too close, she pictured grabbing them by the hair, forcing their heads back, and sinking her fangs into their vulnerable throats. She pictured drinking her fill, then leaping to the next helpless human.

She could drink a dozen people dry within minutes, despite the size and strength of some. She might be young and weak for a vampire, but she was far stronger than the average human. There'd been a few times she imagined slaughtering a bar full of patrons and making herself drunk on their blood. She probably wouldn't even get a bruise.

"It'd be fun but not worth it," she reminded herself, and she thought about how much most of the people at Pounders had reeked. "My next job needs to be something where I don't have to deal with people."

Maybe the two shifters chasing her away from Pounders was a blessing in disguise. At least she wouldn't have to deal with Phill ever again. If there was anyone she was tempted to make a meal of, it was that man. And all his regulars. Honestly, there wasn't a single man there worth saving.

She'd kill them all and revel in it. Justice for all the people those degenerates probably abused. It would be amazing until she was inevitably tracked down and slaughtered herself.

Vampires didn't have an organizing body like wolf shifters, witches, druids, or pixies, but they all agreed that humans finding out about their existence would be bad. There was only one thing that made all vampires work together; hunting down a rogue vampire who no longer kept their secret. If she went around biting people in public or killing indiscriminately, she'd end up being hunted down by her own kind.

Hundreds of years ago, humans decided vampires weren't real, and the vampires would like to keep it that way.

She was a perfect example. Two years ago, she had no idea any of these creatures existed. Now she was a vampire herself and exposed to the hidden world of magic that lived side by side with the mundane human world. With all this newfound knowledge, she felt confident to call bullshit on the whole thing.

All those romantic movies about vampires being seductive and protective were shit. They were abusive, sadistic assholes! Except to their flock of course. For those few individuals they shared pieces of their souls with, vampires were gentle and loving. Both vampire and flock would die to protect each other.

Everyone else was fair game. When a vampire met you for the first time most were only interested in knowing one thing: what would you taste like?

Even the people they hired to organize their finances, clean their homes, and cook for their flock could end up on the menu if the vamp was feeling particularly snacky. With the ability to put humans and most non-humans into thrall, no one would even remember being bit. Thrall was one of a vampire's strongest weapons and something she couldn't truly use yet.

"I did get that guy to tip me a twenty yesterday," she consoled herself. Urging customers to tip better was a far cry from having them completely under her control, but it was progress.

Suddenly the bag of blood disappeared from her hand. She'd been staring right at it. One moment it was there and the next it was gone. She froze as fear spiked through her body, making her heart pound. There was only one thing that could've caused the blood to disappear without her seeing it.

Damn, and here she was thinking this night couldn't get any worse.

Imani

She took a second to brace herself before speaking.

"Hello, Vincent," she said, letting her empty hand drop to her side but not turning to face the vampire who'd created her.

"Is this all you have to eat?" he asked with exaggerated concern. She heard him rubbing a thumb over the plastic blood bag. "It's a rather paltry amount."

Taking a deep breath before turning, Imani reminded herself that Vincent let her leave a year and a half ago. It was unlikely he was here to hurt her after that much time. All she needed was to stay calm and find out what he wanted.

Did vampires do welfare checks? No, it was more likely there was a nefarious reason for his visit.

Vincent was standing in the middle of her dingy, rundown, converted garage apartment with a familiar disdainful expression on his face. As usual, he was dressed in understated elegance. Everything on him, from his perfectly styled hair to his Italian shoes, looked deceptively simple but screamed of wealth. Simon and Opal, the two humans who made up his flock, both dressed and acted as if they'd been born into wealth. The three of them together never failed to turn heads when they went out in public, but very few would witness the truly vile monsters they were.

Every person the trio ignored had narrowly escaped torture and possible death. Imani was one of the unlucky few who had caught their attention.

"This place is…" Vincent's voice trailed off as he focused his eyes back on her, the bag of blood still held in the palm of his hand. Her instinct was to snatch it away from him, but she knew from experience that wouldn't work. The moment she moved, he'd simply do the same thing he'd done to take the bag in the first place, put her in thrall.

He was so powerful he'd put her in a state of total submission before she even knew he was in the room. She'd heard a rumor he was the oldest vampire on the West Coast and nothing she'd experienced so far pushed her to believe anything else.

"This place is a hovel," he finished. "It stinks of the nagas who own it. It's hard to imagine putting up with the smell saturating everything. The accommodations certainly don't make up for the stench. You have nothing but a bed, a table, and a chair. Even for a lowly human, these would be deplorable conditions."

She knew better than to clap back. "I don't notice the smell. Besides, I don't need much."

"I remember that about you," he replied. "You never demanded things, unlike my sweet Opal who is always fawning over something new." He spoke as if they were good friends. As if they shared delightful memories of the blue-eyed brunette that had taken pleasure in making Imani beg for the bagged blood that sustained her.

Unsure of what to say, Imani tried being direct. "Why are you here?"

Vincent didn't move, but she saw his aura flair a split second before she felt his power against her skin. It took effort, but she didn't wince at the feel of thousands of needles stabbing all over her body. The worst part was that he wasn't even putting much effort into hurting her.

"I don't believe it's your place to ask *me* questions," he answered, his tone deceptively mild. "Now, I ask again, is this all the blood you have? Is there more squirreled away in that little box?" He nodded his head at her dorm fridge.

There was no point in lying. "That's everything."

The needles of power pressing in on her vanished. A reward for her good behavior. She didn't sigh with relief or move. She knew from experience that remaining still and impassive was her best option right now.

"Only this one bag." He looked down at the unit of blood in his hand. "How hungry you must be. This isn't much more than a light snack. When was the last time you ate?"

"This time yesterday," she responded, then lied through her teeth. "I'm due at work soon, so you might want to tell me why you're here."

"Work?" he repeated, tilting his head slightly as if the word was in another language. "You labor for others?"

"I'm a bartender," she answered. *Or was,* she added silently.

"Is that how you're paying for this?" he asked, holding the bag of blood up a little higher.

Her mouth watered as she focused on the red in his hand. She was forced to swallow a few times before she could speak.

"Yes, that's how I pay for my meals. My work also pays for this apartment and gas for my motorcycle. You know, all the stuff the average person needs," she responded then winced when she heard the sarcasm in her tone. She braced for reprisal, but none came.

"How very demeaning," he responded, pity clear in his voice. "An apex predator reduced to being a barmaid. That's a far worse punishment than anything I could do to you short of execution."

She couldn't let that one go. "How can you think working a regular job is worse than what Opal and Simon did to me?"

He looked genuinely confused. "Why would you say that? I fed you well and protected you. My flock and I lavished you with all the latest clothing and accessories specifically selected to complement your dark skin. You spent your days sleeping on a luxurious bed in an opulent room. You had a life most couldn't even dream of and yet you walked away from all of it when given the opportunity. It's puzzling, no?"

Biting her lip until she tasted blood, Imani barely managed to keep from screaming at him that none of that made up for the way they'd abused and tortured her for six months. Thankfully, Vincent was accustomed to conversations with a slow cadence, so he didn't become impatient when it took her a few minutes to respond with something that wasn't going to get her punished.

"Freedom is important to me."

"Ah, yes," he responded with a nod. "The ephemeral American freedom. That statement shows your youth. I was born hundreds of years before Europeans stumbled upon this landmass. Simon and Opal became my flock before then as well. Perhaps that's one of the things they found so amusing about you, the importance you placed on freedom over safety and comfort."

She didn't bother pointing out that his "safety and comfort" included lots of pain and humiliation at the hands of his flock. In Vincent's eyes, his flock could do no wrong, and she should be grateful they paid any attention to her at all.

Vincent gestured around the room using the hand holding the blood. "If this is what freedom is, perhaps you're ready to rejoin my household. Your room is as you left it, and Opal saved all your clothes in hopes you'd come back."

"Y-you want me to come back?" she stuttered. This wasn't what she was expecting at all. When he'd let her leave, she'd assumed she'd never see any of them again.

"*I* don't want you to return," Vincent said with a slight frown. "But Opal and Simon miss you terribly. They began pressing me to bring you back after the fourth attempt to make another vampire failed."

"Fourth?" Imani croaked out. Successfully turning a human into a vampire was rare. The process required the vampire to drain the human. When they were on the verge of death, the vampire fed the human his own blood. This was repeated for days until the human either died or turned.

Imani had vivid memories of being turned. Vincent kept her under thrall so she couldn't move but allowed her to be fully aware of her body and surroundings. Her body grew cold as he drank from her the first time. When her vision dimmed, she'd assumed that was it; she was going to die. Then he'd forced open her mouth and poured his blood in, setting her body on fire from the inside out. It was as if lava flowed through her veins and as much as she'd wanted to scream, she couldn't even whimper.

When the pain started to dissipate, he'd done it again. And again. She'd lost count after the third time. Eventually it worked. The pain stopped and was replaced with extreme hunger and blood lust. Weak and under Vincent's supervision, she'd been forced to beg Simon and Opal for every drop of blood she received.

When they got tired of the begging, they moved on to humiliation. Then inflicting physical pain. Injuries still hurt, even if her body was capable of healing quickly.

The thought of Vincent murdering four other humans while trying to turn them into vampires made her stomach churn. Those poor people.

"Before you, I'd never attempted to create a vampire," Vincent mused, as if they were colleagues talking about a pernicious math problem. "The ease with which you transitioned from cattle to vampire made me think others had exaggerated how difficult it was. Now I see that I'd accidentally picked an excellent candidate. Well, not me. My flock chose you. Perhaps they could sense something I couldn't."

Imani shook her head, sending her long magenta braids flying over one shoulder. "I'm not going back."

Vincent focused on her hair with a frown. "What is this style? We had your hair tamed so nicely. Why would you artificially lengthen it with this gaudy color?"

She knew he'd heard her but was ignoring what he didn't like. She tried something else. "Do you really want another vampire living in your home? Sharing space with your flock?"

Vincent's shoulders stiffened. It was subtle, and if she wasn't so familiar with him, she wouldn't have noticed. "Of course I don't. If you recall, I was the one who sent you away. But my sweet flock wants you back. I have no choice but to bring back their most prized toy. Hopefully they'll grow bored with you within a few decades."

Oh, sweet baby Jesus, this wasn't going in any direction she wanted.

"I don't want—" Before she could finish that sentence, Vincent had crossed the room in a blur of motion. As much as she hated showing weakness, Imani shrank back as his imposing figure loomed over her.

"You'll be coming home with me, no arguments," he intoned. He wasn't using thrall yet, probably because he was enjoying her fear. "You can leave all these things behind. None of it is appropriate to our life and perhaps the next denizens of this place will require rags."

Imani quickly doubled down on her earlier lie. "But I have to go to work. I'm expected."

For some odd reason, Vicent felt very strongly about fulfilling obligations. He insisted all good faith contracts, promises, and commitments be fully satisfied. That is until he got hungry. Then he might drain you dry instead of listening to your investment portfolio. She'd seen it happen to a hedge fund manager.

She needed right now to be one of the times when he felt it important to act "honorably" and let her go to work. She needed him to leave without her, giving her a fighting chance at running away. Escaping from his mansion with his staff of wolf shifters and heavily barred doors and windows would be nearly impossible.

"Expected?" he repeated, his face going perfectly blank and his body still.

"Phill, the owner, doesn't have much staff so if I don't show up tonight, he'll have a lot of issues," she pushed, throwing more obligations out there. "He's how I was able to rent here, and I owe rent to the nagas who own this apartment."

The implication was that Phill was part of the naga slither that owned her apartment, making the obligation more powerful. She'd pay for it if Vincent caught her in the lie, but it was a gamble worth taking.

"This apartment belongs to the Gorman Slither," she added, naming the largest slither in San Diego.

Vincent grimaced. "Nagas can be surprisingly insidious. It might be wise to err on the side of caution. Very well, I'll extend you this courtesy. Go in and explain to the barman naga that you can no longer work there after tonight and you'll be leaving this place behind. In two nights, I expect you to rejoin my household." He dropped his eyes to take in her jeans and tank top. "This delay might work out for the better. I'll have an outfit delivered here for you to wear and send a driver for you. Make sure your appearance is appealing for my flock."

It was hard, but she continued to meet his gaze. "Yeah, I'll tell Phill I'm quitting after tonight."

"You should refuse any payment he offers," Vincent instructed. "It's the least we can do. I'm no doubt depriving him of his only competent servant."

Giving up on any semblance of being a calm, emotionless vampire, Imani nodded her head rapidly. She probably looked like a bobble doll as she worked very hard at not looking at her backpack full of cash laying on the bed where she'd flung it. "I'll even leave my tips behind."

He gave a sharp nod of approval. "Very good, *zaya*."

She tried really hard not to react to the Russian term of endearment, but he must have seen the hatred and fear on her face. During her six months in his house, he hadn't called her *zaya* very often, but when he did, it was usually followed by a punishment. Just hearing the word made her stomach knot and her body push her to run.

I'm working on it, she told the instinct driven part of her brain. *Keep it together and we'll be getting away from him soon.*

He paused, and she thought he might be about to leave when he leaned down and put his lips to her ear. "I know you're thinking of bolting. The moment I walk out that door, you plan to pack your things and run away. Working for the nagas is nothing but an excuse, isn't it?"

"No," she protested. "I woul—" She gasped as he moved faster than she could follow. Straightening, he wrapped a hand around her throat and easily lifted her off the ground. Feet kicking uselessly in the air, she grasped his wrist and tried to pull free.

"Don't lie to me, *zaya*," he said, holding her effortlessly as she struggled. "I'm your maker. Even if you manage to travel far away, I'll be able to hunt you down. There's no place you can hide from me." Was that true? Could he find her wherever she went simply by the fact that he'd turned her?

A malicious smile curved his lips. "Maybe you should run. It's been a long time since I've had a challenge and you're a clever little rabbit." He shook her as he spoke. She clawed ineffectively at his arm, her vision dimming. This wouldn't kill her, but that didn't stop her body from telling her it was dying from lack of air.

"And once I catch you, I'd get to punish you. Perhaps I'll rip your tongue out. When it grows back, I'll rip it out again.

Wouldn't that be fun? I could keep doing that until I'm bored and then I'll pour silver in your mouth so it can't grow back. Vampires don't need tongues to live. In fact, it might help you live longer if I removed yours. I'd be doing you a favor, in a manner of speaking."

When he let go, she fell into a heap on the floor. Gagging and gasping, she kept her gaze down on the floor and concentrated on not panicking. Having an attack right now wouldn't be helpful.

"You have twenty-four hours to end your employment and settle your debts with the Gorman Slither. I don't want them coming to my home and demanding recompense for you. If you need further money, call me." He pulled a phone out of his pocket and tossed it down on the floor near her leg. "I will not have my reputation tarnished by a mere pet."

She remained perfectly still and kept her eyes on the floor. It was an effort, but she didn't react to his words or the phone clattering down next to her.

When she remained silent, he crouched in front of her and waited until she lifted her eyes to meet his gaze. "You will come back. You will entertain my flock for as long as they want. Your choices are to walk into my house on your own two feet or for me to drag you home covered in silver chains and missing a tongue."

He licked his lips as his eyes lazily trailed down her body. "Actually, your dark skin would look beautiful in silver. The constant burning and healing would be a bonus, wouldn't it? Now I'm even more eager for you to run."

Smirking, he tossed the undamaged bag of blood down next to the phone. This entire time, he'd held it carefully enough to not accidentally crush or puncture it. Even when he had her by the throat.

"Enjoy your paltry meal," he taunted. "Don't consume anything more than this. Opal will enjoy it if you arrive hungry."

With that, he turned and left, not bothering to close the door behind him.

Imani

Even after Vincent was gone, Imani stayed on the floor until she felt steady enough to get to her feet. Once she could stand, she started packing. There was no question about her next move—*run!* Run fast, run far, and don't look back.

If Imani was being honest, she didn't know why she'd stayed in the first place. Sunny San Diego seemed like a poor choice for vampires to call home, and yet Vincent had mentioned that there was an inordinately high number of them living in the large, dense Southern California county.

She should head north, maybe to Washington, or even all the way up to Alaska. They had winters that were dark all day and during the constant sun of summer, she could hibernate like a bear. She'd feed until she was ready to burst like a tick, then find a nice cave to barricade herself in and sleep the summer away.

It was a testament to how horrible the last two years had been that the idea of being trapped in a cave for several months at a time sounded like heaven to her.

"At least there isn't much to leave behind," she muttered, looking around the studio. She'd be able to carry everything important in a backpack and duffle bag.

It was short work packing her two bags, and she was zipping the overfull duffle closed when her phone rang. Seeing

Briar's name flash on the screen made some of her tension slip away. Tapping the phone, she started talking right away.

"Hey, girlfriend," Imani said, trying to keep her voice light. "I'm a little busy right now, but I'm glad you called. I'm leaving town, and I'm not sure when I'm going to be back so don't bother coming by Pounders anymore. I'll tell you when I'm in town again."

Assuming she survived that is, but there was no point in burdening Briar with that thought.

"Leaving?" Briar asked with worry in her voice. "You told me just a few days ago you were struggling to buy enough blood. We had that whole fight about me buying blood for you. How are you getting the money to leave?"

Imani blatantly ignored the money question. "You know how it is. I just need to get out of town for a few days. Maybe I'll ride up the coast."

She wasn't surprised when Briar didn't buy it. "No way you're taking a vacation. Tell Auntie Briar what's going on. I can help."

Imani fought with herself. She'd been raised by a strong woman who refused to lean on anyone, even her devoted husband who'd died far too young. The need to be that strong warred with the knowledge that she was dealing with things her mother could never have dreamed of.

Hadn't her mom always said a woman's friends were invaluable? After she'd been turned and allowed to leave Vincent's estate, Imani had lived a socially isolated life because she was too scared to contact anyone from her old life.

Briar made her believe she didn't need to do this alone. After having a long chat in the alley behind Pounders several months ago, Briar continued to visit her at least once a week. One time, she'd brought her friend Maddy and a wolf shifter named Mikey. Briar had been determined to be part of Imani's life and maybe even find a place for the vampire among the diverse group of Mikey's welcoming pack, Lobos Gris.

It could be time to trust a little and embrace a new community of friends.

"Imani? You still there?"

"Yeah, so, I might be in some trouble," Imani admitted, feeling a little dizzy with relief from getting to talk to someone.

"Tell me what's going on," Briar demanded. Imani could hear talking in the background and then Briar's muffled voice. "I'm talking. Shut up or leave." Then she was back. "Imani, do you need me to come get you?"

"No!" Imani said quickly. The last thing she wanted was to be in the same vehicle as Tobais. Being in the same room with a more powerful vampire made her skin crawl; sharing a space as small as a car sounded like a nightmare.

She knew better than to ask Briar to come alone. And there was no way Tobias would let his human partner be alone with another vampire. Every time Briar visited the bar, Imani had felt Tobias lurking outside the building. Briar, Memphis, and Tobias's relationship was still new and had a shaky start Tobias might never get over. Letting his vulnerable human flock member leave the safety of his house alone at night wasn't going to happen.

"If you don't want the three of us showing up, then you better start talking," Briar warned. "And don't think I can't find out where you live."

Briar's threat made Imani chuckle. "Yeah, yeah, you're a big-time scary hacker," Imani teased. Damn, it felt good to banter.

"And don't you forget it. Now, what's going on?"

"I need to hide for a while," Imani admitted. "And I should probably leave San Diego altogether."

"Hide?" Briar questioned.

"There are a couple of guys looking for me," Imani explained. "And my maker showed up and wants me to move back in with him and his flock."

"Oh, hell no," Briar barked. "You're not going back there. Pack your shit up and get your ass to our place. You can stay with—"

An angry voice and the crack of something wooden breaking in the background came through the call. Imani winced. Those were the sounds of an angry vampire.

"Okay, maybe that's not the best idea," Briar said. Imani could hear Memphis speaking soothingly to Tobias in the background.

"You know better," Imani chided gently. "Tobias won't be able to handle another vampire living in the same house. Leaving the state is the better option."

Saying those words out loud made a strong melancholy wash over her. The thought of getting on a freeway and heading north filled her with a deep sadness she couldn't explain. The urge to stay in San Diego was strong. What was wrong with her sense of self-preservation? Why wasn't a vindictive vampire with a sadistic flock enough to squash any feeling of reluctance at leaving?

It was official, somewhere along the way she'd gone certifiably insane. Does one hold funeral services for their sanity?

"You can't stay here," Briar announced, pulling Imani out of her thoughts and back to their conversation.

Imani snorted. "You think?"

"I've got a counter proposal," Briar continued. She wasn't one to give up easily, or ever. "Tobias has property all over the place. I'm sure there's an empty house or condo you can use. And because he's a vampire, you know it'll be secure from the sun. It's a win-win. You get to stay in San Diego, and we don't lose anymore furniture to one of Tobias's temper tantrums."

Tobias's affronted voice came through the phone with perfect, chilly clarity. "Vampires don't have temper tantrums; we display dominance."

Briar's voice got a little distant, probably pulling the phone away from her mouth. "Well go show your toddler dominance to the backyard where there isn't any furniture I'm attached to. I really liked that table. It was the perfect height for fucking."

There was a beat of silence before Memphis's roar of laughter crackled through the cheap phone along with Tobias's reluctant laughter a second later. Jealousy at their joy and love made Imani suck in a breath. She'd probably never have a flock of her own. Even if she found them, she had nothing to offer. Penniless vampires didn't attract flocks.

There was a reason no one writes romance novels featuring poverty-stricken vampires. Why put up with their kind if they couldn't at least provide luxury?

"Ignore Tobias. He probably needs a nap," Briar declared into the phone. Imani could easily picture the woman fearlessly facing down Tobias with her trademark smirk. "Anyway, back on topic. You stay local by living at one of Tobias's properties. You'll be hidden from your maker and you don't have to risk trying to travel. I don't want you stuck on the road near dawn. A lot of bad shit could happen to you, Imani. And bonus, you get to hang out with me sometimes!"

"Is that a bonus or a threat?" Imani teased. Briar didn't get a chance to answer as Tobias's voice came through the phone clearly.

"I know you can hear me, Imani," Tobais said in the background. "Briar speaks the truth. You are welcome to inhabit any of my empty properties. It would make my Briar happy and be a good compromise to having you in my home."

Imani looked down at the backpack sitting next to her duffle. It had the meager cash from her stash and what she'd stolen from Phill. "I can pay rent."

"I dare you to try and see what happens," Briar retorted. "Besides, I like collecting favors. I'll find you a place to live for a while and then you'll owe me."

"I have no money, no power, and no influence. What the hell can I possibly do for you?" Imani laughed, feeling on the verge of tears.

"It doesn't work that way," Briar argued. "My favors aren't a one-for-one, equal-exchange thing. I might ask you to help someone else out in the future and you'll do it 'no questions asked' because I helped you now."

Imani could easily see Briar building a network of friends by doing stuff like this. No wonder she was so close to the Lobos Gris Pack. Briar had the communal instincts of a wolf shifter.

"Yeah, okay," Imani agreed. "I'll owe you."

"Great!" Briar cheered as if Imani were doing her the favor. "Give me a minute and I'll call you right back. You still riding that little motorcycle?"

The first time Briar's mate Memphis had seen Imani's battered DRZ400S, he'd called it a toy. She'd rolled her eyes, pointed to his Harley and asked what he was compensating for. He'd laughed, then bullied her into letting him service her Suzuki and even slapping on a new set of tires. She'd tried to refuse, but he wouldn't let her say no.

"What do you think, I went out and bought myself a Rolls Royce with all the cash I rake in?" Imani scoffed.

Briar wasn't fazed by her sarcasm. "Okay, so still on two wheels. I can come over to help you move anything that needs a bigger vehicle."

"No need," Imani was quick to assure her. "Everything I own fits on the bike."

"Shit, you live light," Briar commented. "I could take some lessons."

"From what Maddy says, your t-shirt collection alone could fill a room," Imani teased. "I'm not sure living light is in your nature."

"It's not that bad," Briar defended, but Imani could hear the laughter in her voice. "Whatever, I'll get you an address in a few. Hold tight 'til then." Before Imani could say anything else, Briar ended the call.

Dropping down to sit on the bed, Imani looked around the apartment. She was paid through the month. After she was gone, it would be a simple matter of calling the nagas and explaining she wasn't coming back. There were still three weeks to the month. They'd probably be able to get an occupant in less than a week.

There were way too many other preternaturals out there like her, in desperate need of a safe place to stay. It meant they were willing to put up with high rent and deplorable accommodations for a modicum of protection.

Safe spaces were something she'd always been obsessed with, even before being turned.

One of her big dreams was opening her own club. A place women could come to drink and dance and not have to worry about guys being obnoxious or spiking drinks. In her perfect club, she'd have bouncers and staff ready to kick people out if they were misbehaving at all. At this magical bar, the women's bathroom would be huge and opulent, and the guys would get one stall and a trough urinal—outside in the alley.

Imagining her dream club always made her smile, but now she had a second life goal. She wanted to create a safe place for powerless preternaturals to live. Maybe an apartment-like situation where everyone could have their own unit. Or should it be more like a dorm to encourage the individuals to bond with each other so they could form a community of misfits and outcasts?

Not that she'd be able to do that anytime soon. But if she survived, she'd eventually be as powerful as Vincent. With that level of age and ability, she'd be able to amass a fortune quickly. That was a goal that only needed her to survive now to achieve later.

The phone buzzed with a text from Briar.

Briar: *I've got a house for you to use for as long as you want. It hasn't been used for years.*
Imani: *Years? How many we talking?*

There was a bit of a pause before Briar's answer came through.

Briar: *Ten-ish. But I'm sure it's in good shape. The guy who was in charge of Tobias's estate while he was missing for a decade was a douche, but he took good care of Tobias's stuff.*

Imani shivered at the reference of what Tobias had gone through. Trapped in a hidden room in a basement and bound with magical chains for ten years was something only a creature as powerful as Tobias could survive. It had been dumb luck when Briar had stumbled on him and then called Memphis in to help rescue the starved vampire. Now Briar and Memphis were Tobias's flock. If anything remotely threatened them, Tobias shed the thin veneer of humanity he wore most of the time and slaughtered the threat without remorse.

Briar: *I can meet you there? Help out if the place is a little dusty and needs a good cleaning.*

Imani was quick to refuse.

Imani: *No need, I'm sure it'll be fine. I'm not worried about a few spiderwebs or a layer of grime. There has to be at least a pack of rampaging dust bunnies to scare me.*
Briar: *I'll send an army of robot vacuums to back you up. Let loose the vacuums of war!*

Chuckling to herself, Imani found a gif of a Roomba with googly eyes to send to Briar. Brair sent the same gif at the same time! She really adored this woman. They were destined to be good friends. In another life, Briar might have even been a member of her flock, but Tobias found her first.

The next text from Briar was the address, the code to get into the gate, and another code for the front door. The house was still in San Diego County, but far from the dense city center. It would work as the perfect hiding place while she figured out her next move.

She sent a gif back with a dancing computer saying thank you, then grabbed her stuff. Time to start fresh. Today was the first night of the rest of her eternity.

Imani

After securing the duffle to the back of the bike, Imani gathered her waist length braids and tucked them inside her textile motorcycle jacket. Once that was zipped up, she slung on her backpack and pulled on her helmet.

Throwing a long leg over the supermoto, she sat down and slipped her cell into the holder mounted on her handlebars. It was quick work to set up the mapping app with her destination and approve the route without looking.

With that set up, she pushed the bike up off the kickstand and heeled it out of the way. A nudge to the shifter pedal with her toe slipped the bike into neutral. The key was already in the ignition. She twisted it to the on position and hit the starter, giving the bike a little throttle at the same time. With the engine still warm from her ride from the bar the Suzuki came to life easily, and made fussing with the choke unnecessary.

She tapped the bike into gear with her left toe, twisted the throttle, and released the clutch. She pulled out of the short driveway in front of her converted garage-studio and steered onto the streets. The mapping app sent her to the nearby I-5 onramp that wrapped around in a long 360 corner and included nice banking all the way.

Leaning the bike as she swept through the onramp, she made the turn into a double apex. Rounding the last of it, she twisted the throttle as she straightened up. By the time she was pushing the small 250cc engine toward freeway speeds, she was grinning widely. There was nothing like riding to make her feel free, no matter what other shit might be going on in her life.

Five years ago, she'd gotten into motorcycles. After one supermoto class, she'd been hooked on the versatile style of riding. Several years of supermoto classes and track days made riding the bike second nature. This was the only part of her former life she was able to keep. Not once in all those years of track days and honing her riding skills had she considered that a motorcycle would become her primary mode of transportation.

The truth of the matter was that life after death was expensive and motorcycles were cheaper than cars.

The map on the phone guided her through several freeway interchanges until she was getting off the I-15 at a familiar exit. To her delight, it looked like the "optimal route" included Highland Valley Road, a small, twisty, two-lane road that many motorcyclists and sport car enthusiasts visited on weekends.

"Oh yeah, baby!" Imani shouted to herself, her voice unnaturally loud echoing around in her helmet. The late hour meant few cars would impede her enjoyment of the tight and curvy road. While most riders would shy away from riding this fast at such a late hour, enhanced vampire vision allowed her to see the road at night with no streetlights as well as humans would see during the day.

It was roads like this where her supermoto shined, including the occasional sandy or dirty section where her tires threatened to lose grip. Riding supermoto was about learning to manage the motorcycle's tires' grip on all kinds of surfaces. Feeling the back tire try to slide out only made her grin wider.

Before she knew it, she was at the super tight turns that marked the end of Highland Valley Road's twisties. Easing back on the throttle in the straight section, she pulled in a deep breath. She'd been working so much that it'd been a while since she'd ridden for the joy of it.

Maybe it was a good thing that her life had gotten disrupted. She hadn't been living, only surviving. With Briar's help, she might be able to plan a better life from here forward.

She hadn't paid any attention to the mapping app when she'd first put in the address. She'd been much too distracted by her anxiety and the driving need to *leave*. Then she'd hit the first twisty road and didn't care where she was going. Now, as the app guided her deep into the rural area of San Diego's east county city of Ramona, Imani started to have reservations.

She wasn't going to complain no matter what the property turned out to be. But she really hoped she didn't end up in some broken-down trailer with no electricity except for a generator. Ramona, like much of San Diego, was an eclectic mix. While most neighborhoods were a combination of poverty and wealth, Ramona was a mix of wealth and rural. Horses, goats, and other livestock were a common sight along with wineries and upscale neighborhoods.

Following the directions she pulled into a narrow, private drive that wound its way up the side of a mountain. Keeping her pace moderate, she steered the Suzuki around unfamiliar bends. Her phone stopped getting a signal, making her hope she was close. The mapping apps weren't always reliable in these areas, and she might have to backtrack to figure out where she'd made a wrong turn.

She finally got to a wrought-iron gate, punched in the code, and motored in. It was only another hundred feet further before she could see where she'd be staying. No broken-down trailer or old converted farmhouse for her.

Before her was an enormous Mediterranean style house with a red-tiled roof, white stucco walls, and arched windows. She gaped as she parked the bike under the drive-through portico in front of the elaborate entrance.

Thumbing the kill switch, then twisting the key to off, she took her time dismounting and removing her helmet. The place was dark and the area quiet, but that didn't lessen her caution.

Turning in a circle, she took in what she could see of the property. She couldn't be sure, but she thought Tobias might own the entire darn mountain because she didn't see any lights until she looked all the way down the mountainside to the far-off main road she'd come from.

"Why do I feel like some obnoxious dude should be coming through the front door and telling me to get off his property in a snooty voice?" she murmured. Leaving her helmet hanging off the bike's mirror and her duffle strapped to the back, she made her way to the front door.

As with the gate, the code to the door worked, giving her access to the house. Although she didn't turn on any lights as she stepped inside, she could see almost all the details of the luxurious home. The place was immaculate with what looked like custom-made furniture and original art on the walls.

"Damn, this place is dripping," she said to the empty house.

Letting the door swing closed behind her, she located a bank of switches and flipped them all on. Tasteful recessed lighting illuminated everything, including the portico behind her. Sliding her backpack off her shoulders, she set it down on a table that was probably worth more than every car she'd ever owned put together.

A quick tour revealed six bedrooms, all with en suite bathrooms, a massive kitchen that was probably every cook's wet dream, a four-car garage with a Lexus, and a…

"Well, damn. Now I do have a Rolls Royce," she said with a laugh, running her fingers over the Phantom. Not that she'd use it unless the circumstances were dire, but still, a girl could dream.

"What kind of monster is Tobias to have all you beauties stored way out here with no one to appreciate any of you?" she asked the cars. There must be caretakers or various services that came out because the house and cars all looked clean. Not a cobweb or dust mote in sight. She wasn't going to need a Robot Vacuum Army after all.

Her phone buzzed. Surprised, she pulled it out to find she had full bars now. That was good because she hadn't seen a landline yet.

Briar: *I've got food coming to you, so don't eat the messenger.*
Imani: *This place is intense, and I get a meal plan? I'm not sure I'll ever be able to pay back this favor.*
Briar: *I know how you'll pay me back. You'll forgive me.*

Briar's words made the hair on the back of Imani's neck stand up. What the hell did she mean by forgiving her?

Before Imani could question Briar further, there was a knock at the door. That had to be the bagged blood. Briar must have ordered it as soon as she'd sent Imani the address. Eager to get her hands on it, she rushed to the front door. Throwing it open, she expected to see one of the guys from the service that provided blood for most vampires in San Diego.

That wasn't who was at the door.

The sight that greeted her made her freeze and suck in a shocked breath. The same two guys she'd run from only a few hours earlier at Pounders were there! Normally she was quick to act when presented with a dangerous situation, but the bizarre sight of these two familiar men sitting cross-legged on the stoop of the house had her both shocked and baffled.

A glance down revealed a cooler at her feet with a note on top. These two couldn't possibly be regular blood runners, the nickname for individuals hired to deliver blood bags to vampires. That was too much of a coincidence.

Briar's text about forgiveness hit Imani. Anger flashed through her at the thought of her friend's betrayal. Caution kept her from turning tail and running. The two men might be sitting, but they were both shimmering with powerful shifter magic. They'd be able to shed their human forms and chase her down before she made it halfway to the garage.

Was she going to have to fight? Maybe she could wound them enough to get away. But then it would be daylight in only a few hours. Could she find a motel room this time of night? Would she be forced to sequester away in someone's garage or garden shed and hope that no one found her while she was helpless?

All these thoughts swirled in head along with the barely suppressed panic.

"Don't run!" The bigger one begged, his voice loud and desperate. He didn't move to stand up, but his face looked deeply afraid. What could he possibly be scared of?

"What the fuck do you want?" she asked. She succeeded in making her voice strong, but her body betrayed her by taking half a step back. The pale one hadn't spoken yet but watched her with intense glowing amber eyes and a heavy scowl. She was pretty sure he wanted to eat her.

Bigger spoke again, his olive skin a sharp contrast to his pale companion. "We only want to talk. My name is Mac, and this is Lex. If you read the note, you'll see that Briar, Tobais, and Memphis have vouched for us. They've also pledged their protection to you. If we do anything you don't want, they'll hunt us down on your behalf."

Imani scoffed. "I'm supposed to trust a piece of paper? I might not be an old vampire, but even I know pledges have no value unless there's a blood exchange.

"Tobais is willing—" Mac didn't get a chance to finish his sentence. The scowling Lex jumped to his feet and rushed her with a loud snarl. "Lex, no!" Mac shouted, but his friend didn't listen.

"Can't let her disappear!" Lex roared as he charged her.

This shifter was exceptionally fast. His speed coupled with her consuming too little blood made her an easy target. She tried to run but didn't even make a full turn before this Lex person was on her. His arms wrapped around her chest like bands of steel. He lifted her off her feet as if she weighed no more than the small cooler he'd knocked over to get to her.

"Let go, you big bastard!" she screamed. Even though it wouldn't do any good, she kicked and struggled anyway.

"Stop moving," Lex growled. Because she'd been half turned when he grabbed her, her left side was pressed to his chest, her arms trapped at her side. The guy was nothing but solid muscles.

"Lex, please," Mac cried out, scrambling to his feet. "Let her go, love. You're scaring her!"

Memories of Simon and Opal calling each other pet names as they tortured her flashed through her mind. White hot rage filled her. They might kill her, but she wasn't going down without a fight.

"I'll never be a victim again!" she screamed.

Then she struck with her only available weapon, her fangs. Her position in his arms gave her access to his neck and, without hesitation, she sank her fangs into the fat vein easily seen through his pale flesh. Letting her hunger take over, she pulled from him without care of limiting the flow. Hot, powerful blood filled her mouth and the rest of the world faded.

Outside of the vampire who'd made her, this shifter had the most powerful blood she'd ever tasted. After only a few pulls, her veins started burning with potent magic as her body absorbed his energy. All thoughts of struggling left her. With a moan, she closed her eyes and focused on sucking at his neck.

The guy didn't cry out, curse, or try to make her stop. The powerful arms holding her gentled, and one hand moved to her head. She thought he'd grip her hair to wrench her face away. That didn't happen, instead his broad hand cradled her head, holding her. Encouraging her.

"That's it," Lex murmured to her. "Take all you need from me."

If it were any other circumstance, she'd think they were intimate partners, not prey and predator. He should be trying to rip her off him, not urging her to drink.

"I can feed her too," Mac said. She heard him move and when she opened her eyes, mouth still attached to Lex's throat, she saw the other guy standing close. His expression was—aroused?

He rubbed a hand over his neck, as if trying to draw her attention. "Please, love. Take from me too."

What the fuck was going on?

Buzzing like she'd taken a bunch of tequila shots in a row; she unhooked her fangs from Lex's neck. His hand fell away from the back of her head. The arms around her went from restraining to embracing.

Strangely, she didn't feel the need to flee or fight. A bone deep contentedness swept through her, adding to the drunk effects of the blood she'd imbibed.

When she turned her head to take in Mac, Lex nuzzled the side of her face with a little huff of happiness.

"Beautiful," he murmured in her ear.

"Yes, she is," Mac agreed, his eyes locked on her lips. She felt something trickle from her mouth. Reaching out, he swiped a thick thumb over her chin and pulled back to show her a smear of blood. Lex's blood. They both focused on his thumb.

Then he made the least threatening growl she'd ever heard.
Really it was more of a huffing purr than a growl.

"Suck," he demanded and placed his thumb over her
lips. He didn't press down and force the digit into her mouth; his
touch was only a whisper of connection inviting her to part her
lips.

Opening, she drew his thumb into her mouth. The taste
of Lex's blood combined with this male's skin made lust explode
through her.

Both men groaned. As shifters, they could probably
smell her arousal. What was going on here? How had she gone
from wanting to evade and escape to biting and embracing?
Nothing was making sense.

One thing was clear though, she needed these men to
keep touching her and all of them were wearing way too many
clothes!

Mac

Mac had never been so turned on. Watching Lex's eyes roll back, and his face go slack with pleasure as Imani fed on him, sent blood rushing to Mac's cock. Then Imani had let go of Lex's neck and looked up at him with blown pupils and pure lust in her soulful brown eyes.

He fell into those perfect eyes, unable to look away.

Without realizing what he was doing, he put his thumb to her lips. Her hot, wet mouth closing over his skin had sent a wave of heat crashing over his body. The intensity made his legs want to fold under him.

There were so many things he wanted to do all at once that he froze for a moment, unable to move.

"Smells so good," Lex murmured, licking a patch of skin under her ear, making her jerk and causing Mac's thumb to pop out of her mouth. "Want to lick you all over."

He watched as a small trickle of blood seeped from one of the punctures on Lex's neck. Jealousy hit Mac hard. He wanted to provide her with precious sustenance. He needed to know he was nursing her as much as Lex. Bending over a little, he craned his head to the side and presented her with his neck.

"Feed from me," he demanded. "I might not be a chimera shifter, but my blood is strong."

She blinked slowly, confused. It was as if he was speaking an incomprehensible language.

"Feed from me," he repeated, pushing his neck close to her face. He couldn't see her expression any longer, but he could feel her lips brush his skin and her hot breath fan across his pulse point. "Take me inside you. Nourish yourself."

She tried to move her head away. Mac saw Lex keep her in place with the hand still cradling her head.

"Do it, beautiful," Lex urged. "Taste him too."

That was all the encouragement she needed. With a needy sound, she struck, her fangs sliding painlessly into his flesh. Each pull of her mouth felt like she was sucking at something deeper inside of him. Her magic flowed across his skin, raising gooseflesh and making his heart pound with lust.

"That's it," Lex whispered. "Take what you need. We're yours. We belong to you."

Mac wanted to agree with Lex, but he couldn't make his mouth work. Moaning, he closed his eyes, focusing on the pull of Imani's mouth. Her magic washed down his body, like hands caressing him.

He was dimly aware of Lex shifting his hold on Imani. Soon her body was pressed into his. Without thinking about it, he wrapped his arms around both her and Lex. It felt good to hold both of them. Lex made a sound that was probably a chimera version of a purr but sounded a lot more like a diesel engine with a timing issue.

The three of them stayed like that—frozen in a perfect moment in time. The lust raging through Mac was tempered by his feelings of affection and nearly giddy relief at having Imani safe in their arms.

It was Imani who ended the moment. Extracting her fangs with care, she brought her head up to look him in the eye. Her mouth was slightly open, and she looked dazed.

"I'm full," she whispered, clearly shocked. "I've never been full. I didn't know I could feel full."

"We'll always keep you fed," Mac promised, and Lex's weird purr got louder for a moment in agreement. "You'll never be hungry or alone again."

Lex's purr made her look over her shoulder at him. Mac followed her gaze to see Lex's head nestled against her back with his eyes closed and a small smile on his lips. Mac had never seen the chimera's face so relaxed before. Sensing eyes on him, Lex looked up with a dopey smile.

"You're mine," she murmured. "You're both mine."

"We are," Lex rumbled before dropping his head back down to rest against her.

"I never thought…" her voice trailed off, her tone wondrous. Mac understood; he'd never thought he'd get one love let alone two.

Turning her face back to him, her eyes dropped to his neck, brows furrowing. Mouth turned down in a frown, she wiggled a hand free from between them to gently touch the bite mark.

"I hurt you," she whispered, her mouth twisted in pain and confusion. "Why did I hurt you?"

"You didn't hurt me, love," he assured her. "Far from it. Your bite is a fucking aphrodisiac."

Her brows smoothed. "You're not lying to me?"

"Never," he murmured, pressing his lips to her forehead before pulling back to meet her eyes. "In fact, I'm gonna need you to bite me more. Sink those fangs into me, please. Anywhere and everywhere, preferably when we're both naked."

Lex's rumbly purr grew louder for a beat before he spoke. "Yes, naked biting. Can we start doing that right now?"

Although Imani's expression didn't change, Mac could hear her heartbeat speed up. Then her smell blossomed. It was a delicate scent full of feminine desire. Lex took a deep breath in through his nose and made a small growly sound. The chimera must smell it as well.

"Need to taste you," Mac whispered. "Please, Imani. Let me lick your pussy."

"I, uh," she ran a tongue over her lips, drawing Mac's attention to her mouth. He couldn't wait any longer. Lowering his mouth to hers, he licked across the seam of her lips, begging to be let in. With a soft sigh, she opened for him.

Fuck, she tasted good. There was a faint trace of his blood, but the rest was all her. He could spend hours, no, days, kissing this woman. Imani moaned into his mouth, letting him know she was enjoying their kiss too. Her body melted into his embrace and her sweet, perfect scent further perfumed the air.

Lex's hand reached around and slid up his shirt to touch the bare skin of his lower back. The feel of Lex touching his skin while he kissed Imani was too much and not enough all at the same time. Lust exploded inside him, heating his skin and shutting down his ability for higher reasoning.

He needed all three of them out of their clothes and touching *now*!

Breaking the kiss, he pulled his head back to look Imani in the eyes. "I'm going to strip," he warned, not surprised at the deeper timbre of his voice. "Then I'm going to take your clothes off. Tell me now if you don't want it."

"Yes! Good idea, no more clothes!" Lex agreed eagerly, pulling his hand out from under Mac's shirt. They both turned to watch Lex. An unexpected chuckle bubbled up Mac's throat after watching Lex completely strip in less than five seconds. He even got his lace-up combat boots off.

Mac had been around Lex while they were both naked several times when they'd worked together in the past. Because he'd assumed his love would never be reciprocated, he'd always been careful to keep his eyes trained somewhere else or only on Lex's face. With the change in their relationship, he gave himself permission to look.

The sight of Lex without clothes took Mac's breath away.

Lex might be short compared to his seven-foot height, but he wasn't small. He was probably about six foot two or three inches, with a good amount of heavy muscle covering his body and a surprising number of scars. Mac had his fair share of scars, especially on his left side where an IED had gotten him. Despite their ability to heal quickly, most shifters still scarred. Except chimera. It was rare to see scars on one. Lex must have suffered grievous injuries to end up with marks like those.

Other than the scars, this male was perfect. Unlike his furry brother Memphis, Lex had very little body hair. A smooth, densely muscled chest led down to a ripped abdomen and finally a gorgeous, long uncut cock rising out of a tidy nest of light brown hair.

Actually, that was a little too perfect. Did his boy manscape? He'd have to ask Lex later when he wasn't busy swallowing convulsively because his mouth was watering. Between the smell of Imani and the sight of Lex, Mac was sure his dick was about to punch a hole through his pants.

He and Imani must have been staring too long because Lex made an impatient huffing sound. "Mac, Imani, your turns!"

Mac set Imani on her feet and stepped back. He gave her a small smile before focusing on stripping out of his own clothes. He wasn't as graceful or quick as Lex, but he didn't take his time either.

When he was finished, he stood still and let Imani and Lex get a good look at him. He was heavily muscled, but unlike Lex, he had some fat on his body. There were no defined washboard abs, and he wasn't manscaped. His chest was covered in a pelt of soft dark brown hair that led to a thick happy trail all the way down to his junk. He'd never been self-conscious before, but now that he was standing next to the cut and corded Lex, he worried they might find him lacking.

Imani was still fully clothed, her eyes moving across every inch of his skin. His raging erection flagged as his anxiety rose. If she wasn't stripping, she must not want him. Maybe she only wanted Lex? He was the more ripped of the two of them.

What if he'd been mistaken, and he wasn't part of Imani's flock? Could he have gotten his feelings for Lex mixed up in his head with belonging to Imani?

Miserable, he reached down for his shirt. "I'll go down and get the truck. You two have fun."

Before he could pull the shirt back on over his head, Lex tackled him. It wasn't a gentle take down either. The shirt went flying and his back hit the floor, forcing the air out of his lungs. While he caught his breath, Lex got comfortable sitting on his belly. A few drops of pre-cum from Lex's erection dampened the hair on Mac's sternum. Between that and the proximity of the rest of Lex's powerful body, Mac's cock perked up again.

"You got sad," Lex declared, his expression a combination of confusion and upset. "I could smell it. You got worried, then you stank of sadness and then you wanted to leave. Did I do something? I can fix it but tell me exactly what I did wrong."

"You didn't do anything wrong," Mac assured the chimera. "I think I might have gotten myself worked up in the wrong way. I don't think Imani wants me like she wants you."

Lex scoffed. "Bullshit." Looking over his shoulder, Lex motioned for Imani to come forward. "Tell him. Tell him he belongs to you too."

For a brief moment she froze with a slightly overwhelmed look on her face. Sure she was about to reject him, Mac opened his mouth to demand Lex let him up so he could leave. Before he could make a sound, her back suddenly snapped straight, and she leveled fierce eyes on him.

"Keep him there, Lex," she ordered as she crossed the small distance that separated them. Sinking to her knees next to him, she ran her fingers through his hair until she could grab onto a good chunk of it. Her grip was firm but not painful. She forced his head to the side and brought her face close to his ear.

"You don't get to leave me," she whispered to him, her words heavy with intensity and magic. "You and Lex are both mine. My flock. My creatures. Do you understand? *Mine!*"

Her voice deepened to an inhumane growl on that last word, and he felt her magic pulse through him. He blinked as both lust and love exploded deep inside him.

"Yours," he agreed, feeling drunk on the power she was pulsing. From what Briar, Tobias, and Memphis had told them about Imani, she wasn't supposed to have this level of magic yet. They must have been wrong because he could feel it heating his skin, sending sparks of pleasure up and down his spine.

Lex felt it too. The chimera hissed, his dick jumping and slapping back down on Mac's skin.

"Me too, right?" Lex asked, his voice bordering on a whine.

Without releasing Mac's hair, Imani sat up and grabbed Lex by the back of his neck. "Yes, you too," she agreed. "You both belong to me. Now and forever."

The words felt heavy and meaningful.

"Kiss me?" Lex begged.

Letting go of Mac's hair, she held Lex's face still and put her lips to his. Her kiss was aggressive, and Lex melted. Mac noted the chimera kept his hands to himself like a good boy. For as aggressive as Lex was with him, the strong and skilled chimera was acting like an obedient submissive with Imani.

Submissive. A revelation metaphorically struck Mac upside the head.

Outside of a fight or merc assignment, Mac always told Lex what to do when they were together. No matter what Mac ordered him to do, Lex did it without comment or complaint, even giving Mac his half grin when praised. Mac had always assumed Lex simply didn't want to be bothered making choices when he wasn't at work.

That was wrong. Lex had probably been desperate for Mac to demand more.

It wasn't that Lex hadn't wanted him for all the years they'd been friends, it was that Lex was submissive. So submissive, in fact, that he couldn't bring himself to ask for what he wanted.

How fucking clueless could a sloth bear be?

Feeling bold and in desperate need to touch, Mac reached up to grab Lex's gorgeous dick in one hand and rested his other on Imani's jean covered thigh. The two were still kissing, but Lex jerked, then moaned as Mac stroked his cock. Slippery beads of pre-come leaked from the head, which Mac used to help massage the turgid flesh.

When Imani ended the kiss, Lex kept his eyes closed, his breathing uneven and his body tense. When she moved her gaze down, their eyes met.

"We should go upstairs," she murmured. "Where there are rooms with big, comfy beds. Wouldn't that be nicer than here on the floor?" Lex whimpered but didn't speak.

"Yes," Mac agreed, feeling breathless and needy.

She dipped her head slightly. "I'm glad you agree. Does that mean you'll follow me upstairs?"

"I plan on following you to the ends of the earth," Mac vowed. "Upstairs is only the first step."

Lex

"Get off me, Lex," Mac ordered him as Imani stood up and stepped back. When Lex didn't move right away, Mac grabbed him by the hips and heaved him into the air. Lex easily twisted in the air and landed crouched next to Mac.

"Hurry up, you two," Imani demanded, a salacious smirk on her face.

Lex stood but couldn't make himself step forward until Mac was standing up too. He wanted to make sure Mac didn't try to go anywhere.

When Mac moved to get dressed and leave, it had been like a knife to Lex's heart. He hadn't even realized what he was doing until he found himself sitting on Mac. It was the most aggressive he'd ever been with the sloth bear.

Now that Mac understood the three of them belonged to each other, Lex felt his aggression bleed away, replaced by a bit of uncertainty, making him unsteady and hesitant. This wasn't a firefight in the middle of the jungle during an ambush; it was so much more complicated. Lex didn't want to make a wrong move that might displease Imani or Mac.

Heaving himself to his feet, Mac faced him, then snaked a hand out to grab Lex by the back of the neck. Mac's hold was forceful to the point of almost being painful. Lex loved it. The touch made him feel grounded and safe. He never wanted Mac to let go.

"March," Mac rumbled and used his grip to guide Lex up the stairs, following Imani. She led them to a bedroom. The king size bed was covered in a thick comforter and a dozen decorative pillows. Imani started tossing pillows off the bed and only stopped when she'd excavated down to the comforter. After she'd pulled that down with a flourish, she looked at them.

"Hop in," she urged.

"We should undress you first," Mac countered, and Lex nodded his head with a sound of agreement. It was nice having Mac naked, but he wanted both his mates without clothes.

Imani looked down; her expression mildly surprised as if she'd forgotten she was still dressed. She reached for the hem of her shirt but before she could start pulling it up, Mac stepped forward with his hand on Lex's neck still guiding him.

"We'll do that," he insisted, dropping his broad mitt away from Lex. Without Mac's firm touch, Lex felt adrift for a moment, but then Mac nudged him. "You should get on your knees and take her shoes off."

The clear direction helped. It felt good to sink to his knees and let both Mac and Imani tower over him. He could hear them kissing as he untied Imani's boots and loosened the laces. He appreciated the practical and durable footwear as he tugged on her pant leg to get her to lift so he could slide the right boot off. After he removed her black sock, he couldn't help himself; he massaged her delicate foot before setting it down.

Resisting the urge to start kissing her feet, he tackled the laces on her left boot. About the time he'd gotten that off, her shirt dropped to the floor next to him. Looking up, he watched Mac start kissing down Imani's neck and shoulder. At the same time, he shifted one finger into a claw and cut through the front of her bra.

Imani pulled back with a gasp, then laughed. "Don't do that again," she warned him even as she pulled the ruined garment off.

Mac grumbled something unintelligible and went back to kissing along her collarbone. Lex was caught for a moment by the beautiful sight of the giant, scruffy Mac compared to the elegant Imani. They were perfectly exquisite in their different ways. Both of them made his heart pound and his hands itch to touch.

"Get up here, you pale bastard," Mac grumbled with a soft smile when he noticed Lex staring.

Scrambling to his feet, Lex stood with his head bowed a little and waited. He couldn't explain why, but it didn't feel right to look Mac or Imani in the eyes. With his eyes down, he had a clear view of a dark-skinned, delicate hand circling his hard dick and tugging gently.

A larger hand gripped under his chin and lifted. The pressure didn't stop until he was looking Mac in the eye. "I need you to say something if anything becomes too much."

Lex tried to nod his head, even though it was a lie. He'd never utter a word if it meant they might stop.

Mac frowned, let go, and stepped back. "I'm serious, Lex," his deep voice rumbled. "I'm not going any further unless you promise you'll tell us if something hurts."

Lex didn't say anything. Making everything stop was the exact opposite of what he wanted.

"Lex." Mac's one word held a lot of warning, making fear sour Lex's stomach. He tried to say something, but the words got caught in his stomach.

"What's going on here?" Imani asked, pressing herself against Mac's side so she could face Lex. "Why do you look so scared, Lexie?"

Lexie. If it was anyone else, he'd fucking hate the nickname, but from Imani it sounded soft and affectionate.

"He's submissive, but I'm worried he won't use a safe word if we give it to him," Mac told her, making blood rush to Lex's face. He had pitifully little sexual experience, but even he knew what a submissive was. Could that be why he was fighting the urge to drop back down to his knees and why it felt so right when Mac handled him roughly?

"I read submissives are sometimes scared of rejection, so they'll stay quiet almost no matter what the Dom does," Imani commented. "Is that what's going on here, Lexie?"

Moving his gaze over, he met Imani's eyes and tried to think how to answer her without causing trouble. The silence stretched.

"Let's go at this a different way," Imani murmured. "You're mine, right?" He nodded his head. He was hers and Mac's. Heart, body, and soul. Now and forever. "It would make me happy if you agreed to use a safe word."

Lex couldn't take it anymore; he dropped his eyes back down to the floor. "I'll say something." The lie caused his voice to sound hoarse.

"I'm a shifter too," Mac reminded him. "I can smell your lie."

"You guys can smell lies," Imani murmured. "That's good to know."

"Only on people we know well," Mac explained. "And you're going to have to tell me what you're reading that involves submission and dominance."

"Sure thing," Imani agreed with a lighthearted laugh. "I've got a whole stack of romance books with some great scenes we might want to try out."

As they talked, Lex moved a little closer to them. If he could touch his mates, maybe he could get them to stop talking about safe words. Reaching out, he placed one hand on Imani's hip and another on Mac's chest. Neither of them rejected his touch, making some of his earlier anxiety melt away.

"Lex, tell me what I want to hear and mean it this time," Mac warned. Lex stepped closer until his body was flush with both of theirs. Goddess they felt good against this skin. He wanted to kiss and lick every part of them.

Mac's hand came up in a flash and grabbed him by the throat. He gasped but didn't struggle and let his arms drop to his side. He could still breathe but swallowing would be hard. His eyes flew up to meet Mac's, and he saw both kindness and determination in the sloth bear's gaze.

Imani put a hand on Mac's forearm, scowling. "Don't hurt Lexie."

"He needs to pick a safe word and promise to use it," Mac countered. "He thinks he can lie or avoid the issue. A little force might help him lean into his needs."

Lex was having a hard time understanding Mac. The moment Mac grabbed his throat, a wave of hazy calm swept over him. His heartbeat had slowed a little and his body relaxed into the sloth bear's solid grip. Not so much that he'd strangle himself, but enough to really feel Mac's strength.

Could he get Mac and Imani to bite him at the same time? Mac didn't need to feed on him, but the bear had enough control to only shift his jaw and teeth. He could sink long canines into Lex at the same time Imani impaled him with her fangs.

Fuck, that sounded hot!

His eyes jumped between Mac and Imani. "Please bite me. Please," he begged. Because Mac was still holding his neck, his voice was a gruff whisper, but the sloth bear didn't let go.

"Lex, you know what I need you to say," Mac reminded him.

"You can use the stoplight system," Imani suggested, petting a hand down his chest and then curling her fingers around his cock. Her touch made him shudder, then she made him groan when she pulled away. "Green for good, yellow for slow down, and red for stop. It's easy Lex. Go on, say it so we can go back to having some fun."

"Green," Lex croaked.

"More, Lex," Mac demanded as he started to squeeze. Lex felt his air cut off, but he didn't struggle. Darkness started to eat at the edges of his vision, and he suddenly realized what Mac wanted.

"Yellow." The word had almost no sound, but Mac released his grip and grabbed Lex into a hug.

"Good boy," he praised, kissing his forehead and rubbing his hand up and down his back. "That's what I wanted."

An immense sense of relief washed over him. He'd been afraid they'd force him to say red and there was no way he was uttering that word. Red meant stop and stopping was the last thing he ever wanted either of them to do.

Imani pressed against his back while looking over at Mac. "You're not going to make him say red?"

"We can work with yellow," Mac assured her. "And asking him to say red might stress him out too much. I think the three of us are going to be together for a long time so we can work on that later. Now into bed, love."

"As long as you're planning on joining me," Imani agreed, and Lex felt her warmth move away.

Releasing him from the hug, Mac turned Lex around and gripped the back of his neck in one hand. That hand guided him to the bed where Imani was already lying down, her gorgeous body spread diagonally across the large bed.

"Who's first?" she asked, opening her legs suggestively.

"Everyone," Mac answered, making her blink in confusion. Mac pushed him forward until he was forced to climb onto the bed on all fours. The pressure from Mac's hand didn't stop when he was between Imani's legs. Mac followed him onto the bed and kept pressing until Lex lowered his head; his mouth was almost touching the soft, black curls between Imani's legs.

"Lex is going to lick that sweet pussy while I get to kiss and touch both of you," Mac explained as he finally let go of Lex's neck. Lex rolled his eyes up to make sure this was what Imani wanted. When he saw eagerness on her face, his hesitation vanished. He buried his face in her sex like a starving man.

She was already turned on and wet, so his tongue was quickly coated in her succulent juices. Her moan only made him more eager. When he found a spot that made both her legs jerk, he knew that was the spot to focus on.

"Can I touch you here, love?" Mac asked, his fingers trailing down Lex's crack and over his back hole. Lex made an eager sound and pushed his ass up in encouragement. Any touch was a good touch right now. Mac chuckled. "Easy, love. I'm going to make it good for you."

The large shifter withdrew his hand and got off the bed. Lex would've protested, but Imani started breathing hard and grinding herself against his face. Her movements distracted Lex, making him focus on her building pleasure.

"Harder," she demanded. He pressed his lips and tongue more firmly against Imani's little nub of pleasure, careful to keep his teeth from digging into her soft flesh.

"Need more!" she called out and then Mac was back, kneeling on the bed next to her. She grabbed at him with frantic hands and dragged his face to hers.

Looking up the length of Imani's torso and chest, Lex watched them kiss as if they were long-lost lovers finally reunited.

In truth, wasn't that what they all were? Souls who'd been waiting to meet? Keeping their incomplete hearts dormant and safely tucked away until their matching parts came together to form a whole and harmonizing love.

Shit, that sounded poetic! He needed to remember to tell his mates those words later, when his mouth wasn't so busy.

While he watched and continued to lick and suck on Imani, Mac covered one of her breasts with a single hand. When the sloth bear squeezed gently, Imani moaned into their kiss, making Lex want to do more.

Careful to keep his face buried in Imani's sweet sex, Lex drew his legs up under him a little and shifted her legs over his shoulders. She made a little gasping sound but didn't resist the way he shifted the angle of her hips. Mac stopped kissing Imani long enough to look down and see what Lex was doing.

Moving slowly so either of his mates could stop him if they wanted, Lex reached up with a hand and sank two fingers into Imani's hot core. Imani sucked in a breath, then moaned. "Yes," she breathed. "Like that. More like that."

Mac gave him an approving look before going back to kissing Imani and toying with her breast. Lex closed his eyes, focusing on pleasuring Imani. Except for the fact that he wasn't touching Mac, this moment was one of the most perfect he'd ever experienced.

Imani's muscles started to tense up, telling him she was getting close. He could hear Mac growling all kinds of sexy words to Imani as her heels dug into Lex's back.

"*Yes!*" she cried out, back bowing as she came. Hoping to draw out her orgasm, Lex kept sucking and touching her until she sobbed out a "stop," and pushed his head away. Sitting up, he lowered her legs to the bed and surveyed his panting mate.

Mac kissed her a few more times while Lex watched. He wasn't one for taking pictures, but he found himself wishing he had his phone to snap a few images he could squirrel away and treasure in the future.

"I hope you don't think we're done," Mac rumbled, sitting up and grabbing Lex by the neck. He pulled Lex forward and crushed their lips together. Mac's kiss was forceful and Lex loved it.

"Oh, Goddess," Mac panted when he pulled away. "You smell and taste like Imani and you mixed together. Fucking ambrosia."

Imani huffed out a laugh. "I want some Lexie kisses too," she demanded lazily.

With his grip on Lex's throat, Mac pushed him down. Unsure of where Mac wanted him, Lex maneuvered himself until his weight was resting on his knees and forearms, his hips between Imani's legs and his face hovering over hers.

"Hi, baby," she murmured, then pulled him to her for a kiss.

This. Was. Everything.

Imani

To Imani's utter shock, she wasn't done after her first orgasm. She'd never been a multi-O girl before. Sex had been fun for her, but nothing she couldn't live without as long as she had access to her vibrator and books. Some of her partners had been better than others, but none of them had made her interested in doing anything after she came. Normally, she would be all about rolling over, cuddling up, and going to sleep. Or kicking the guy out of her bed if he wanted to be chatty.

This time was different. Being with these two was different. She was different.

No sooner had she started kissing Lex than she was ready for more. Her body felt energized and needy. The blood she'd taken from both of them made her buzz, like she'd pounded several cans of energy drinks in a row. All her senses felt hyper sensitized, and every little touch caused a cascade of sensation through her.

With Lex lying between her legs and his hard length resting along the length of her slit, she was torn between wanting to continue kissing him and pulling away so she could direct him to fuck her. Hard.

When he shifted a little and rubbed against her, she broke the kiss with a little gasp. Opening her eyes, she found Mac sitting next to them, watching.

"You two are beautiful," he whispered before leaning over and kissing them both in turn. It was nothing more than a light peck on the lips, but the expression on his face was anything but wholesome when he pulled away.

Mac held up a small bottle of expensive olive oil. "We're going to have to improvise tonight."

For a moment, Imani was confused. "What do you nee— oh!" Halfway through that sentence she realized what olive oil could be used for besides cooking.

Mac's grin was decidedly wicked as he shifted his gaze to Lex. The chimera didn't look confused or scared. He was staring at the bottle with excitement. Lex knew exactly what Mac was planning to do and was all for it.

Very slowly, Mac started unscrewing the bottle, making a show of every turn. "Here is what's going to happen. Lex, you're going to keep kissing and loving on Imani. She's going to take that hard cock of yours and do anything with it she wants."

At his statement, she felt Lex's dick jump, as if it was nodding in agreement.

"While you two are playin', I'm going to get your ass nice and ready for me," Mac continued. "You're going to take my entire dick like a good boy. I'm going to make sure it's good and you don't get to come 'til I say."

"What if I want it to hurt a little?" The moment the words were out of his mouth, he looked worried.

Imani reached up and framed his face with her hands, turning his head to look at her. "It's okay if you like a little pain," she assured him. "There's no shame here, remember? Tell me you understand."

A small smile curved his lips and he let out a soft breath. "Yeah, got it. I get to ask Mac to hurt me."

Lex's words and his adorable smile made Imani want to do something she'd never thought would be her kink—causing a partner pain during sex. Before she made him hurt, she had to be sure that was truly what he wanted.

"What if I did it too?" she asked.

His smile grew. "Yes, please." His eyes dropped to her mouth. "More biting, please." His eyes closed, and he shuddered as if imagining what she could do to him. "Or claw me. Slap me. Anything."

Imani felt her fangs ache and descend from her gums. He wasn't even putting much pressure on her clit, and she already felt worked up. This was the most aroused she'd ever been in her life.

She'd read books featuring BDSM, gotten turned on and wanted to try it. Real life attempts didn't turn her on and the partners she'd tried it with left as disappointed as she was. She assumed it was one of those things she liked in theory but not in practice, like eating healthy.

Now she understood why she hadn't enjoyed it in the past. In all the books she'd read, the women were always the submissive partner. They were the ones getting tied up, played with, flogged, and fucked. She'd unconsciously assumed that would be her orientation, but Lex was showing her that wasn't true at all.

She wanted to dominate the fuck out of this man, and he wanted it too.

"Don't forget your colors," she reminded him as she used her hands cupping his cheeks to turn his head slightly. "If I get a hint that you're in too much pain and didn't say anything, it's a red. Everything stops and doesn't start again. Yellow means we'll keep going after checking in. You got me?"

She ran her emerged fangs over the taut skin of his neck. Lex moaned but didn't talk.

"Answer," she demanded, then pressed one fang against his vein but didn't pierce the skin. His blood pounded under her tooth, calling to her.

"I promise to call yellow," he whimpered, and pushed his neck against her fang, trying to pierce himself. Using her hold on his face, she kept him where she wanted him.

"No, baby," she cooed, enjoying the quiet, frustrated sound he made. It was almost a sob. "I decide when it happens, not you. No, you have to wait for it." Lex let loose a loud whimper.

Looking over Lex's shoulder, she saw Mac had moved to kneel behind Lex. She couldn't see what he was doing. This angle wasn't going to work for her. Letting go of his face, she pressed on his shoulders.

"Up on your knees," she demanded. Lex was quick to move.

Mac moved out of the way and watched with interest as she leaned over the side of the bed and retrieved a bunch of pillows. She piled the pillows against the headboard, then reclined. She had to move a couple of them around until she was satisfied. When she was done, she could lie back with her hips elevated a little and her shoulders up higher. Then she settled Lex back between her legs with his dick nestled against her sex. She bent her knees to get her legs out of Mac's way while he was playing with Lex.

In this position Lex's shoulders weren't blocking her view. Now she had a front-row seat to all the things Mac was going to do to their needy partner.

"Good idea," Mac commented as he straddled Lex's thighs. Setting one big hand on Lex's tight ass, Mac rubbed. Lex lifted his hips a little at the same time Mac brought his other hand down hard, leaving a perfect red print on Lex's right ass cheek.

Lex yelped and pushed his hips forward and almost inadvertently slid his erection inside of her. Imani gasped and he moaned. As much as she wanted that, it needed to be on her terms and at her direction.

Imani gripped Lex's jaw, holding him still. "Put your cock inside me," she ordered. "But only the tip, no further than that."

"Just the tip," Mac chortled behind Lex. Imani looked up to meet the big man's gaze, finding herself smiling despite the juvenile nature of Mac's comment.

"Careful or I'll abuse you next," she warned him.

"If that is abuse, sign me up," Mac quipped.

Imani raised an eyebrow at him. "Or I could do to you what you're planning to do to Lex."

Mac didn't even pause before answering. "I'll buy you a strap-on and you can peg me. I've always wanted to try that."

"Deal, but I get to pick the size." At her words, Mac went from looking composed to worried in zero seconds flat, making Imani smirk. "Careful what you wish for," she taunted.

"Yes, love," Mac agreed.

While they'd talked, Lex started a slight rocking motion. A clear sign of his neediness. He hadn't pushed inside her yet, but when she looked down, his expression was strained.

"Such a good boy," Imani murmured and opened her knees a little wider, inviting him in. "Remember to stop."

He eased inside of her, pushing the bulbous head of his cock past her slick, tight entrance. He wasn't too big for her to handle, but he was large enough to make her glad she had total control of the pace.

"Oh god," he cried, body rigid with tension as he went perfectly still.

Imani looked past his face and down his spine to find it wasn't only her causing him to cry out. Mac had a look of absolute concentration on his face as he worked two fingers into Lex's tight back hole. Imani watched with fascination as the large man eased those fingers past the second knuckles. He was gentle and slow, making Lex whimper and shut his eyes tight.

"More, please," Lex begged.

"Easy, love," Mac murmured. Then he must have done something with his fingers because Lex's whole body spasmed.

"There it is," Mac cooed. "There's the prostate. Feels good, doesn't it?"

Biting his lip hard enough to draw blood, Lex jerked his head up and down. Caught by the sight of the bright red against Lex's pale lips, Imani leaned over and captured him in a kiss. Lex moaned and fell into the kiss, whimpering and crying softly into her mouth.

Despite everything Mac was doing to him, Lex's cock didn't slip any further into her. Reaching down, she tweaked Lex's nipple, tugging softly, then harder. His response to the touch was to kiss her with even more fervor.

It was obvious this male hadn't been deceiving them when he'd claimed to want a little pain.

She was worked up enough to want him to slide the rest of the way inside her, but resisted the urge. There was a plan in her head, and she wanted to make it happen in reality. With a tug hard enough to make Lex gasp, she pulled away from the kiss.

"What's your color, baby?" she asked.

Lex's eyes fluttered open and met hers. His pupils were blown, and he looked a little dazed. "G-green," he stuttered, then pulled in a deep breath. "Green-green. So fucking green. All the damn green. I'm so green I'm ready to hulk out."

His ramblings made Mac snort out a laugh and Imani grin. "That's good. What do you say if things are too much?" she pushed.

"Yellow," he answered promptly. "I fucking got it, okay? Green, yellow, red. Let's fucking race!"

Mac made a disapproving grumbling sound. Imani looked up in time to see Mac's free hand come down hard on Lex's ass. "Don't sass us, boy."

"Yes, sir," he moaned.

After making Lex groan and whimper a while longer, Mac withdrew his fingers. "I could work you open more," he murmured as he made a production of slicking up his cock with oil. "But I think you want it to burn a little, don't you?"

Lex didn't answer and Imani got the impression he couldn't speak. Or maybe he was worried about saying the wrong thing. He did make an eager sound that had Mac giving him a happy pat right on top of the red hand mark from earlier.

Pulling Lex's ass cheeks apart, Mac set the head of his massive dick against Lex's hole. Fascinated and more turned on than she ever expected, Imani watched Mac's cock slowly push into Lex.

"Oh, fuck," Mac moaned as he slowly slid himself all the way inside Lex, one millimeter at a time. Lex's eyes were closed tight, and his mouth was open in a silent cry. For a brief second, Imani worried he was in pain, then he started mumbling "green" over and over again.

"Shhh, baby," Imani whispered to him. "We won't stop."

He stopped repeating the word and started breathing hard. His body was coated in sweat from the strain of remaining still under the onslaught of sensation. Imani had to admit, she was feeling needy for movement herself.

Once Mac was fully inside Lex, he let out an explosive breath. "Lex, you're gripping me tight. Relax around me, love."

"No," Lex refused. "No leaving me."

Mac petted down Lex's back and Imani brought her lips to his ear. "Relax," she repeated Mac's word, then added her own. "No one's leaving you."

"Feels so good," Lex mumbled. "Don't want it to stop."

"I won't," Mac promised and continued to stroke his hand up and down Lex's back. "There, that's it, love."

Imani was about to start ordering both men around when Mac gripped Lex's hips and pushed him forward.

"Oh!" she gasped, then moaned as Lex's cock sank into her. He was a good size, and she was ready for him. His thickness rubbed against her clit as he filled her, making pleasure zing up her spine. "Oh yeah, right there."

With his dick buried in her and full of Mac's meaty shaft, Lex let loose with a loud moan. He'd screwed his eyes shut again and was holding his trembling body rigid. For a breathless moment, the three of them stayed like that. Connected in a more intimate way than Imani had ever been with anyone else.

Imani watched Mac's hands tighten on Lex's hips. She reached down and put one of her hands on his. Raising his gaze to hers, she saw Mac's eyes were as blown as Lex's, but his expression wasn't glazed or overwhelmed, it was adoring.

"You're both so perfect," Mac whispered.

"All of us are," she countered. "Now start moving or I'm going to murder you!"

Huffing out a laugh, Mac pulled himself partially out of Lex. Whimpering, Lex tried to follow, but Mac easily held him still. Once he'd mostly withdrawn his cock, Mac stopped and seemed to brace himself. Then guided Lex back with his grip on the smaller man's hips, pulling him out of Imani. With a measured pace, Mac used his grip to press Lex forward and back into Imani.

While Mac and Imani remained still, Lex was going to move with them.

"I didn't think this could get better," Imani moaned.

Mac grunted, his entire focus on guiding Lex's movements. At first, Lex was stiff and jerky, but he quickly smoothed out. It wasn't long before Mac let him increase the pace. Breathing hard, Lex thrust into Imani then pushed back to take Mac's dick like the good submissive he was.

Sweet tension built in Imani with every drag of Lex's cock over her clit. She was already sensitive from the first orgasm. This second one was looming and ready to strike. For a moment, she thought to hold back and delay to heighten the pleasure for all of them. Then she saw how desperate both Mac and Lex looked. They hadn't had a first orgasm to take the edge off; they'd been hard and needy the whole time.

She could play with making them both wait another night. Right now, it was time for them to fly.

"Follow me!" she demanded, grabbing Lex's jaw and forcing his head to the side, baring his neck and that fat, pulsing vein. She wasn't gentle when she sank her fangs in.

Magic and power flooded into her with his sweet blood. She didn't want to take too much, but the perfect taste of him made her greedy. Lex cried out, and for a second she thought he was hurt. The increase in the pace of his hips told her differently.

Her pleasure crested. Screaming into his neck, she heard him begging in a mishmash of words. Lex's movements turned desperate, and his hips snapped back and forth between her and Mac.

She could hear the panting breaths from both shifters. Then Mac roared, signaling his orgasm. Within seconds of Mac, Lex's body shuddered, and Imani felt warmth flood her channel.

Taking a last swallow of Lex's blood, Imani extracted her fangs and flopped back on her mound of pillows. Lex went limp on top of her, leaving Mac on his knees looking stunned.

"Holy fuck," Mac breathed, sitting back on his heels and running a shaking hand through his hair.

Lex's blood warmed her skin and pleasure was still ricocheting through Imani, making forming words difficult.

"Agreed," she managed to get out. Then she shut her eyes and hugged her legs around Lex before letting them flop to the bed on either side of him. Lex was already snoring.

Mac

Mac sat there and stared at his mates. They needed to be cared for, but he wasn't sure he could stand up yet. That was the most intense thing he'd ever experienced, even including some of the life and death assignments he and Lex had done together. Breathing deep, he focused on calming his heartbeat. Lex made a little sound of contentment and nestled his head on Imani's chest. She breathed out a sigh and draped an arm over his back. Neither of them opened their eyes.

Struggling off the bed to his feet, Mac had to stand for a moment while some of his blood made the long journey back up to his head. Once his vision cleared and his body felt steady, he staggered to the bathroom. After wetting down a washcloth, he returned to the bed and gently rolled Lex off Imani.

"No," Lex whimpered, his hand reaching out to make a grabby motion.

Mac touched his shoulder. "Lay there for a moment, love. Then more snuggles."

Lex quieted and relaxed, allowing Mac to wipe him down. Returning to the bathroom, he wet a second washcloth and did the same for Imani. Once both his mates were clean, he shifted them in the bed so they weren't on an uneven pile of pillows. Then he arranged them together.

Neither one woke up even a little as Mac organized their positions and limbs. Once he was done, Imani was the little spoon and Lex was the big spoon. Taking the spot behind Lex, Mac made himself the biggest spoon and laid one of his arms across both his mates.

Pulling their combined scents into his nose, Mac dropped into a contented, deep sleep.

Mac

Mac woke up hungrier than he'd ever been before. Not even the time he'd spent three unexpected days hidden in a remote jungle of Brazil living on grubs while waiting for the kidnappers to show up compared to this hunger.

Hunger had never woken him up before. His bear pushed him to eat, sending him images of big, fluffy biscuits drowned in a heavy sausage gravy, greasy hash browns slathered in tabasco sauce, and a heaping plate of crispy bacon. Oh, and waffles. His bear wanted a stack of golden waffles dripping with syrup.

His bear was fond of human food, but then again, what bear wasn't?

Stomach rumbling, he looked over to find his mates had shifted position in the night. Imani was curled up on her side facing him with Lex acting as the big spoon behind her. The sight of the two of them sleeping made him momentarily forget his hunger. They looked peaceful and gorgeous.

Imani's long braids were tucked into a lavender colored satin bonnet she'd insisted on getting out of her bag. It minimized damage to her hair during the night but even more important for them, the bonnet also kept Imani's magenta braids safe from him or Lex rolling over on them and trapping her. One of Lex's arms was wrapped around her chest, his other arm was under her head. That couldn't be a very comfortable pillow, but the soft smile on her lips told him it didn't matter.

He hadn't been left out of the cuddling. Both of her hands were wrapped around one of his hands, loosely holding onto him. When he'd rolled away in his sleep, she must have reached out to grasp him and only found his hand. The blatant affection made his heart pound a little.

He wanted to wrap his big arms around both of them and draw them tightly against his body, making Imani the meat in a shifter sandwich. If only his stomach wasn't empty and his bladder overly full. Time to take care of his body then get back to his slumbering mates.

Moving slowly to keep from waking Lex, he sat up and looked at the room's large windows. All three of them were covered in metal shutters. He vaguely remembered hearing them deploy and felt a little ashamed at being so caught up in sex that he forgot to worry about Imani and the sun.

Thankfully, the house was set up to protect a vampire or Imani might have been in real trouble when the rising sun beamed down right onto their bed. The near disaster was a good reminder to him. They were going to need to secure safe housing for Imani once they left here.

Standing up, he silently made his way to the bathroom down the hall instead of the one attached to the suite. He didn't want to wake Lex with a flushing toilet. After doing his business, he made his way downstairs.

The kitchen was massive with tons of pantry space and two refrigerators, but not a single bit of food anywhere. Not even an old can of soup or stale sleeve of crackers.

"Crap," he muttered. They'd driven Lex's truck here. Unwilling to give Imani the time to run, they'd left the vehicle hidden among some boulders and tall Oleander bushes off the main road and hiked up the hill through the trees.

Unconcerned with his nudity, Mac stepped out the front door into the midday sun. He walked past the carport and found a good vantage point to survey the property. From where he stood, parts of the winding drive down the mountain were visible, but he couldn't see the truck from here.

It wouldn't take him long to get back to the vehicle. Because they'd gotten hot and heavy on the ground floor last night, his clothes were still in a pile behind him with the truck keys in the pocket of his jeans.

He wasn't going to die of starvation, but his empty belly wasn't comfortable either. Lex would be equally famished when he woke up. The need to provide food for his chimera mate made him want to leave long enough to find a fast-food place and bring back a mountain of burgers and fries, but he didn't know this area at all. Both their phones were still in the truck so he couldn't even look at a map to see how far away the nearest source of food was.

There was an alternative. He could get something delivered. Extending his arms over his head, he stretched and thought about how much it would cost to get DoorDash or UberEats to deliver all the way out here. Even if he was going to do that, he should probably move the truck at least or it might get noticed and vandalized by bored rural teenagers. And he should retrieve his phone and send Briar a text telling her everything had worked out.

He was still stretching when strong arms wrapped around his waist and lifted him up. "Wha—?"

"No leave!" Lex growled, his voice closer to animal than human. Why was Lex's animal so close to the surface?

Mac didn't struggle, but his heartbeat kicked up. "I wasn't going anywhere, love. You can put me down."

Lex put him down, but before Mac could move, the chimera swung him around and put a hard shoulder in Mac's belly.

"Oof!" The air rushed out of Mac as he folded over Lex's shoulder. Standing up with Mac's long body draped over shoulder, Lex easily strode back into the house, kicking the door closed with his heel.

Torn between amusement and alarm, Mac tried to reason with Lex. "Easy, Lex. I'm not leaving you. I'll never leave you. But maybe I should go grab the truck."

Lex didn't stop his progress up the stairs. "Imani's asleep."

"I know, love. She's a young vampire. She's got to sleep during the day. It's not her fault, she can't fight it," Mac reminded him.

A huff of impatience came out of Lex. "Guard."

"Oh, sure," Mac agreed as Lex crested the stairs. "You need to guard her. Of course. But I could still go—"

"Guard both of you!" Lex growled.

That made Mac laugh even though it caused his belly to hurt where it was resting on Lex's shoulder. "Right. You need to guard us both. I got you. But I'm not in danger, I promise."

"Guard," Lex repeated, his voice more a chimera growl than human. Mac was alarmed for a moment. Was Lex going feral? That wasn't supposed to happen to chimeras.

"I know you feel like you need to protect us," Mac started, hoping to find a way to reason with this version of Lex.

"Bad bear, no leave," Lex muttered.

When he finally set Mac down, they were standing next to the bed.

"In," Lex ordered, pointing to the bed. His expression was fierce, and his eyes were glowing gold.

"If I'm quick, can I go get the truck?" Mac hedged. "I need my phone to order food. Aren't you hungry, love?"

"No," Lex answered, his body tensing up as if ready to wrestle and subdue Mac. Gone was the submissive Lex from earlier. This was a version of the man barely in control of his animal, and chimeras weren't known for obeying orders.

Mac knew Lex would never hurt him, but he also didn't want to cause the chimera any unnecessary stress. Giving up on getting to eat anytime soon, Mac flopped onto the bed. He couldn't wake Imani up if he tried, so it didn't matter if he wasn't careful.

"Good mate," Lex praised with a smile. He got into the bed, pushing Mac to scoot closer to Imani. Once he was spooning the beautiful vampire, Lex snuggled up against Mac's back. Throwing an arm over Mac's waist, Lex put his face against Mac's skin. The smaller man felt unnaturally warm, worrying Mac until he remembered something important about chimera shifters.

"Lex, are you in rut?" Mac asked.

"Love," he insisted without answering Mac's question.

Mac stifled a chuckle. "Are you in rut, love?" he amended.

This time Lex answered. "Soon."

"Shit," Mac muttered. When chimeras found their mate, they'd go into rut. It usually lasted a few days, but from what Mac had heard, those few days were a wild ride. There was no way they were going to last without food.

The minute Imani woke up, she could distract Lex, allowing Mac to make a break for the truck. Once he had their phones, he could at least get food delivered.

Except Lex might attack the humans trying to deliver the food. Maybe begging Memphis or Briar to drop food by would be a better option.

At least they wouldn't need blood for Imani. He and Lex could feed her all she wanted. In fact, he looked forward to it. The thought of feeding her made his cock plump. Ignoring that along with his growling stomach, he relaxed his body and let his mind drift.

It was going to be a long day, hopefully he'd be able to sleep through most of it.

Lex

Lex couldn't sleep. He should be exhausted, but he felt keyed up and twitchy, probably due to the onset of his rut. The beast he shared his body with was tense and… joyful?

Focusing inward, Lex found his inner chimera ecstatic. They'd been lonely for so long that finding one mate would have been cause for celebration, but now having two was a windfall they never expected.

Smiling, Lex listened to Mac snoring softly next to him. He probably shouldn't have been so forceful with his bigger mate but waking up to find Mac gone had sent Lex into a panic. Only getting him back into the room with Imani made him feel better and settled his beast. He couldn't understand why Mac had been so set on leaving the house. They had everything they needed here. Shelter from the sun for Imani, a nice soft bed, and…

Lex's feeling of contentment vanished with one thought—food.

Mac had tried to tell him, but Lex was distracted by his animal's instincts. What was he going to do? He needed to provide for both his mates. Imani would be easy, but Mac would need more. He's eaten plenty of meals with the sloth bear and knew he had an appetite to rival anyone else Lex had ever met. His large mate was going to need plenty of sustenance to remain content. How could he provide it?

Hunt.

His beast had the right idea. He'd scented deer last night when he and Mac hiked up the hill. In his chimera form, he could easily track and take down a deer and bring back the entire carcass for his bear. The thought excited him. He could provide for both his mates; blood for one and meat for the other.

There was one problem; he'd have to leave the house to hunt. Could he risk leaving his two mates without his protection? It's true Mac was big and strong but still not as deadly as he was. Very few could match a chimera shifter, especially not one as well trained as Lex.

He wished they had some guns. He'd feel better if he could leave Mac with a few weapons while he went out hunting. How quickly could he track, kill, and bring back a deer? How long could he leave his mates alone and vulnerable without a single weapon?

Doing a quick circle of the house to judge how far away a deer might be would give him a better estimate. If they were too far, he'd figure something else out.

Decision made, he eased out of the bed with his normal stealthy grace, then hurried down the stairs. His focus was so intense that he jumped and growled when a cell phone on the floor started buzzing. Looking down, he saw Briar's name on the screen.,

Briar, Memphis's mate. A female. A friend of his mates and an ally.

Picking up the phone he clumsily swiped to answer it with his big fingers. Fuck, he hated phones at the best of time.

With his rut imminent, it was twice as hard. It took him two times to successfully answer the phone.

"Imani?" Briar's voice asked, her tone worried. "You okay?"

"Asleep," Lex grumbled.

"Lex?" Briar sounded a little more confident.

"Me, yes," Lex answered. "Daylight. Mates asleep."

He wasn't the most gifted with words to begin with, but right now he might as well be the poster boy for caveman speak.

"Does that mean you're all doing good?" Briar asked. "No one got their throat ripped out or anything?"

Incensed at Briar's implication, Lex growled.

"Sorry! I didn't mean anything by that," Briar rushed to assure him, then her voice became distant. "Hey, no I've got this," she argued with someone else.

"Don't growl at her, you meathead," Memphis shouted into his ear. He must've taken the phone from Briar. Lex's answer was to growl at Memphis. He didn't have time for this nonsense.

"Need things," Lex demanded. "Lots of foods."

"Why do you sound like an idiot?" Memphis asked, his tone confused. "You're talking like someone—"

Lex didn't have time for this. Giving up, he interrupted Memphis. "Going to hunt. Fuck off." Before he could drop the phone back on the ground, Memphis got his attention.

"Oh shit, no, don't hang up!" Memphis shouted quickly. "Rut! You've gone into rut. Why didn't I think of that sooner?"

"Stupid," Lex answered easily.

"Love you too, asshole," Memphis shot back. "Sit tight. I'm going to get a shit ton of food and blood up there. Don't leave the house until you've got control of your beast."

"Going to hunt," Lex repeated.

"If you want to, sure," Memphis agreed. "But wouldn't you rather stay with your mates instead of chasing down a cow?"

"Deer," Lex corrected.

"Or a deer," Memphis agreed, his tone softening. "I'll bring you a bunch of stuff instead. You're not alone, brother. I'll take care of you so you can guard your mates."

That sounded good to Lex. They might not always get along, but he trusted his brother implicitly. "Yes."

Memphis blew out a loud breath. "Great. Try to keep your beast reined in, yeah? No need to go scaring some random, clueless humans."

"Ask him if Imani is pissed at me." Lex heard Briar's request in the background.

"She's asleep, Babydoll," Memphis answered before Lex had to say anything. "She'll be dead to the world till the sun goes down."

"Shit, right, I forgot. Well, tell Lex that there's a year's supply of beer in it for him if he can convince her to forgive me," Briar pushed.

"Do you comprehend how much Lex drinks?" Memphis asked with a laugh.

Lex couldn't understand why Imani would be angry with Briar, but it wasn't something he was going to get involved in. His mate could decide who she wanted to like or dislike without his input. All he needed was to know who she wanted him to rip apart.

"Done, bye," he said loudly before hanging up the phone on the sound of Memphis's protests.

With the phone still in his hand, he made his way back upstairs. Setting it on the nightstand with a soft click, he slid back into bed with his mates. Later, when he could leave them in a more secure location, he'd bring Mac a nice, tasty deer, moose, or elk. He'd hunt down anything his mate wanted. It filled him with all kinds of satisfaction to picture Mac's sloth bear ripping into a freshly killed meal, meat still warm and bloody.

The thought made him smile as he drifted off to sleep.

Imani

Imani was dead to the world, trapped in the dreamless sleep caused by daylight. With the sunset came awareness, but not all at once. Every evening for the last few years, she'd woken slowly by stages. For the first few minutes, she wouldn't be able to move or even open her eyes. She could only listen to the world around her. Then her limbs would come alive, and she'd be able to walk, but there weren't any fine motor skills. It was only after the last light of the sun was entirely gone that she regained full control of her body.

This night was slightly different as her ears woke up to an explosion of sounds.

Roaring. Crashing. Breaking glass. The sounds of fighting slightly muffled by distance.

Trapped in a body that wouldn't move, all she could do was strain her vampire hearing, trying to figure out what was going on. It sounded like a war was happening!

"What the fuck?" a voice next to her cried out in confusion. A man's voice—Mac. Memories flooded back to her. Right, she'd fallen asleep with Mac and Lex, two shifters that had fed her and then given her the best sex of her life.

No one answered Mac's cry, and she felt the bed move as he got up. Magic washed over her skin; he'd shifted into his bear form. Large, clawed paws thumped and clicked across the wood floor; then she heard him thunder down the stairs.

"Lex!" The single shouted word came from outside. Everyone but her was outside now.

Another roar sounded. It was like nothing she'd heard before, vibrating through her very bones. Something big and scary was out there and she was lying here, helpless. She needed her body to finish waking the fuck up!

She focused on moving her eyelids. *Open, damn it!* she ordered them but was rewarded with only a twitch.

The roaring had gotten quieter, but only because the sounds of fighting were louder. She heard Mac shouting but couldn't make out the words past the fear raging through her. It was incomprehensible, but in one simple day, these two men had become infinitely important to her. She needed to get up, not so she could run away from the danger but to jump into the middle of it. There was a battle going on and they needed her!

Finally, her eyes popped open. A second later she was able to sit up. Usually, she was a little shaky and sluggish when she first rose from her daytime sleep. Not this time. With shocking agility, she rose from the bed in one fluid motion.

Standing in the middle of the room, she gazed at a giant hole that had once been a window. It wasn't only the glass that was missing, but the frame and a good portion of the wall had all been destroyed.

Turning her back on the ruined wall, she rushed downstairs. She paused long enough to pull out a massive shirt from the pile of clothes on the floor at the bottom of the stairs. Tugging it on over her head, she wasn't surprised to find it fell all the way to her knees. Both her flock were big boys and made her feel petite despite her five-foot ten-inch frame.

Ignoring her bare feet, she wrenched open the heavy front door and rushed outside. Following the sounds of violence, she sprinted around the house. With a gasp, she came to a stumbling halt once she had a clear view of what was going on.

There were three shifters fighting in their animal forms. One was easily recognizable as some kind of bear, but the other two were creatures she'd never seen before. Both the unfamiliar shifters had lion's heads and manes with spikes protruding from humps of muscles on their backs. They also had identical long, scaled, and segmented, armored tails with a stinger on the end. But that's where the resemblance stopped.

The one closer to her was shorter, with a more lion-like body and a reddish coat with a shaggy mane that extended down his chest and under his belly. The other one had a body more like a moose, with long legs, hooves, and a big barrel body. These had to be chimera shifters. One had to be Lex and the bear must be Mac. Now she had to figure out what chimera was Lex.

As she watched, the bigger monster kicked out a leg, sending the bear shifter tumbling. Oh, hell no! She wasn't letting either of her men fight this tall fucker without her help.

"You messed with the wrong vampire!" she yelled. A strong show of bravado had helped her in the past when faced with creatures more powerful than her. If she wasn't going to run, then her first weapon was intimidation.

All three of the shifters stopped fighting and backed away from each other. As she marched up, the bear rushed to her and put his big furry body between her and the other two. Stepping up next to him, she placed a hand on his side, comforting them both. He let out a little huff but didn't take his eyes off the monster. She could feel his chest heaving under her hand and could smell blood coming from him. He'd gotten hurt.

Possessiveness flowed through her. Mac belonged to her. His blood. His body. His everything was hers!

"These two are mine!" she announced, not only to the enemy chimera but to the world. The words felt right, and something she'd been missing fit into place. "Leave before I kill you for touching them."

Lex growled at the bigger chimera even as he slunk backwards to stand on her other side. Unlike the bear, she didn't smell any blood on him. She still wanted to attack the giant beast for daring to hurt her flock but restrained herself. The three of them weren't guaranteed a win, and she wasn't risking either of them on an uncertain outcome.

"What the fuck is going on?" a female voice from behind Imani called out, making her and the two shifters turn. Briar was walking around the house holding several grocery bags in each hand. "I know I was supposed to wait, but I got bored and—"

She didn't get a chance to finish that statement. The bigger chimera let out an ear-splitting roar and vaulted over Imani and her mates, landing halfway between them and Briar.

Startled, Briar dropped the bag she was holding and flinched back. "Woah, why is everyone wearing their fur? Are we under attack?"

"Run!" Imani called out, afraid for her friend. Briar was human and probably didn't understand how much danger she was in. "We'll hold him off."

"Run?" Briar repeated, confused. "Why would I run from Memphis?"

Now it was Imani's turn to be startled. "Memphis?"

Briar nodded her head and pointed at the shifter facing off with Imani, Lex, and Mac. "Yeah, that's Memphis. Why the hell is everyone so riled up?"

As she spoke, Memphis was snarling, snapping his tail in the air, and stomping at the ground as if trying to drive them away from Briar, but he wasn't attacking.

A massive hawk appeared out of the sky. Swooping down in front of Memphis, the hawk shifted into the form of a very pissed Tobias. Because he was a vampire instead of a true shifter, he remained fully clothed when he shifted, making his appearance immaculate despite his method of travel. His hair wasn't even mussed.

Imani could only hope to be that powerful someday.

"Get away from my flock!" Tobias snarled.

Blinking at the strange turn this evening took, Imani held up her hands palms out. Next to her, Lex growled low in his throat and tensed. She moved a hand to rest on his back, trying to soothe him and keep him at her side.

"We were here first," she said, working on keeping her territorial impulses from overwhelming her. More than with Memphis, she wanted to attack Tobias. Having another vampire so close to Lex and Mac was redlining her protective instincts. "Your flock decided to invade our territory."

"We aren't invading anything," Briar called out, stepping around Memphis's massive, shifted form. The big beast moved sideways to keep her from passing him. With a sigh of annoyance, Briar stopped trying and talked loudly around

Memphis's bulk. "We were delivering supplies. Memphis said Lex is in rut, so he's gonna need plenty of food."

"Rut?" Imani murmured. She'd never heard of that before.

"Chimera shifters go into rut when they find their mate," Tobias explained coldly as he stepped back to stand next to Memphis. He hissed in anger when he saw blood on the shifter's shoulder. "Which one of you did this?"

Memphis swung his big head over to nuzzle Tobias's hand. Taking advantage of the distraction, Briar moved to stand at Tobias's other side.

"Let's all take a breather," Briar suggested, peering around Tobias to get a look at Memphis. "Remember what Memphis was like when we first got together? Lex is having the same issues."

"Perhaps," Tobias answered. "But it doesn't excuse them from attacking my flock."

"No really, it's our bad," Briar insisted. "We shouldn't have even stopped, just kept driving and tossed the food at the front door on our way out."

The image of Briar leaning out the window of a moving car while hurling bags of groceries at the front door of the fancy house made a grin curl Imani's lips. It was something she could see the woman doing while cackling with joy at the same time.

Without warning, Tobias was in front of her, grabbing her by the neck. His age gave him vampire speed, making it seem as if he was teleporting from one place to another.

Momentum moved them until her back hit the house, knocking the breath out of her. Reflexively, she grabbed his arm, but there was no chance she could pull him off her. He might not be as powerful as Vincent, but he wasn't far off.

"You think threatening my flock is amusing?" he hissed, his fangs lowered and his eyes blood red.

A violent fight behind him broke out, but she couldn't look past those glowing red eyes. His humanity had bled away; he wanted to kill her.

Still in his fur, Mac wrapped his mouth around Tobias's arm and bit down. Without hesitation, the vampire let go of her throat to throw the shifter off, ripping both his sleeve and the flesh underneath. The bear went tumbling but was quick to get back to his feet and charge.

The need to protect Mac pushed Imani to move. Before Mac could reach Tobias, she tackled him, sending them both to the ground. Grabbing a handful of his hair, she wrenched his head back, intending to sink her fangs in and rip his throat out.

She didn't get a chance. The older vampire flipped them over so he was kneeling on her belly with his hand back on her throat. He held her down with ease as he kept his focus on the oncoming bear. His body was tense, and she could tell he was ready to rip the oncoming shifter to shreds.

Before the bear could reach them, a jet of cold water hit Tobias. Sputtering, he let go of Imani. He held up both hands in an attempt to block the water. With his hand off her throat, she could grab Tobias and toss him off her. He landed on his feet several yards away, hair plastered to his skull and dripping water.

Scrambling to her feet, Imani saw the bear had stopped in his tracks and was staring at something to her left. Looking over, she found Briar with a hose spraying the two chimera who were still battling.

"I think we all need to cool off and calm the fuck down!" she shouted with a grin that could only be labeled as evil.

Briar's aim was excellent. She managed to hit both shifters full in the face with her jet of water, one right after the other. Gasping and making sounds like a cat being baptized, the shifters broke apart. The taller one did a full body shake to get the water out of his eyes. The smaller one crouched to attack but was hit by another barrage of water.

"Don't even think about it, Lex," Briar shouted, following his retreating form with the water. She didn't stop until he backed far away.

Movement made Imani look over to see Tobias striding toward her. She braced for his attack, but Briar was quick with her hose. She turned the stream on him before he got his hands on Imani.

"Damn it, Tobias. Stop! Imani's a friend, and this is all just a big misunderstanding. I thought humans could be illogical, but you guys turn into nothing but instinct and attack everything. You can speak like six languages. Try using one of them first!"

With vampire speed, Tobias appeared next to Briar and gently plucked the hose from her grip. She didn't fight over her improvised but effective weapon. Flicking back her chin-length turquoise hair with a sweep of her hand, she glared up at him.

"Are we done?" She sounded like a mother talking to a toddler having a tantrum.

"Almost," he agreed. Without looking away from her, Tobias aimed and fired the water at Lex who was creeping back over to Memphis.

Lex let out an indigent yowl and jumped back. If Imani wasn't so keyed up, she might have laughed. Mac ambled forward and nudged Lex. Giving up on attacking Memphis, Lex let Mac guide him back to Imani's side.

With Mac and Lex standing next to her and the others at least thirty feet away, she could relax a little. Mac had a few wounds, but there wasn't much blood darkening his black fur, and Lex didn't seem to have a single scratch.

The other trio was now huddled together, and Briar was talking in low tones with animated arm movements. Tobias's expression was neutral but Memphis, still in his shifted form, was hanging his head like a chastised dog.

While they talked, Imani looked over at Lex, marveling at his animal body. "Damn, boy, your shifted form is pure menace."

Lex met her eyes and tilted his head with a little whine, as if he was unsure if her words were a good or bad thing. Leaning close, she sank her fingers into his wet mane.

"We're good, Lexie," she murmured. "I get you. This world is a tough place; better to strike first."

With a huff, Lex ducked his head and bumped his broad lion face into her chest. There was a soft huff behind her and then a bear's face was poking over her shoulder. Reaching up, she wrapped a free arm around the bear's head and turned to give him a peck on the side of his snout.

"We're good too," she assured Mac.

The sound of a throat clearing pulled Imani's attention off her shifters and over to Briar. The woman was standing in front of Tobias and Memphis with a hopeful expression on her face.

"Right, so, everyone apologizes for getting into a fight," she said, gesturing with her thumb behind her. "We should've known better than to do anything that might set Lex off, especially Memphis."

She rolled her eyes back at him. The chimera looked away, avoiding her gaze.

"We're going to leave now," Briar continued. "We'll have everything you guys need delivered to the gate down at the bottom of the hill. You've got my number, so call or text if there's anything I forgot to order for you. Stay here as long as you need, even after Lex's rut is over. He doesn't have a place down here, and I don't know if Mac's place is big enough for the three of you. Tobias doesn't use this house anyway. Hell, he'd forgotten he owned it until I was asking him for a place you could stay."

Imani shifted her eyes to Tobias to gauge his reaction to Briar's offer. The older vampire met her gaze unflinchingly. "It's true. I have no use for this property. It's one of many I own. If it makes Briar happy, you can have it."

Implied in those words was the threat that if they did anything to make Briar unhappy, Tobias would have no mercy. Imani nodded her head to let Tobias know she understood everything he was telling her.

"Good job," Briar praised, her tone only halfway sarcastic. "You almost didn't sound murdery." She tugged at his wet sleeve. "Time to go. Want to ride with us or fly home?"

"Ride," he answered succinctly as he let Briar pull him around the house to the main drive.

Imani and her mates remained where they were as Briar led Tobias and a still shifted Memphis away. There was the slight feel of magic on the night breeze, then Memphis's human voice was loud with indignation.

"No!" he wailed. "Fucking Lex made me shift through my vest. We just got this one last week."

"With the number of times you've destroyed your vests, we might be single-handedly keeping Frank in business," Briar declared, humor in her voice.

"I already have one waiting. I ordered two the last time," Tobias said, voice full of loving amusement.

"Come on, big man. I've been stashing spare clothes for you in all the vehicles," Briar urged, their voices faded to indistinguishable noise after that. None of them moved, not even when a vehicle started up and drove away. It wasn't until they heard the faint sound of the gate opening and closing at the bottom of the hill did Imani relax. Leaning heavily against Lex, she realized how badly she was depleted.

"I need to sit," she mumbled as the world tilted around her. "And I'm gonna need some blood."

Mac

With fast, seamless magic Mac could never match, Lex shifted from his animal form to human and grabbed Imani before she could slide to the ground. As Mac pulled his bear back into his body, Lex cradled Imani to his naked chest.

"What's wrong?" he asked, looking up at Mac with real fear in his expression. This was the first time Mac had ever seen this kind of fear on Lex's face. Anger, concern, calculation, discomfort, or glee were common expressions, but never fear.

"I think she needs blood," Mac answered. "She hasn't drunk from us yet tonight and she had to expend a lot earlier."

"Fuck," Lex muttered and looked over to Mac. "House," he ordered and wouldn't move until Mac started walking. Forget that Mac was bigger than Lex in their human forms, or that they'd first met while working as mercenaries. Lex was unsettled and in full protector mode. He saw Mac as his mate, not a capable fighter. Mac wasn't insulted. It was a chimera thing.

"Why don't you sit on the couch?" Mac urged, holding the front door open. He didn't want to go back up into their room. Lex had destroyed the wall by jumping out the window in his shifted form and Mac had done more damage following.

After Imani felt better, he'd scout out another room and move furniture around if he had to so they could keep the big bed. For now, the couch would work.

To the left of the front door was a large seating area with an L shaped couch and several matching ottomans. Lex eased down on the couch only after Mac had shut and locked the door.

Cradling Imani on his lap, he looked up at Mac. "Need knife."

"Knife?" Mac asked as he joined Lex on the couch, leaning over so he could get a better look at Imani's face.

"She needs blood, but she can't bite. I'll cut and drip blood into mouth," Lex explained. It was obvious he was struggling to use words.

"Right, I'll grab one," Mac agreed, rushing off to the kitchen. When he returned, he didn't pass the knife to Lex's open hand. Taking a seat on the couch at Imani's head, he sliced his wrist and eased it between her lips.

"Fine," Lex grumped. "Me next."

Imani made a soft moan and sealed her lips around the small cut and sucked. It hurt, but the slight pain paled in comparison to the deep satisfaction he felt. Draping his free arm over her, he placed a palm on Lex's shoulder. The moment he made contact a soft wave of magic washed over him, making his head loll back. By the way Lex sucked in a breath and Imani jerked, they must have felt it too.

A sense of euphoria filled him, plumping his dick with blood and making his skin feel hot. Was this what it was like for other triads? How did they ever separate for any amount of time?

Then another wave hit, and this time Mac could tell it had originated from Lex. What they're feeling had to be a side effect of the chimera's rut. His beast was supercharged and looking for release in any way possible, if not sex, then sharing magic energy.

The magic made Mac's body melt into the couch. Imani let go of his wrist and rolled onto her back, mouth open and breathing deeply.

"I've never felt so good," she murmured, eyes closed, and body relaxed into Mac's and Lex's laps.

"Same," Mac agreed.

"Yeah," Lex grunted.

The three of them lay like that for several minutes, floating in the magic, until Mac's stomach let out an obnoxiously loud rumble. There was a beat of silence before both Imani and Lex started laughing.

Chagrined, Mac felt his face getting hot. "I think I'm a little hungry." As embarrassed as he was by his body's demands for food, he was also pleased at the sound of his mates' laughter.

Imani ran her hand up his chest and then cupped his cheek, drawing his attention down to her. "I don't think there's any food in the house, but I'll run out and get you something. What do you like?"

"Memphis and Briar brought us food," he reminded her, warmed by her care.

"Another vampire and his flock brought you food," she murmured with a frown. "It's my job to care for you. I haven't done anything right. All I do is take from you. It's not right. You should have a stronger vampire."

"No!" Lex growled loudly enough that his deep voice echoed in the large room. He was clutching her legs now and glaring.

"What the hell?" Imani asked, looking at him with concern and wariness. Mac worked on keeping his expression calm and easy.

"We won't leave you, Lex," he assured the chimera. Without breaking eye contact with Lex, he spoke to Imani. "Remember, Lex is in rut. It's going to be hard for him to be separated from us. That's why he jumped out the window and attacked his brother, even though deep down he knows Memphis would never hurt us. He isn't thinking clearly right now."

"Right," Imani said, drawing out the word. "Saying he jumped through the window is a bit of an understatement, isn't it? He took out a chimera-sized chunk of wall, like one of those old cartoons."

"And that illustrates my point," Mac agreed. "He's not usually so impulsive. The Lex I've worked with in the past is cool and calculated. It's the rut making him act weird. He'll calm down after a few days."

"Could he be a danger to himself?" Imani asked, looking worried. "Should I try to command him? My ability to hold people in thrall barely works on humans; it probably won't do anything to Lex or you."

"I can hear," Lex pointed out, looking annoyed. "I'm right here."

"Could've fooled me," Imani muttered, making Mac laugh and Lex's scowl lighten slightly.

"I'm chimera," Lex declared, his eyes the color of molten gold. "I protect vampire and little bear."

Mac snorted out a laugh. "Whatever." Lex looked like he was about to argue, but Mac kept talking. "Love, I was hungry earlier, but now I'm starving. If I don't eat soon, I'm going to shift and start digging up grubs."

"Grubs?" Imani questioned with a wrinkled nose.

"Don't knock 'em until you've tried them," Mac answered with a smirk. "They're juicy and pop when you bite down. So tasty!" Imani's disgusted expression made him laugh and Lex chuckle. "We have to appease our animal half too. At least I don't go hunting deer like Lex."

Waving a hand in the air, Imani stood up. "Sure, fine, eat grubs or hunt down Bambi, but later. There's perfectly good food probably going bad outside. Let's get that and feed you guys right now."

Mac stood also. "And I should rundown to the main road and get Lex's truck."

"No!" Lex was up and standing between her and the door in flash. To Mac's relief, she didn't look worried or threatened by Lex's overbearing behavior, only frustrated.

"Lex, baby, we need to feed Mac," Imani reminded him gently as she pulled the last of her long braids out from under the shirt she was wearing.

He recognized the shirt as the one he'd been wearing yesterday. She looked damn sexy wearing his oversized shirt. The hem went all the way down to her knees and the neck of the garment slipped over one shoulder. The sight made him want to give her more of his items to wear. How adorably sexy would she look in one of his hoodies? She'd swim in it and be surrounded by his smell. That made it even better, like marking her with his scent. Was it weird that he wanted her to wear something of his all the time?

Was this a new fetish?

"You two stay. I'll be quick," Lex insisted, snapping Mac out of his thoughts and back to the situation at hand. Before he or Imani could say anything, Lex grabbed a giant wood and glass display case full of china and carried it to the front. The sound of crashing and breaking ceramics filled the room as he slammed it down, effectively blocking the front door.

"This isn't our house," Mac reminded him with a wince.

"Damn, now I'm gonna owe Briar another favor," Imani muttered before speaking up. "Lex, it's going to take me years to pay for the hole in the wall upstairs. How about we keep the damage to a minimum from now on?"

When Lex looked over at him and Imani, his chimera's eyes were glowing brightly. The beast was riding him hard, and Mac knew better than pushing him any further. He wouldn't hurt them, but he could make their life uncomfortable while Lex's beast sought to "protect" them.

"Don't leave!" he repeated, then turned and stacked more heavy furniture in front of the door.

Once Lex decided the door was blocked well enough, he turned and rushed at them. Mac wasn't surprised when he felt Lex's arms wrap around both him and Imani. Without much effort, he picked them up. Neither of them bothered to struggle.

Imani sighed. "Lex, what do you think you're doing?"

"He's going to make us safe," Mac grunted as Lex carried the two of them upstairs. Bypassing the room with the destroyed wall, he carried them into a smaller room with a queen-sized bed. Setting them both on their feet, he backed up and gave them a stern look.

"I do things. You stay," he ordered before striding out the door then slamming it shut. Mac could clearly hear the sounds of more heavy furniture moving and delicate things breaking. Lex was barricading them in the room.

Imani leaned against him with a tired sigh that was half chuckle. "So much for not breaking more stuff."

Mac slung an arm around Imani and hugged her to his side. "I wouldn't worry about it. Tobias is loaded. But if it really bothers you, I'm pretty handy. Lex and I should be able to do most of the repairs on the wall, and then we only need to worry about replacing broken furniture and knickknacks."

"Some of those knickknacks probably cost more than my bike," Imani commented.

"I saw your bike. I doubt it would even cover the light bill here," Mac teased.

She smacked him playfully in the ribs. "Why you all got to be picking on my bike like that? I dare you to keep up with me when we're on a tight and twisty." Before he could respond, she pointed to the room's closed door. "Wait, how the hell does he think he's getting out of the house if he barricaded all the doors downstairs?"

"Shifter," Mac reminded her. She didn't resist when he led her over to the only window in the room. "I think he's going to take the same exit he created earlier."

Looking out, they could see a bit of the back area where Lex had attacked first and never asked questions. The sound of things being moved around inside the house eventually stopped and soon after, Mac and Imani watched Lex jump from the second floor to the ground. He was still in his human skin and naked.

"That boy's gonna cause an accident," Imani commented. "Or get arrested."

"No one will see him," Mac assured her.

"You don't think anyone's going to notice a big, muscled, naked, white dude running around?" Imani challenged. "I know it's dark out, but it's not that late. Plenty of people are probably still driving around down there."

Turning her away from the window, Mac led her to the bed. "Don't worry about it, love. If Lex doesn't want to be seen, then he becomes damn near invisible. It's almost like the guy can make shadows appear in broad daylight and disappear into them. I don't know if it's a chimera thing or a Lex thing, but I've never known anyone as good as Lex at going unseen."

"Tell me about you and him," she demanded as he sat on the bed, his back against the headboard. When he tugged, she followed and settled between his legs, propped up against his chest. "I feel like I've known both of you forever, but also as if we've only just met. It's weird."

"It's the vampire instinct," Mac explained. "You can sense that we are your flock, making it feel like we've always been and will always be yours."

"Yeah, something like that," she agreed. "But I still want to know about you guys. All the standard stuff and all the secret stuff you don't tell anyone. I want to know it all."

"Only if you'll do the same," he countered.

"There isn't much to tell," she demurred. "Two years ago, I was human and did human things. Then Vincent turned me, and my life has been about surviving and not much else."

He didn't like that answer. "Your days of only 'surviving' are over. And don't think I didn't notice how you phrased that. The fact that you were once human doesn't make you less-than any of us. Tell me about what you were doing before you were turned. I want to know all about your human life."

"I wasn't hanging out with shifters, vampires, fae, or pixies," she answered with a half laugh.

"That you know of," he was quick to point out.

She nodded her head, rubbing her cheek against his chest. "No, you're right. I was probably bumping hips with some of your kind on the dance floor and never even knew. That would explain why some of the people I've danced with never seemed to get tired."

Mac latched onto the wistful note in her voice. "You like dancing?"

"Not liked, I loved dancing." The longing in her voice broke his heart. "The best places were crowded, loud, and frantic. I'd go out every Friday night, dance till two or three in the morning, then sleep all day Saturday."

The thought of Imani surrounded by a crowd of predatory males, human or preternatural, made Mac's blood pressure rise. "You'd do this by yourself?"

"Almost never."

Imani's answer didn't make him feel better. "Did you have a boyfriend or lover you'd go with?" A horrible thought occurred to him. "Did you have a husband?"

"None of the above, so you can calm down all that tension I feel. Going out was for me and dragging a guy along would mean I'd have to take care of him. That was too much effort. I had a small group of friends, and we'd all go out together to watch each other's backs. You know, make sure no one got drugged or if they drank too much, we made sure they got home. Except there's not much even the most dedicated girl-gang can do when up against a vampire using thrall."

Mac hugged her tight. "I can't change the past, but I promise you now; we'll go out dancing and you'll have as much fun as you used to. Your life is changed, but far from over."

Imani

Waking up surrounded by large, muscled, snoring males had become a common experience for Imani over the last five days. A glance up showed the shutters were still in place, telling her it was daylight outside.

Wait, it was daylight, and she was fully awake? This was something new and a welcome change. She didn't even feel lethargic or forced to wake in stages!

With the guys still fast asleep, she tried to figure out why she'd woken up. Not that she was going to look at her new ability to wake and move before the sunset as troublesome, but it did raise questions. Could it be due to Lex and Mac keeping her so well fed?

Not only was she sated on a regular basis, but she was consuming powerful blood. Every time she drank from them, magic rushed through her body. Each day she felt a little stronger, faster, or more in touch with her vampire side. Although she'd never condone it, now she understood why some vampires preyed on shifters; their blood was amazing!

She tried to feel guilty, except the boys loved it. When she didn't bite them during sex, they'd complain. If she bit one, the other would be there, waiting for his turn. It was as if she was giving them blow jobs instead of sliding her fangs into them.

Although, judging by the moaning, shuddering, and begging they did while she fed, that analogy might not be far off.

Being awake was nice, but there was no point in getting up until the sun had set. Besides, there was always time for snuggles. Wiggling in Lex's grip, she tried to roll over and put her back to Mac. Lex grumbled in his sleep and tightened his hold on her. It was a familiar scenario, and she knew exactly how to fix it.

Looking over her shoulder, she spoke gently. "Baby, I'm not getting up, but I want to roll over. Let go so I can move, and I'll cuddle up nice and close, 'K?"

The chimera's eyes fluttered open, his expression sleepy and unfocused. Unlike the last few days, his eyes were no longer a glowing, molten gold. They were a beautiful amber, his normal eye color while in his human skin. It could only mean one thing: Lex's rut was over.

The moment their gaze met, something powerful rose up in Imani. A magic she'd never experienced before blossomed inside her. It crackled across her skin, snapping and popping loud enough to rouse Mac. She was vaguely aware of the bear shifter sitting up, but she didn't spare him a glance. Her entire focus was on the chimera.

Lex's eyes widened. "Imani?"

Brushing off Lex's loosened hold, Imani sat up. Her vampire instincts pushed hard, making it impossible to speak. Lex sat up facing her, his expression worried. Some part of her told her she should comfort him, that she was acting strangely. That part was a small, quiet voice and easily ignored by the vampire instinct roaring inside her.

Taking hold of the back of Lex's head, she drew him forward until they were almost touching. Looking into his worried gaze, she reached deep inside herself and ripped something loose. Power created a bright bubble around them, lighting up the room in jeweled purple and blue as she shoved what she'd torn from herself into Lex.

His mouth dropped open, and he sucked in air. "What've you done?" he wheezed out. "I've never felt like this."

Gritting her eyes against the intense pain, Imani panted and let go of Lex.

"What's going on?" Mac asked from behind her.

"I don't know," Lex answered, rubbing his chest. She knew she hadn't hurt him; not like she was hurting herself. Her vampire instincts wanted her to pull a piece of him and draw it into her, but she ignored it. What she'd done to herself hurt, and she wouldn't expose either of her shifters to that pain.

For as long as she lived, they would never suffer if she could help it. They were her flock. They belonged to her, fully and completely. Forever tied to her with pieces of her soul housed inside them.

Yes, that's what was going on, she was giving him part of her soul. It would allow them to live the same unnaturally long lifespan as her. The agony of ripping sections of her soul apart was small compared to the bone deep satisfaction that they would have an added defense against death.

"Imani, love, talk to us," Mac begged, petting her back. Sparks of magic crackled under his touch, sending fissures of power down her spine. "Shit, I've never seen anyone bleeding magic like this."

"I can feel her," Lex said, sounding a little shaky. "She's inside me. Like a presence in the back of my mind. It must be a flock thing, right?"

"Could be," Mac answered as she turned around to face him. She gripped him as she'd done to Lex and held him close, staring deeply into his concerned eyes.

Lex scooted around her until he was sitting next to both of them. "I think she's about to do the same thing to you."

Mac looked eager but worried. "Don't hurt yourself, love."

She was in absolute torment, but all the pain was worth it. Enduring this anguish gave her a strange sense of pride along with the gratification of providing her flock with something no one else could ever give them: herself.

Holding Mac steady, she ripped another piece from her soul and wrapped it in heavy magic. She could feel her strength flagging, making her panic a little and shove it hard into Mac. The big shifter's head went back, and his spine bowed, his mouth opened in a silent scream.

She let go of his head and watched closely. She could tell she'd caused him discomfort but hoped it wasn't too bad.

Nothing like the misery currently eating her from the inside out. Dropping her head down and blinking hard, she fought the part of her that was still pushing to take from her flock instead of only give.

"Mac?" Lex shouted, panic clear in his voice. "Mac, talk to me."

Panting, Mac slumped down. "I'm fine, I think. Fuck, what a rush. It felt like I was hit by a massive dose of adrenaline and electricity at the same time."

"I don't think she was as gentle with you as with me," Lex commented.

She wanted to explain, but she still couldn't talk. There was a roaring in her ears so loud she could barely hear them. She was severely weakened by giving away pieces of her soul and refusing to take theirs in exchange.

"Love, can you look at me?" Mac asked, putting a gentle hand under her chin to urge her eyes up. Her head weighed a thousand pounds, but she managed to raise it enough to meet his gaze. Her vision was hazy and narrow, making it hard to focus on him.

It was Lex who spoke next in a scared growl. "Why are her eyes white, Mac? What's going on?"

"I don't know," Mac answered, sounding as fearful as Lex.

She wanted to comfort them, but all that happened was her eyes rolled back in her head and she slipped into blessed unconsciousness.

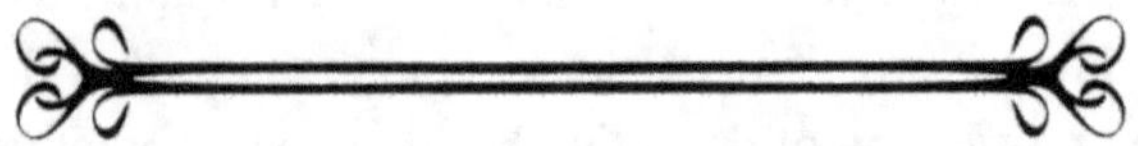

Mac

When Imani went boneless on the bed, Mac's first instinct was to try to rouse her, but he hesitated.

Frantic with worry, Lex was on his knees hovering over Imani, straightening her limbs and rubbing her skin. "This can't be good. We need to do something."

As much as Mac wanted to agree, he was at a loss on how to help. "I've only ever dealt with a vampire once before, and that was all business. I've never seen one do this before. Could it be because she's young? Maybe she wore herself out, like when she was fighting Tobias."

"White eyes," Lex reminded him grimly, then started looking around the room. Because the queen-sized bed had been far too small for the three of them, Lex and his beast had taken it upon themselves to fix the situation.

First, he'd pushed the original furniture in the room out of the way, or simply broke it apart in the case of the bed and dumped the bits and pieces into the hall. With the rut riding him hard, he hadn't been in the frame of mind to listen to anyone. Mac had tried to reason with him, but Lex wanted a big bed for his mates and the way he did it was the most efficient, if destructive.

Then Lex dragged the California King mattress from the other bedroom and situated it in the middle of their new room. Then he'd gone from room to room and picked out specific pillows for reasons he couldn't explain and placed them all around the mattress. When he was finished, it looked more like a nest than a bed.

Mac had stood back and watched, only interceding when Imani looked torn between being annoyed or laughing at the whole situation. When Lex started breaking bed posts like twigs, Mac was forced to distract Imani with cuddles and kisses until Lex was done. No one liked seeing perfectly good furniture ruined, but there was no reasoning with a chimera in rut.

Looking into Lex's eyes, Mac could tell by the lack of bright gold color that the chimera's rut was over. That might have been a relief if they weren't faced with a new challenge; figuring out what was wrong with their vampire.

Lex ran a hand over Imani's head, petting the unconscious woman. "I know they get white eyes if they're starved of blood, but that takes years."

Mac rubbed over one of Imani's bite marks on his neck. "It's not possible for her to be starved of blood with the amounts we've been feeding her. This has to be something else."

Tilting his head to the side, Lex leaned a little closer to Imani. "We need to do something; her heartbeat is getting sluggish." He glanced over at the window. "And the sun's setting. It should be speeding up, not slowing."

Scrambling off the bed and to his feet, Lex barreled out of the room before Mac could even comment. With Lex out of the way, Mac leaned in close and listened to Imani's heartbeat for himself. What he heard caused a spike of fear to go through him. It'd never gotten this slow, even during her deepest daytime sleep.

Whatever was wrong with her had to be related to what she'd done to Lex and himself. Not only could he feel her presence in his head, but he also felt more powerful than before. With the magic coursing through him, he knew he could shift faster, had more strength, and was probably faster to heal.

He'd give it all back if Imani's heart would return to a normal pace and she'd open her eyes and smile at him.

Lex barreled back into the room with a phone clutched in his hand. Mac could hear it ringing as the chimera dropped into an empty spot on the bed on the other side of Imani. He held the phone out between them as the person on the other end picked up.

"Lex?" Memphis's voice sounded sleepy. "What's up? Are you finished with your rut?"

Lex ignored his question. "Imani's sick. Her eyes are white, and her heartbeat is getting slower even though the sun's almost down."

"Tobias is here. Let me put the phone on speaker," Memphis responded, the sleepiness vanishing from his voice.

"Did I hear correctly?" Tobias questioned. They could hear Briar and Memphis talking softly to each other in the background. "Did you say her eyes are white?"

"Yes," Mac answered. "Is she dying? Does she need blood?"

"When did she feed last?" Tobais asked. "Was it a substantial meal?"

"She fed from both of us just before we all went to bed for the day," Mac explained. "That's got to be a good-sized meal for one vampire, right?"

"Yes, quite substantial," Tobias agreed in a grim tone. "If she's fed that recently, then it isn't starvation. There's only one other thing that could be causing this. Did you refuse to let her take parts of your soul when she did the exchange?"

Both Lex and Mac echoed that last word. "Exchange?"

There was a brief pause and Mac could tell it was a shocked silence. "To create our flock, vampires exchange pieces of their souls. We take a small part of your soul and give you a bit of ours in return. It ties a vampire and their flock together. We extend your life to ours and you ground our humanity so we don't become mindless monsters."

"How do we fix this?" Lex demanded. "If she gave us parts of her soul and didn't take ours, how do we make her do it now?"

"You can't," Tobias answered simply.

Mac couldn't help the shocked sob that tore from his throat at the thought of losing Imani. "Help us," he begged. "I'll do anything. You can drain me dry. Have everything I own. I don't care but save her."

While Mac was focused on pleading, Lex's expression hardened. "If she dies, I'll hunt you down and destroy you."

To Mac's shock, Tobias's response was bland and cruel. "Even if you survive her death, you won't be in any state to challenge me."

Furious talking started up in the background, and Tobias sighed heavily. "Calm yourself, Memphis. I'm not going to let that happen."

Those words gave Mac hope. "Can you help her?"

"I can," Tobias answered. "But it won't be pleasant for anyone. I'm going to shift and fly to you. My flock will not be following me. In this volatile situation, I don't trust either of you to maintain your composure. It won't do anyone any good if either of you attack Memphis or Briar."

"Fine," Lex agreed. "But hurry."

Tobias's answer was to end the call. Both Mac and Lex stared at the phone in silence for several seconds. Then Lex tossed the phone aside.

"If figures my brother would end up with an asshole," he grunted.

"Because Memphis is a dick?" Mac asked, trying for a joke.

"No, because he's the nicest of us Grangers. He's the one everybody called whenever hikers got lost or a kid wandered into the forest. Up in Bend, that happened way more often than it should've. He never charged a cent for the kid rescues and had a sliding scale for hikers. He might look scary with the beard, leather, and motorcycle, but he's a cinnamon roll."

"Cinnamon roll?" Mac echoed as he picked up one of Imani's limp hands and held it between his bigger, rougher mitts.

Lex mirrored his movement with Imani's other hand. "Yeah, because he's soft and sweet. He's a leather wearing, scruffy cinnamon roll." Lex looked down and Mac could see tears glistening in his eyes. "Tobias is going to save her, right?"

"Of course." Mac tried to project the confidence he didn't feel. "He's powerful, especially now that he's got Memphis and Briar as a flock."

"If she leaves, I'm going with her," Lex declared.

Mac didn't need to ask what he meant and had only one response to give. "Same."

Lex

Lex heard Tobias land in his bird form. It was easy to distinguish from a real flight animal as the shifted vampire's bird form moved without a bird's normal fluid efficiency. If he had any doubt, it was resolved when the sound of flapping was replaced by a wash of magic and the sound of human feet striking the ground and running several strides to deal with the residual momentum.

"Tobias is here," Mac said unnecessarily and turned his gaze to the door. Both of them watched the open bedroom door. It wasn't long before they heard the front door slam open. It had barely been working after Lex abused it while he'd been in rut. It was one more thing in a long list of damages he'd caused to the formerly immaculate home.

It was that thought that made Lex say the first thing that popped into his head the moment Tobias appeared in the doorway. "I broke a lot of shit, but I've got money. If it's not enough, I can earn more. I'll replace everything I broke. I'll rebuild the whole house or buy the place if necessary."

His declaration made Tobias stop in his tracks, and Mac looked over at him with a confused expression. "What does that have to do with anything?"

"I believe Mr. Granger has remembered who owns this property and is worried about reprisal for abusing my hospitality," Tobias answered dryly as he finished walking into the room. Once he was at the bed, he dropped to his knees next to Imani's head and lifted an eyelid. She didn't react at all.

"Shit, I hadn't thought of that," Mac grunted. "I agree with Lex. We can make this right."

Tobias waved off the concern. "I don't care. I'd let the three of you turn the place into a pile of rubble if it made Briar and Memphis happy. Having your vampire die and you two following will make both of them very unhappy." With a grave expression, he let go of Imani's eyelid and looked up at them.

"This is bad," he told them. "To save her, and by extension the two of you, I'll have to do something extreme."

"Extreme?" Lex repeated, feeling lightheaded from fear. "Explain."

"I'm going to cause both of you a lot of pain," he answered. "I'm going to have to rip out pieces of your souls and push them into Imani."

"Do it!" Mac insisted.

Tobias shook his head. "You need to understand what this means. I have no link to either of you, I'll have to do it with brute force instead of finesse. Both of you must remain still, and I'm sure it goes without saying that you can't attack me during the process, no matter how much it hurts."

"I can take the pain," Lex assured him and held out a wrist. "Do you need to bite me?"

Tobias looked down at his offered wrist with a slightly revolted expression. "Good god, no. All I need is to touch all three of you at the same time. Move over there and sit like this," he instructed, motioning Lex to sit next to Mac on Imani's other side. Then Tobias had both him and Mac put their hands side by side on Imani's sternum.

Tobias placed one hand over both their hands and then laid his other hand on Imani's forehead. If the situation wasn't so dire, Lex would hate having Tobias touching his sleeping and vulnerable mate. Right now, all he felt was desperation.

"If either of you break contact before I'm done, you're all dead," Tobias reminded them.

Mac wrapped his free arm around Lex's shoulder. "We won't."

Lex leaned into him a little, thankful for the comfort. "We can endure anything for Imani."

"Very well," Tobias said and closed his eyes. "Brace yourself and try not to scream too loud."

One moment all of Lex's pain was mental, a breath later he was sure his beating heart was being pulled out of his chest.

It was as if an invisible hand had dug in between his ribs and was trying to scoop out his heart whole. Screaming wasn't an issue because he couldn't pull air into his lungs. His vision started to gray out both from pain and lack of oxygen. Passing out would be a relief, but if he was unconscious, he might break contact with Imani. He focused on forcing air into his lungs and staying in position.

Imani jerked under his hand. He looked down to find her eyes were open and no longer white. Now they were the color of blood. Her lips pulled back in a snarl, revealing long, white fangs.

"I won't let you hurt them!" she snarled.

She didn't understand what was happening. Lex longed to comfort her, but the best he could do was keep himself sitting upright with his hand steady under Tobias's. Next to him, Mac's body shook, and he knew the bear shifter was also struggling to stay conscious.

"Imani, you will calm down," Tobias ordered.

Lex felt strong magic fizzle over his skin at Tobias's words. He must have been pouring a lot of power into trying to put the younger vampire into thrall. With the amount of magic he was using, she shouldn't have been able to fight him, but she kept trying to claw his hand off them.

"My flock!" she screamed. "Mine!"

"As I noted when we first met, you're unusually powerful for someone so young, but that's not a good thing at the moment," Tobias grumbled, his voice strained. "Quiet yourself and let me finish what you started."

The sensation of having his heart pulled on subsided slightly as Tobias focused on thrusting magic at Imani. Lex could see the moment Tobias was able to put her in thrall. Her body relaxed, and her eyes stared blindly at Tobias. The elder vampire looked visibly shaken as he let out a jagged breath.

"She has the abilities someone decades older would've accumulated," he muttered. "When this is all over, we better be allies or live very far apart." Tobias said more words after that, but roaring in Lex's ears prevented him from hearing anything. The slight reprieve from the pain was over, and when Tobias swung his gaze up, Lex was hit by a wave of agonizing power.

During a fight years ago, Lex was impaled in the chest by a silver dagger. He managed to kill the man, but then he'd fallen to his knees and slumped over. He hadn't even had the strength to pull the dagger out. Although his heart was managing to beat around the dagger, the silver was steadily poisoning him. He would've died within the hour if Mac hadn't gotten to him. Until now, he'd thought that was the most pain a person could endure.

He'd been wrong. The pressure on his heart grew to such intensity that he was sure it had to be partially out of his chest cavity by now, attached only by stretched thin veins and arteries.

At least that's what it felt like.

Then something popped. It was like a piece of his insides came loose and flowed out of him. There was a sudden sharp bite of agony, as if he was being ripped in half. He heard Mac scream. Dear gods, he wanted to do the same but couldn't make a sound. There was no breathing or thinking, there was only pain.

Then everything went blessedly numb.

Was this what it felt like just before you died? He was surprisingly calm. Only a soft concern of leaving Mac and Imani to fend for themselves crossed his mind, but there was no terror or push to fight.

Was this the flop trauma response he'd heard about? Instead of fighting, freezing, or fleeing, a person gave up and accepted what was going to happen. He'd heard it was a place where the heartbeat slowed, and you disassociated. Could someone disassociate from pain when in flop?

Whatever was happening, at least he didn't hurt anymore.

When Tobias's hand lifted off his, Lex managed to squint open his eyes. Tobais looked worn out but relieved.

"It's done. And not a moment too soon." Tobias leaned over Imani's body to put his face right in front of Lex. "Breathe," he commanded.

Magic hit Lex, and he sucked in a breath. That first breath reminded his lungs how to work, and he started sucking in air like a swimmer surfacing after being under a second too long.

"There. That's better," Tobias said, looking satisfied. "Now I understand why you were so quiet. I thought it was self-control, but you simply had no air to use for screams."

Still gasping, Lex looked down at Imani. She appeared to be asleep, face relaxed and breathing normally. He could hear her heart beating now, steady and strong. Her color looked good, and he was sure if he peeled her eyelid back, he'd see her eyes were back to their beautiful dark brown color instead of white or red.

Turning his head, he found Mac slumped over. His poor sloth bear had passed out from the pain. Tobias had been wise to hold the men's hands down on Imani's sternum so he could make sure the contact didn't break even if he or Mac couldn't remain upright.

"He's fine," Tobias assured him. "All you and Mac need is sleep and a good meal when you wake up." The vampire looked down at Imani with a slight frown. "She'll need a lot of sustenance as well."

When Tobias's eyes rose to meet his, the vampire looked intrigued, as if he was figuring out a puzzle. Lex's fuzzy brain couldn't figure out how to form words with his mouth, so he slowly blinked as the vampire spoke.

"I only now realized I hadn't arranged for blood to be delivered here, and I know Briar and Memphis didn't see to it either. That means Imani's been taking from you and Mac. Normally, we don't drink from our flock. Probably because most vampires take humans as flock members. Even after we share our souls with humans, they're still comparatively fragile. You're both such strong shifters that she couldn't hurt either of you by taking blood. I think part of her recent growth in power is due to being well fed by you and Mac. I suggest you continue to encourage her to drink from you."

Lex felt a sloppy grin form on his face. He was starting to feel loopy, probably a reaction to the sudden absence of pain after being in such agony.

"Fucking love it when she bites me," he slurred.

Tobias laughed. "I don't doubt it."

Lex tried to blink, but his eyes wouldn't open back up. He fell over and had the vague sense of Tobias moving him around. There was the sound of more shuffling then his mates were on either side of him. Assured they were all going to live, he let himself slide into unconsciousness.

Imani

Mac and Lex were both sleeping deeply. Mac was on his back with Lex lying on top of half of Mac's chest. Their continued sleep allowed Imani to sit on the edge of the mattress and gaze at them while she thought.

Guilt swamped her at how much pain her shifters were forced to endure because she was inexperienced. If she'd simply given into her vampire impulse earlier, there probably would've only been a bit of discomfort. Instead, she'd resisted and passed out, forcing Tobias to rip at her flock's souls.

How could they want to be with her after that? Her role was to protect them from threats, but what if she was the biggest threat? There were only fuzzy half memories from what Tobias had done several hours earlier, but she heard him say one thing very clearly.

We don't drink from our flock.

Looking back to her time with Vincent and his flock, she'd never seen him take from Simon or Opal. The significance of that hadn't registered until now. She'd been biting Lex and Mac without regard for their safety. Other vampires didn't do that to their flock. They might want it, but what if she was the equivalent of poison, slowly killing them with her natural inclinations?

On top of feeding off those who were supposed to be the most precious to her, she almost killed them quickly by botching their soul exchange. Shame filled her.

A small voice reminded her that Vincent had never explained the intricacies of taking a flock. Teaching her how to be a vampire had been beneath him. All he cared about was that she entertained Simon and Opal like a good little toy. None of that assuaged her guilt. She'd locked these men to her without any regard for what they might want. It's true that they felt a pull towards her and believed she was their fated mate, but now she'd chained them to her for eternity. Consent was never even discussed.

"You're thinking really loud," Lex mumbled. Sitting up, he rubbed a big hand over his smooth head and yawned. "Man, I'm hungry."

"Me too," Mac agreed as he sat up and grabbed Lex in a rough hug. "Morning, love."

Lex gave the big bear shifter a sleepy smile. "Vampire morning," Lex assessed with a glance at the unshuttered window. The dark night outside was clearly visible. "What is it, like one or two in the morning?"

Imani picked up the nearest phone and tapped the screen to life. "It's almost two."

"If I'm waking up, then it's morning. That means I want breakfast. Let's make French toast," Mac rumbled with a rough voice, probably due to the screaming from earlier.

She couldn't hold it in any longer. "I'm sorry." The words rushed out of her at the speed of her guilt. "Neither of you got a choice. I can fix it though. We can find a witch to separate us. She could return your souls. We don't have to be bound."

Both men froze and stared at her. Mac looked confused while Lex looked hurt.

"You don't want us?" Lex asked. "What did we do?"

"How can you want to be with me?" Imani screeched, feeling desperate and torn. She needed to make this right between them, but at the same time the thought of them taking her up on her offer made her go cold. "I've been drinking from you and vampires aren't supposed to do that. And then I almost killed all of us. It's bad enough that I'm a shitty vampire with no control or power. I can't even protect either of you. Even worse, now I'm the biggest threat of all! I could've killed us."

Mac's face relaxed. "You're not a shitty vampire. You're fucking brilliant. Tobias is even scared of you."

Imani forgot her guilt long enough to scoff. "Bullshit. I've got nothing compared to Tobias's power."

Lex shook his head. "You're leaving out the *yet*. You're not as strong as him *yet*. But you will be and probably within the next few decades. You have him worried enough that he wants to stay on your good side for reasons beyond your friendship with Briar or because Memphis is my brother."

"That still doesn't make up for the fact that I put both of you in grave danger," Imani reminded them, feeling morose. "It wasn't another vampire, a pack of shifters, a troop of pixies, or a gang of tooth-pullers that almost ended your lives. I almost killed us. That has to make you guys want to leave me."

"There is nothing you can say to make me afraid of you," Lex countered. "People I didn't even know have tried to kill me. Why would I run from your love?"

Imani blinked at that comment, a little thrown. She was still trying to figure out how to respond when Mac broke the brief silence.

"I think what Lex is trying to say is that we didn't die. Sure, it wasn't pleasant, but we're still all here. And it's not like we have to share souls every other day. It's a one-and-done deal." He rubbed his chest over his heart, drawing her eyes to his soft pelt of chest hair. "And I love feeling you. It's this soft warmth in my chest and a humming happiness in my brain. It's hard to describe, but it feels right. Perfect. As if I wasn't whole before, but now I am."

"What he said," Lex commented, earning him a laugh from Mac.

"That was lazy, love," Mac teased. "You're not in rut. You can use your damn words."

"Why? You do it so much better," Lex shot back, looking mildly disgruntled. Then he turned his gaze on her, expression softening. "You're not getting rid of us and if you try to hire some witch to undo our binding, I'll tie you to the bed and tickle you for an entire night. You've never experienced tickle torture until you've been tormented by a chimera's tail."

Before Imani could respond, Mac started speaking. "Remember when we first got here, and Lex tackled you? You forgave him because you knew he wasn't thinking straight. Then he went into rut and got even more crazy. You wouldn't hold any of that against him, would you?"

Put like that, Imani had to agree. "I suppose not."

"Then why would we blame you? Especially if we wanted to be bound to you as much as you wanted to bind us," Mac continued, still rubbing his chest above his heart in slow, broad circles. "I feel full. Full of contentment and security. I've never experienced anything like it before, and I have you to thank for that."

Lex nodded and touched the back of his head. "I can sense you in my head. It's like a soft, happy humming. It makes me feel seen."

His words made Imani do an internal survey of herself, something she'd avoided. She could feel the shifters in both her heart and her head. Love and devotion. Adoration and loyalty. All the various positive emotions were mixed together and thrumming through her like rippling waves of warm tropical water. That's how she knew there was more Lex needed to tell them.

"What is it, baby?" she asked. "What do you need to say?"

He took a deep breath and let it out slowly. With his hand still on the back of his head, he dropped his gaze to the bed. He mumbled something she was sure wasn't English.

"Lilly show?" Mac repeated, making a small smile flash across Lex's face.

"Tywyllwch," he repeated. "It's Welsh."

Imani was lost. "Is that a species I don't know about?"

"No, it's me," Lex answered. "The Anwyl Pack uses Welsh as their pack language, and they gave me the nickname Tywyllwch. It means darkness."

That didn't make anything clearer. "You're really pale to be called darkness. Is it an oxymoron?" she questioned. "Like giving a big guy the nickname Tiny?"

"If it is, then Memphis must be Tiny Man," Mac joked. "He's almost as big as me."

Lex didn't even crack a smile. If anything, he lost the slight softness in his face as he continued to focus stonily on the bedcover. "I got the name because of what's inside me. I've done things. Killed a lot of people. That's what I've been hired to do. You should know that. You should know that I'm not worthy of you."

"Lex, you haven't—" Mac started to say, but Lex looked up, his gold eyes swirling with power and cut Mac off.

"No," he snapped. "You don't know what I've done."

Imani wasn't sure what to think. She knew in her heart Lex wasn't an evil man and that made her ready to forgive Lex anything. If his guilt was anything like hers, she needed to understand what he was saying fully before he'd believe her when she said it didn't matter.

"Tell us about it," Imani urged.

"Don't hate me," Lex whispered, dropping his gaze again. Imani couldn't take it anymore. She scooted into his lap, surprising Lex. He was quick to wrap his arms around her and nuzzle his face into her braids. She saw Mac move until he was sitting behind Lex and wrapped his long bear arms around both of them.

Lex let out a long breath and relaxed a little.

"We could never hate you, love," Mac murmured.

"Never," Imani echoed. "Talk to us, please."

"Where do I start?" Lex asked. "My first kill or the most recent one? I have too many sins to count."

"Tell me about how it all got started," Imani demanded.

"In Bend," Lex started.

"Bend, Oregon, where you grew up?" Mac asked.

Lex nodded his head slightly. "The place always felt too small and happy. Everyone was so content. Half of my brothers have found their mates and settled down to raise families. I felt like I never really belonged. I think it was my chimera pushing me to find my mate, but I didn't realize that 'til now. Anyway, a guy was on a skiing trip with a bunch of friends and got into a bar fight. I was working as a barback and broke it up. The guy was impressed and offered me a job. I left the next day."

Imani could easily picture Lex as a young man, new to adulthood, and trying to figure out who he was. "How old were you?"

"Nineteen," Lex answered. "I wasn't even old enough to work at the bar, but Henning, he's the second oldest of my brothers, was managing at the time and paid me under the table. He and his mate own it now. Mom pushed me to go to college, but I hated school. I hated sitting indoors for so many hours a day. My family wasn't mean about it, but they definitely felt like I needed to pick a direction. Chimeras are supposed to focus on making money while they're young so when we find our mate, we can support them and our children. Chimeras tend to have big families."

"Yeah, you're one of eight, right?" Mac asked.

"Yeah, second youngest," Lex answered. "It's Kingston, Henning, Memphis, Paris, Nashville, Jackson, me, then Knoxville."

Imani blinked for a moment, thrown off. "Wait, what's your full name?"

"Lexington. Um, we're all named after towns and cities in Tennessee."

Imani raised an eyebrow. There was no way she would let that explanation end there. "Why?"

"It was Mom's thing. She's from there and was really proud of the state but won't go back because she had a big fight with her family about marrying a chimera. They were some of the rare humans that know about preternaturals. That's all she'd tell us, and Dad won't talk about it either. I think there was even an attempted kidnapping by her family to get her away from Dad. And I know one of her brothers lost an arm fighting when Dad came for her. Honestly, Dad must have been holding back because he could've easily wiped out her entire family without breaking a sweat."

"And then she went and had eight boys. Your mom must have the patience of a saint," Imani murmured. "Were there so many kids because she kept trying for a girl?"

"No," Lex responded. "She knew we'd all be boys. Chimeras don't have female children. Or at least not outside of legend. We chimeras always find our mates with other species.

That's one of the reasons I was eager to leave when I was nineteen. With so many siblings finding their mates, I was scared I'd never find mine."

"But you were so young," Imani mourned. "When I was nineteen, I was in college and the farthest thing from my mind was building a family."

"I'm a chimera, though," Lex was quick to point out. "We think differently."

Imani pushed Lex to continue his story. "What happened after you left with…, what was his name?"

"Edward," Lex supplied. "He'd been in the Marines and saw how much private contractors make. When he got out after four years, he formed his own group. By the time I met him, he'd been doing it for fifteen years. He was the one who started my training, then sent me off to a couple of training programs. I was good. Really good. And not just because I have shifter speed and strength. I was better than the other non-humans in training."

"Did Edward know about you?" Mac asked. "Was he one of us?"

Lex gave a derisive snort. "He was human and didn't have a clue. Later I realized he was…what's it called when you have highs and lows? Like you get really sad or really excited? There'd be times when no one could do anything right and times when we were all perfect employees. You never knew which version of Edward you were getting."

"I think you're talking about bipolar disorder," Imani supplied. "But whatever was wrong with him sounds like it wasn't being monitored by any professionals. That couldn't be good for the people under his command in the company. Especially if you guys were going into dangerous situations."

"Yeah, you're not wrong," Lex agreed. "But he wasn't so bad. Most of the jobs were guarding people going into unsavory areas. Violence was rare because Edward would usually use double the number of people that other companies would use for the same kind of assignment. He never wanted us to shoot first, but if fighting started, we were expected to be merciless. Losing a client wasn't an option. The first three years were good. He elevated me to team leader and gave me the hardest assignments. He even talked about letting me buy into the company and becoming a partner. I thought this was it; I was going to make big money. I wanted to be able to shower my future mate with riches. I was so eager I ignored what was going on with Edward."

Mac made a soft, inquisitive sound. "What do you mean?"

"He started acting erratically. Losing his temper at non-issues or laughing off something important. Some days, I could smell cocaine on him. I made all kinds of excuses in my head for his behavior. I was an idiot."

Mac made a sound of sympathy. "We're all really good at ignoring things we don't want to see."

"But I should've said something," Lex argued.

"What opened your eyes?" Imani asked. "What happened to make you acknowledge what was going on?"

"We had an assignment in a rural area of Brazil," Lex answered, his voice remote and unemotional. "It had something to do with lead mining, but I wasn't really paying attention to that part. Anyway, we were ambushed. Landmines in the road took out the lead vehicle. An RPG took out the truck behind mine, blocking the remaining three vehicles on the narrow rural road."

Mac hissed out a breath. "Land mines and RPGs? You could've been killed outright."

Lex nodded. "Heavily armed militia came out of hiding on both sides of the road and opened fire. All the humans died immediately, but three of us were shifters. We took rounds and were hurt, but we got out and ran into the forest. Once we were hidden from sight, it was easy to shift and evade the militia. I was hit the worst and couldn't keep up with the other two."

Imani couldn't keep the anger out of her voice. "They left you?"

"Of course," Lex answered, as if being abandoned was a given. "I'm a chimera."

"Even chimeras can die," Mac pointed out. "If you took enough bullets to keep you from traveling, that militia could have found you and finished the job."

"As if," Lex muttered, then spoke louder. "But they didn't, and the guys were able to get home to their families. It all worked out."

"What happened after they left you?" Imani asked. This story filled her with a weird anxiety even though he was sitting here, alive and well. "How did you survive?"

Lex gave her a little kiss on the top of the head before he started talking again. "It took about a week for my body to push out all the bullets and to heal enough to leave the jungle. There were wild pigs in that area, and they were easy to drop down on and pretty tasty too. There were also plenty of naturally growing fruits to forage, so I was well fed. The capybara were cool to hang out with while I was convalescing. They didn't care about my shifted form and they're sweet. Like giant, cuddly, inclusive guinea pigs."

Imani didn't have to look at Mac to know, like her, he was trying to figure out what to say. Through their bond, Imani could feel Mac's horror at the thought of Lex wounded and alone deep in a remote jungle far from home. She could also feel Lex's unconcern at the whole situation. Out of everything he'd told them about, this didn't rate on his scale of importance. It was stark evidence of how little he valued himself.

It broke Imani's heart and made her determined to convince Lex of his worth.

"Once I was healed enough," Lex continued, "I searched the jungle and found the militia. I was angry at them. I was angry at the world. I didn't leave a single one of them alive."

He paused, as if waiting for their condemnation.

"Good," Mac grunted. "Saves me from having to go down there."

Lex shook his head, blinking hard and still refusing to look either of them in the eyes. "It turns out the militia were basically a gang. I don't know much Portuguese, but I understood enough to find out the militia had been exploiting everyone in the area. They'd demand protection money from the locals and take whatever they wanted. They considered the mine in their territory, so they demanded money or a cut of the profits from the owners. That's why the owners hired us. The militia took their refusal to pay as a challenge to their authority and decided to make an example out of us."

"Sounds like you were doing everyone there a favor," Mac asserted. "You freed the locals from a real danger. That militia would have bled everyone dry eventually."

"But I didn't know that at the time," Lex countered. "They could've been family men trying to keep the mine from exploiting local labor or any number of things. I didn't find out about all the shit they were doing until afterwards. It made me think, you know?"

"Think about what?" Imani asked.

"About what kind of people were hiring us. How many of the people or facilities I'd been sent to protect deserved to be destroyed? Had I killed good people while shielding bad ones? The worst part was that I knew Mama would be so disappointed in me. She never said anything, but she probably guessed I was doing shady shit. I thought she was respecting my privacy, but that wasn't it. She didn't want to know if one of her sons was evil."

"Shut the fuck up!" Imani snapped, making Lex flinch. When he tried to move back, she wrapped her arms around his neck, locking him in place. She reined in her raging emotions and rubbed one hand up and down Lex's back in a soothing motion. "I'm sorry, baby. I didn't mean that to come out so harsh. Calling yourself evil was just wrong though."

"I don't think it's far off the mark," he mumbled, relaxing into her embrace.

Mac spoke up, his rumbling voice full of compassion. "You started at nineteen and this happened four years into working for Edward. That meant you were the ripe old age of what, twenty-four?"

"Twenty-three, I was a month shy of my birthday," Lex mumbled, risking a glance at Mac. Imani saw him smile and nod before Lex closed his eyes and nestled his head back into her embrace.

"You were so young, Lex," she murmured. "You were trying to figure out who you were and as much as you looked up to Edward, I don't think he was the best guy."

"Imani's right," Mac added. "At twenty-three, I was still living with my dad and focused on nothing but chasing tail."

Mac's confession made Imani snort. "The truth comes out."

"I was a total hoe," Mac agreed. "But both of you are benefiting from my vast experience."

Lex huffed out a laugh. "You never hit on me."

"I'd gotten pickier by the time we became friends," Mac answered. Imani raised an eyebrow at him and Mac flushed a little, probably realizing how that sounded. "I mean, I wanted you. I always wanted you. But I'd never seen you with a guy, so I figured you were straight."

"You never saw me with a girl either," Lex pointed out. "I've never been with anyone until you two."

Mac

Lex's confession made Mac go still with shock. He stopped petting Lex's side and looked over his shoulder to meet Imani's gaze. She was as wide eyed as his.

He had to clear his throat a few times to get the words out. "Are you telling us you were a virgin?"

"Yeah," Lex answered. His tone was way too casual, as if it was an everyday thing to run across a thirty-two-year-old virgin who was so damn hot in bed he nearly lit the sheets on fire.

"You mean no sex with a guy, right?" Imani pushed. "You've slept with women though."

"No one," Lex clarified. "I've kissed a few people, but nothing more."

"I feel honored and a little ashamed," Mac admitted.

"Ashamed?" Lex repeated, confused. He looked up at Mac. "Why?"

"Baby, the three of us did some pretty advanced stuff for a virgin," Imani answered for Mac.

Swallowing hard, Mac worked on talking past his emotions. "If I'd known, I would've gone slower. Been gentler with you." The thought of how debauched he'd been with Lex their first time together made tears burn the back of Mac's eyes.

"Fuck, I penetrated you, love. I shouldn't have done that for your first time. That's something you ease a partner into."

Overwhelmed by his own shame and worried about making Lex feel trapped, Mac tried to withdraw. To his shock, Lex laughed. "Don't be a drama bear."

Imani snorted out a laugh. "I'm getting that put on a shirt."

"Excuse my concern about treating my mate well," Mac huffed. He'd frozen in place when Lex had laughed. Feeling playful, he returned to his bear hug position and then squeezed until both Lex and Imani started wiggling.

Imani exaggerated her attempts to pull in a breath by wheezing. "Can't breathe."

"You don't need to, vampire," Mac replied with a chuckle.

Lex managed to wiggle an arm around and grab hold of Mac's foot. "Loosen the hold or I start tickling," he threatened.

Knowing the chimera didn't make idle threats, Mac loosened his hold, a broad smile across his face. "You know my weakness, love."

Lex let go of his foot and snuggled down into the embrace, pulling Imani close against him. The expression on the chimera's face was one of absolute contentment. "I've never felt this safe."

Mac's heart melted. "You'll always be safe with us."

"Always," Imani echoed. They all enjoyed the cuddles for several minutes before she spoke again. "I don't understand why you didn't realize Mac was your mate earlier. You've been friends for a while."

"Six years," Lex answered. "After Edward's death, his group was dissolved. But I'd made a lot of contacts, and I put myself out there as a free agent. I was smarter this time; I researched the people who wanted to hire me. That's why I was willing to work with Mac. I didn't turn up any dirt on him and everyone I talked to said he was the one to have guarding your back."

"The first job we worked together was that kidnapping one, right?" Mac asked.

"Yeah, that's the one." When Imani made a questioning sound, Lex elaborated. "A guy's kid had been kidnapped and was being held for ransom. Problem was that this group had a reputation for killing the hostage even if the ransom was paid."

Memories surrounding that assignment suddenly had new meaning to Mac. "There were six of us and you insisted I partner with you. I always thought it was because I was another shifter."

Lex lifted his cheek from where it was resting on Imani's head and met Mac's gaze. The molten amber of his chimera eyes were dark and affectionate. "The moment we met, something felt right. Like a puzzle piece falling into place. I'd never felt so calm or centered before, outside of battle anyway. Especially after you stood up to that Wilson guy."

It took Mac a moment to remember Wilson. "He was the one giving you a hard time because you didn't say much when we were all getting to know each other?"

"Yeah, you told him to leave me alone, then you pulled everyone's attention to you by telling that story about the last time you rode in a helicopter and vomited into another guy's backpack. They all started teasing you and forgot about me. I felt saved."

"I didn't save you. I just helped out a little. You're the one who saved me when that lion shifter got the drop on me," Mac murmured. "You give so much and ask for so little."

"Not true," Lex argued with a slight grin. "You gave me a key to your place and said I could crash there anytime. Remember last year when I showed up while you were asleep?"

Mac laughed. "I'm not likely to forget it. You scared the shit out of me."

"What happened?" Imani asked. "Share the funny!"

"I woke up in the middle of the night to take a piss," Mac explained. "When I went to put my feet on the floor, I stepped on Lex instead."

"You jumped so high your head put a hole in the ceiling," Lex continued. "The upstairs neighbor called the cops."

Mac snorted. "Don't exaggerate. I put a dent in the drywall, I didn't pop all the way through. I still had to talk to the cops, but they thought it was hilarious that a visiting buddy had made me scream loud enough to wake up the neighbors."

"Even after all that, you didn't take back the key you gave me," Lex continued after Imani's laughter had died down. "I was still welcome. That's a gift, Mac. You're a gift. With everyone else, I feel like I have to constantly earn the right to be around them. As if I have to keep reassuring them that I'm not dangerous or going to turn feral. But never with you."

Love and affection washed through Mac even as something occurred to him. "Why did you bed down on the floor in my room instead of the couch? We were so busy with the angry neighbor, your laughter, and the cops that I never thought to ask."

Lex closed his eyes and lifted his head up only to let it thump back against Mac's chest. When he spoke, it was barely audible. "Rough assignment. I just needed to be close to you."

Mac didn't ask what happened. He and Imani had probably already pushed Lex enough for now. But when his eyes met Imani's, they made a silent agreement. They were going to make sure Lex understood he deserved to be loved.

"My sweet Lex, your dark days are over," Mac said, hoping Lex heard the absolute conviction in his voice. "We are your dawn, and we'll make sure you get to bask in the light."

Lex

"Can this conversation be over now?" Lex asked. His body felt fine, but his mind was a tempest of emotions and half-formed thoughts. "Mac, I'm super fucking happy with the sex. It was great, and I can't wait for more sex. Lots of sex. I like getting my rocks off. It feels fucking fantastic and the cuddles afterwards are just as good. You hear me?"

"Yes, love," Mac rumbled. "I'll stop feeling guilty and make sure you get to come a lot."

"And keep doing all that ordering around and rough stuff," Lex demanded. He was on a roll, might as well make sure they knew where he stood on everything. "I like the rough stuff. Spank me, hell, use your belt. Give me bruises. Please."

Mac made a sexy growling sound, and Lex's chimera practically purred. The thought of their mate manhandling them like he'd done before made his libido come to life. Ignoring his lust, he focused on his other mate's guilt.

"Imani," he continued, "I'm glad to be bound to you. I never thought about being a member of a flock, but now I can't imagine my life any other way. Feeling you in my head, like a warm, comforting presence, is something I never knew I was missing. If you guys are my dawn, then the sharing of souls is part of the light you're giving me. Feeling guilty over giving me something so precious is stupid."

Imani shook her head. "That was damn poetic, Lex. But I caused you so much pain."

Mac made a soothing sound. "You were in pain too, love."

Lex let out a weary sigh. He needed this deep, meaningful, emotional talk over. "It's important to let go of mistakes. If you dwell, you open yourself up to doubt and that could get you killed. We learn, we adapt, and we move forward."

Imani let out a breath and Lex could hear her tension ease. "That sounds very tactical and practical."

"Lex makes a good point. We don't sit around wailing about mistakes; we learn from them. You need to call Tobias and talk," Mac ordered. "He can make sure you have all the important knowledge. He could mentor you."

Imani hesitated. "Maybe."

Lex rubbed a hand up and down her back. "Mac's idea is a good one, but you don't have to do it tonight. It's something we can think about later. The only thing that has to happen right now is food!"

With laughter and smiles, they threw on some clothes and headed downstairs, chatting and teasing like the family they were.

Imani

Imani watched as Lex and Mac demolished almost every bite of food in the kitchen. They'd been getting groceries delivered every day. The amounts being piled at the gate were mind-bogglingly huge, and at first Imani had worried the food would go to waste.

Spoiler alert, it didn't.

While they'd been busy with Lex's rut, she hadn't paid attention to when and what the guys ate. She knew shifters had healthy appetites, but that hadn't prepared her for the number of calories both Mac and Lex needed to consume at each meal. It's a good thing both of them made good money because even with the money she had in her backpack, she couldn't have covered half their grocery bill.

They'd eaten several massive stacks of pancakes each, enough bacon to create a farm of pigs, giant bowls of pre-cut fruit, two dozen fried eggs, and an entire carafe of coffee each. It was only after they'd eaten enough to feed a dozen humans that they'd finally looked full.

Cautiously, Imani sat down across from the guys. She'd demanded they let her make breakfast. They'd protested but gave in to her. Her determination temporarily turned her into a short-order cook. Despite the hard work, she experienced a primal satisfaction in providing food for her flock.

Leaning back in his chair, Mac patted his belly with a contented sigh. "Best meal I've ever eaten."

Lex sipped the last mug of coffee. "Really good," he agreed. "Thank you."

"Do you guys always eat this much in one sitting?" Imani asked.

"Naw," Mac answered. "Sometimes we're really hungry."

Imani felt her eyes bug out as her mind tried to comprehend them eating even more at a single meal. There was a beat of silence before both men roared with laughter.

"Oh shit, you should've seen your face," Lex grunted.

"Totally horrified," Mac crowed. "That was pure terror at the idea of having to feed us like this all the time."

Fighting a smile, she forced her face into a scowl. "And that's the last meal I'm ever fixing! You two can feed your damn selves from now on."

Their laughter died abruptly.

Lex set his mug down and put his hand together as if in prayer. "Aww, don't be like that. I don't know how you did it, but those were the best pancakes I've ever had. Better than my mama's."

Mac nodded his head. "And you got the bacon perfectly crispy and then you fried the eggs in the bacon grease. That was amazing. It was food nirvana. Don't take away food nirvana!"

Giving up on her severe look, Imani was about to reply when she saw a flash of movement out of the corner of her eyes. Mac and Lex must have seen it too because in two seconds flat they were on their feet and putting themselves between her and whatever had passed by.

"I don't smell anything," Lex growled.

Standing up, Imani tried to step up next to them. "I didn't get a good look but something was there. It looked kid sized."

Mac gently urged her back. "Stay there, love. I can't smell it either, which means there's powerful magic going on."

"Charms?" she asked.

"Maybe, or whoever it is has natural masking magic," Lex answered, taking a half step forward and sniffing. "Still nothing. Mac?"

"I can't smell or hear anything," Mac agreed.

"Weapons?" Lex growled.

"Glock in the truck and the knives here in the kitchen," Mac answered without hesitation.

Imani was starting to get alarmed. "I think both of you boys are going in the wrong direction. How about we grab our stuff and leave?"

When both men swung their gazes around, she almost took a step back. Two sets of glowing eyes focused on her with matching expressions of outraged disbelief.

"Retreat?" Lex asked.

"Before we know what it is?" Mac added.

Here was a downside to having warriors as your flock. "It's one thing to face an enemy you can't get away from, but it's another thing to go looking for trouble," she argued.

"There's trouble and then there's *trouble*," Mac argued. "We're going to make sure this isn't the second type of trouble. There could be something using this place as a nest. We can't simply leave it."

"Cleaning out unwelcome inhabitants is the least we can do after doing so much damage to this place," Lex pointed out.

"You're going to help Tobias out by potentially putting bullet holes in his house along with everything else?" Imani questioned. Both men nodded their heads, their expressions perfectly serious.

"If that's what it takes," Mac agreed, then looked to Lex. "I'll grab the gun."

As Mac hurried out of the house in nothing but his pants, Lex strode into the kitchen still buck naked. He pulled a knife off the magnetic strip next to the sink and tested for sharpness, then put it back and picked another. He must have been satisfied with this one because he turned to face her.

"Maybe you could at least put some pants on," Imani urged. "In case there's a family of magic badgers down there and one of them tries to bite your dick off."

A wicked grin flashed across Lex's face. "I don't think there's such a thing, but I promise I'll keep my cock whole and functioning for your pleasure. Besides, I don't want to ruin the set of clothes Memphis dropped off if I have to shift."

"Fine," she declared, throwing her hands up dramatically. "Put yourself in unnecessary danger. But don't expect me to patch you up if it all goes wrong."

"Don't worry, we're tough," Mac announced, striding back into the room with a gun in his hand.

"That's good 'cuz you're acting damn stupid," Imani jabbed. Unsurprisingly, both men ignored her assessment.

All three of them were sure the thing they saw was going toward the back of the house. Mac went first, then Lex with her trailing behind. At the end of the hall was the door to the garage, but catty-corner to that door was another standing partially open with light emanating from it. Imani couldn't remember if it had been closed before, but she could hear the faint sound of something being shuffled around.

Mac and Lex looked at each other and had some kind of silent conversation. Then Mac toed the door fully open. Peering around Lex, Imani saw a flight of carpeted stairs disappearing into a basement.

Without a word between them, Mac started down the stairs with Lex close behind. Imani paused at the top. Part of her hesitated to face whatever was down there. It might be benign, but if it wasn't, she wouldn't be much help. A larger and more insistent part of her pushed her to follow her flock. They might be in danger and her instincts were to protect her flock, even if there was little she could do.

Wishing she'd grabbed a knife she started down the steps as Mac and Lex disappeared into the basement. She moved cautiously, but the sound of Mac's calm voice made her hurry down the last few steps.

"That's not what I expected."

She rounded the corner at the end of the steps and was confronted by a creature she'd never seen before. The thing looked to be about four feet tall, with a wide mouth, rough greenish skin, and dainty nubby horns poking out of their head. The thing reminded her of goblin images from children's book.

With a bar, pool table, dart boards, and giant wall mounted TV, the basement was obviously outfitted as a man cave or adult rec room. Almost every flat surface of the room was covered in stacks of books. The creature was sitting on an overstuffed chair, feet sticking straight out and with piles of books on either side. Stepping around Lex, she saw the creature was reading a familiar paperback book.

"I read *Hail Mary* last year. It has a really good ending. I didn't expect to like it as much as *The Martian*, but I did," she commented without thinking. It was only when Lex and Mac jumped and pushed her back behind them that she realized she might have messed up.

"That's a hobgoblin," Lex whispered to her. "They hyperfocus on one thing and make it their world. If they've decided to nest on your property, you leave them alone. They're not dangerous unless you get between them and their interests."

"What happens if you do that?" she whispered back as the hobgoblin looked up from the book and watched them with intense black eyes.

"We don't know because no one has ever survived that type of encounter with them," Mac answered her, gently nudging her back toward the stairs.

Shit, had she just gotten them killed?

"Don't leave," the hobgoblin ordered, his voice surprisingly loud in the large basement. "You will stay and speak to me about books."

They froze, tense. "Only talk?" Lex asked.

The hobgoblin eyed Lex. "I don't like the taste of chimera, you're gamey. And vampires always taste too much like iron." Then he focused his gaze on Mac. "Bear isn't bad, but if I eat you, the vampire probably won't want to talk to me about books. Tell her to talk to me, and I won't eat any of you."

"Ever?" Mac pushed.

"For as long as you don't try to touch my precious books," the hobgoblin agreed. "I'm Sopek. You're welcome into my nest for the duration of our conversation."

That promise made Lex and Mac relax a little, but she could tell they were still uneasy. "We agree to your terms as long as we can leave unmolested after an hour," Mac responded.

Sopek frowned. "An hour isn't very long, but I will accept it." Setting the book aside, he climbed off the chair and started moving books around until the couch across from the chair was cleared. "Sit," he ordered.

Feeling a little like Alice facing the Queen of Hearts, Imani sat on the couch with Mac on one side and Lex on the other. The men perched themselves on the edge of the seat as if ready to spring up, so she did the same.

Returning to his chair, Sopek looked at her. "Tell me about other books you've read."

"Right, um, okay. I read a lot of science fiction recently and not much else, so my knowledge is going to be a little limited," she warned him.

"Yes, no, that's good," the hobgoblin answered. "I'm reading that genre now." He pointed to the pool table. "Those are the historical fiction I enjoyed." Then he pointed to a corner of the room where the books were stacked in a pillar shape. "Those are high fantasy." He continued to point out all the different genres represented in the room. As the list grew, one thing was clear, this hobgoblin liked to read everything! She couldn't think of a single fictional genre he hadn't collected.

A glance at the books stacked around his chair revealed all types of science fiction. Everything from silly and lighthearted to serious and involved. There were only a few she'd heard about but hadn't gotten a chance to read yet. Being turned had put a damper on her normal voracious reading habits.

"I see you have some classics here," she noted, pointing at a stack of Arthur C. Clark and Robert Heinlein books. Then she gestured to the Bobaverse and Expansion series piled up next to the first. "And some good writers. But you're missing out on some great books by people of color."

"People of color?" Sopek questioned. "What does this term mean?

She pointed at Mac and Lex. "It basically means anyone who doesn't look like these two." Mac snorted out a laugh and Lex nodded but neither commented.

"Yes, more voices are good," Sopek agreed. "The more contributors, the better the words. Tell me about these writers.

Do they write science fiction? That is what I wish to read right now."

"Sure," she answered, feeling more confident. "You could start with Octavia Butler's series *Lilith's Brood* and then read her *Earthseed* series. The *Earthseed* series is more post-apocalypse but still has strong sci-fi elements."

Sopek nodded with interest as she spoke. "Yes, good. Go on."

"I binged the entire *Binti* trilogy in a single weekend. The author's name is Nnedi Okorafor, and she writes a gripping story," Imani continued. "I also like Jordan Ifueko's *Raybearer* duology."

"Continue," Sopek demanded.

She continued to list authors, dipping into fantasy where it intersected with sci-fiction. Because Sopek was interested in everything, she even threw in some philosophical sci-fi.

"*The Three-Body Problem* by Liu Cixin is complicated, but good. That's the first one in the series, but I haven't had a chance to read the other two yet, so I don't know how the series ends."

"When I acquire these books, I'll allow you to read them," Sopek offered.

Lex jerked and Mac made a soft, surprised sound at Sopek's offer. She wasn't sure if it was because the offer was a trap or simply out of the norm for hobgoblins.

She decided on a non-committal answer. "That's nice of you. Do you like sci-fiction romance?"

"Of course," Sopek answered. "Tell me about the ones you've read."

The next hour flew by as they talked about one of Imani's passions—books. After the first twenty minutes of her listing authors and books she thought he might like, they started discussing some of the books he'd read. Sopek was a fast reader who retained an impressive amount of information, making the conversation enjoyable. They even got into a friendly argument over the deeper meaning of *Children of Ruin* by Adrian Tchaikovsky.

"You've given me the promised hour," Sopek announced abruptly in the middle of a discussion about *Seveneves* by Neal Stephenson. "You may leave if you wish."

Imani didn't really get a chance to respond to Sopek. The guys must have been poised for escape because no sooner did Sopek announce the end of the hour then they stood up in unison, hooking an arm in each of hers and lifted her to her feet. Then they ushered her to the stairs with gentle hands on her hips and shoulders.

"I invite you to return," Sopek called out from his chair. "You're a good vampire and pleasant company."

"Thanks, Sopek," Imani called back over her shoulder. Then she was up the stairs and standing in the hall as Lex gently shut the door and leaned against it.

Eyes closed, he thumped his head back against the door and let out a long sigh. "I need a drink."

"Or several," Mac agreed, pulling Imani into a hug. "You're never to go down there again, understand?"

"He seemed nice, and he promised not to eat any of us," she offered, hoping they'd ease up on the restriction. It'd been a long time since she'd gotten to talk about books with anyone. Sopek had been fun.

Mac wrapped his big hands around her biceps and pushed her away so he could hold her at arm's length. His expression was a combination of scared and amused.

"Let me put it this way, remember how you felt when Tobias attacked you? How powerful he was and how helpless you felt?" Mac asked.

She nodded her head and frowned at the memory. "Of course I remember."

"Sopek could obliterate Tobias without having to put that book down. Outside of deities and Nephilim, hobgoblins are unmatched."

She let out a long breath, reassessing the small, green bibliophile in the basement. "I won't go down there."

Lex straightened up from the basement door. "Everybody get your stuff. We're leaving."

He didn't need to tell them twice.

Mac

It wasn't until he was leading Lex and Imani into his place that Mac made a horrific realization. He lived in the quintessential bachelor pad.

His one-bedroom apartment was full of mismatched furniture, messy piles of items on every flat surface, and a few posters he'd tacked to the wall. If they looked in the fridge, all they'd find would be beer and condiments.

No, this wasn't simply a bachelor pad. It was even worse; it was a dorm room. Not only was this place small, but it was beyond messy.

Lex had been here before and never said a thing. But now that they were lovers, Mac felt a new embarrassment at the state of the place. It was even worse to have Imani here. She must be accustomed to nicer things.

She didn't say anything as she surveyed the living room with the ancient couch that tried to swallow anyone who sat on it and the stack of pizza boxes near the front door. The only thing he could see on her face was curiosity, but she had to be hiding disgust.

Having stayed here numerous times, Lex strode to the bedroom without hesitation. Mac let him go as Imani stepped up to stand next to him.

"I guess you don't have people over very often," she teased.

Feeling his face get hot from mortification, Mac hurried into the kitchen and grabbed the trash can. "Let me clean up a little."

Batting off the lid, he started shoving everything in, including piles of clean clothes on the kitchen table that hadn't been folded yet. His lack of discrimination between trash and not-trash quickly filled the bin. Reaching under the sink, he was relieved to find an entire roll of trash bags. There were enough bags here to put most of the apartment in the complex's dumpsters. Honestly, that's where it all belonged anyway.

"Um, are you throwing away your clothes?" Imani asked as she stepped up next to him.

"Gotta make this place presentable," he grunted, knotting the top of a second trash bag full of clean laundry.

Putting her smaller, delicate hands over his, she stopped his movement, but he refused to meet her gaze. "Mac, are you okay? You're acting weird."

Still unable to look her in the eyes, he ran his gaze over the apartment. "You should be in a nice place."

"This is a nice place," Lex said as he strode into the kitchen. "Your bed is a little tight. We're gonna need to order one of those bigger custom ones. Don't worry though, I think we can make it fit if we get rid of one of the nightstands."

Imani looked over at the chimera with a grin. "It's adorable how focused you always are on our sleeping arrangements."

Lex raised a pale blond eyebrow and crossed his arms over his chest. "Someone needs to make sure we're all comfy while we're fuckin' or sleepin'."

"Bed's too small, and this place is too messy," Mac muttered, reality slapping him in the face for a second time. Even if he cleaned up all the garbage and mess, this place would still be a shabby shithole. He couldn't let his mates stay here. "I'm going to buy us a house."

His blurted words made Imani and Lex stare at him in confusion.

"I've got a house up in Bend," Lex commented. "I don't go there much, but it's nice enough. My brother Kingston and his crew built it for me. You don't need to buy one."

Imani looked interested. "I've never been to Bend, and I've always wanted to try snowboarding." Then she frowned. "Though they probably don't run the ski lifts at night."

Lex waved off her concern. "I can take you skiing at night. There's a whole group of shifters that ski or snowboard after dark every few weeks during the snow season. They officially close the lifts but actually keep them open for us. It's so we don't have to deal with pretending to be slow, like the humans. I've only gone once, but most of my brothers love it. It usually turns into a big party."

This sounded good. They could all drive up to the mountains of Oregon, and his mates would never have to see his shitty apartment again. "Great idea, let's go."

When he tried to turn toward the door, Lex grabbed him low on his waist in a hug and lifted him off his feet for a moment. "What's the rush, teddy bear?"

"This place is a dump," Mac grumbled, relaxing into Lex's hold. He didn't struggle to get loose even after his feet were back on the ground. "I should be providing better. I have money, not a fortune, but enough. I could've picked a better place to live. I'm only here because I'm lazy. Let me find us a nice hotel for the day. Then we can figure out how to get to Lex's house."

"We can't leave San Diego yet," Lex argued. "Imani wants to go dancing and there's nothing like that up in Bend."

Lex's care for Imani's joy made shame hit Mac hard. He couldn't provide his mates with a nice place to live, and he'd forgotten about Imani's longing to go out clubbing. Could he do anything right?

"Mac, stop it," Imani ordered, startling Mac. He focused on her, comforted by her gentle smile and Lex's warm hug. "I can see you're tying yourself up in knots. Let's all take a seat and talk, 'k?"

Lex let go of him, and Imani guided him to sit on the couch. No sooner had he sat than the chimera flopped down next to him. Then Lex reached out and grabbed Imani, laying her out over their laps. She laughed and wiggled around until she was comfortable. All the wiggling woke up his dick, but he ignored it. Now was not the time to be sexing Imani up. She wanted to talk, not fuck.

She settled her ass on his lap, her back on Lex's, and head propped up against the arm of the couch. Then she leveled him with a penetrating stare.

"This place is a little messy," she began, making him wince. "But it's nicer than what I was renting before meeting you two."

He glanced around before returning his gaze to her. "That can't possibly be true."

She raised an eyebrow at him. "I don't make shit up." Her no-nonsense tone made him feel better. No, Imani definitely wasn't one to sugarcoat anything to spare his feelings. He could trust her to be honest.

"This right here," she said, waving a finger around to indicate the three of them and the apartment. "Makes me realize we have a bit of a problem. We're insecure in this relationship and so far, we've been taking turns with our fear and doubt. That's not good, though. What if we all end up having a crisis moment together? We could really hurt each other all because we lack confidence in this relationship. That's dangerous."

Mac pulled a deep breath into his lungs, acknowledging the truth in Imani's words to himself. There was a further element Imani didn't know about; Mac was scared. No, terrified was more accurate. He felt so damn lucky to have both Lex and her that he was sure it was all a dream. It was unimaginable he could be this fortunate. He was sure this happiness was built on a house of cards, ready to fail and fold from the slightest pressure.

Imani was right; he had to learn to let that anxiety go and trust his partners.

Lex nodded in agreement with Imani's words. "What do we do?" he asked.

Her eyes shifted back and forth between him and Lex. "First, we stop jumping around."

Confused, Mac felt his brows wrinkle. "Jumping around?"

"Yeah, jumping. As in jumping to conclusions," Imani elaborated. "Don't assume I'm thinking or feeling one way or another. Ask me and I'll tell you straight out what's going on in my head. For example, you need a haircut."

Mac ran a hand through his shaggy hair and felt a tug at the corner of his lips. "You can pick the style."

Imani looked excited. "Can I pick out some outfits for both of you too? I promise not to go crazy or anything. You're both gorgeous men, and those big shirts and baggy cargo pants aren't doing either of you justice."

Interested to see Lex's reaction to Imani's words, he looked over to find Lex was blushing. He felt equally pleased and embarrassed at Imani's compliment. Also, like Lex, he didn't know how to respond.

"Say 'thank you, Imani,'" she instructed them. "This here is our first practice at believing what each other says without reservation or doubt."

"Thank you, Imani," Mac and Lex mumbled simultaneously.

Still red in the face, Lex picked up one of Imani's braids and toyed with it. "We want to get you things too."

"Sure, baby," Imani agreed. "I'm great with going shopping for all three of us. We'll make an evening of it. Get a good meal too. I bet you two wouldn't say no to a steakhouse."

Mac would agree to anything, but Lex spoke up. "Mac likes sushi."

Imani didn't hesitate. "Then we get sushi. Whatever you guys want."

"You'll still feed on us, right?" Mac asked, wanting to make sure she wasn't going to stop taking their blood. "I know we could buy you bagged blood, but you should drink from us."

"That's not going to change," she assured him. "I'm going to let go of that guilt. Other vamps and flocks can do what they want. We get to decide what we do."

"Thank fuck," Lex sighed. His heartful groan made Mac chuckle.

Imani flashed him a smirk. "You like my fangs, don't you, Lexie?"

"We both do," Mac answered for Lex.

His eyes focused on her mouth as Imani parted her lips and ran her tongue over one of her fangs. Blood rushed to Mac's dick at the same time he heard Lex pull in a sharp breath. Mac was about to pull her into a sitting potion so he could offer his neck when she gave him a smile he could only define as evil.

"Here's what we're going to do," she said, her voice full of authority and a hint of magic. "Mac is going to help me pick up around here, and Lex is going to make sure the windows are all properly sealed so I don't get fried tomorrow. After that's all done, you two are going to feed me a nice big meal."

The pure sexuality in her voice told Mac she planned on doing more than simply feeding off them. For a split second, Mac went perfectly still, working to get his lust under control. Lex was the one to act first. He gently lifted her from their laps and set her on her feet.

"Move it!" Lex growled as he got to his feet.

Before Mac could utter a sound, Lex was in motion. He dug out Mac's small toolbox then went about pulling back curtains and measuring window size.

Moving to stand in front of him, Imani put her hands on her hips. "Come on, Teddy Bear. We've got some work to do. And I'm not letting you throw out your clothing. Let's sort that shit and put everything away in its proper place."

Renewed embarrassment helped deflate his erection. He met Imani's eyes with a self-deprecating grin. "I'm trainable," he volunteered. "I promise."

Lex

Lex followed Imani, trying hard not to stare at her lush backside perfectly accentuated in the skintight dress she'd bought earlier in the week. They were walking down a busy public sidewalk and he should be watching for danger, but damn, all he could think about is worshiping that juicy ass.

Movement made him look up. He spotted a guy trying to edge closer to Imani, using the other people passing by as an excuse. Before Lex could whip out a knife and hamstring the guy, Mac was already dealing with it.

"Don't even think about it," Mac growled.

The guy was forced to crane his neck up to look at Mac in the face. Visibly paling, he flinched back, bumping into a few people in his haste to get away. Once the threat was gone, Mac moved his eyes over to Lex. They shared a look before Mac turned his attention back to the sidewalk ahead.

"That was smooth," Imani admired. Lex moved so he was walking next to her. Despite the crowd, it was easy due to the space being cleared by Mac's bulk in front of them.

"You saw the guy?" Lex asked, getting ready to defend Mac if Imani thought the sloth bear had overreacted.

"I saw the guy coming in for a grope," she corrected. "I was ready to shove him before he could grab me, but Mac was quick with the intimidation."

Lex was surprised Imani had noticed the creep. "I didn't think you saw his intent."

"Oh baby, I see all the intent," she countered. "You can't be a woman and go out clubbing without developing a sixth sense for human predators. If Vincent had been human, I'd have known right away he was a slimy bastard."

Frowning, Lex draped an arm over her shoulder as they walked. She snuggled into his embrace, helping to settle his inner beast's constant demand for touch. "You don't have to be so vigilant anymore. Mac and I can keep you safe."

"I'll admit it's nice to have you two, but there's no shutting off the creep-dar," she replied with a half grin.

Ahead of them, Mac slowed, then stopped. He turned sideways so they could see past him. "Looks like the line is around the block."

Lex stifled a sigh at the sight of so many people waiting to get into the popular club. He really wanted to make tonight perfect for Imani. His heart had broken when she'd described her life before being turned. She'd sounded so wistful and sad at the memories of things she couldn't enjoy anymore. He'd vowed he would give her as much of her old life back as he could. A night of dancing, the same as she'd done while human, was the first step.

No, that wasn't correct. Spending the last few days shopping and letting her pick out outfits for all three of them had been the first step. Going out clubbing tonight was the second step. He'd mentally prepared himself for being in a crowded place for hours at a time. But somehow, it was even worse now that they were going to have to stand in line. He hated the delay.

"I've got this," Mac declared and led them around the line and up to the front door. Beyond the simple plastic chain barrier was a club full of writhing bodies, loud music, and good times. Standing in front of the plastic chain was a guy almost as big as Mac and wearing a shirt that had the club's name written across the front. Mac headed right for the male.

"Pike!" Mac bellowed, getting the bouncer's attention. When Pike saw Mac, his face split into a broad grin, hazel eyes shining with welcome. His shaggy dark brown hair was mussed with a section on the back sticking straight up. His employee shirt barely fit him and looked like it might rip if he flexed. Everything about him gave Lex the impression of a Great Dane-I giant body full of enthusiasm and size!

Without hesitation, Pike stepped away from his post to wrap Mac in a hug and pound his back.

"Good to see you, Maccy," Pike responded in a voice nearly as deep as Mac's. With their closer proximity, Lex could smell bear shifter coming from this guy. Considering how friendly this guy was with Mac, Pike was probably a black bear. Unlike the average sloth bear, black bears had reputations for being easygoing and highly sociable.

Pike pulled back and noticed Imani, and then followed the line of her shoulders to Lex. His welcoming smile never wavered. "Who're these two?"

"These are my mates," Mac declared proudly, but only loud enough that Pike would hear and not the humans behind them.

If possible, Pike's smile got even wider. "No shit? That's great!" He opened his arms and Lex realized he was going in for a hug. Dozens of maneuvers flashed through his head. He could grab Pike's wrist and bend it back, forcing Pike to his knees. He could grab the arm and throw the black bear over his shoulder. He could lower his shoulder and drive it into the shifter's belly, then step to the side and kick his legs out from under him.

He probably shouldn't hurt the guy too badly, so he picked a joint lock and dropped his arm from around Imani's shoulder in preparation for the move.

"Lex." Mac's single word was full of warning. He didn't want Lex to hurt his friend.

Reluctantly, Lex abandoned all his defensive plans and let the bear wrap him in an enthusiastic hug. He could see Mac's laughing face and glowered in return. Somehow, he'd make the sloth bear pay for this.

"Mates!" Pike enthused. "I'm so happy for all of you. What a blessing!"

He let go of Lex and reached out to hug Imani. It was only Mac grabbing him in a strong hold that kept Lex from breaking Pike in half as he wrapped long, thick bear arms around her.

"And such beautiful mates too," Pike continued as he released Imani and stepped back to sweep all of them with his sparkling eyes before settling back on Mac. "If anyone deserves happiness, it's you, my friend."

Mac looked touched by Pike's words. "Thanks, man. This is Imani and Lex. I'm proud to say they're my everything now."

"As they should be," Pike responded, nodded to both of them in turn, then placed a hand on his chest. "My name is David Brian Pike, but everyone usually just uses my last name." Focusing on Imani for a second, he cocked his head, then his smile dimmed slightly. "Vampire?"

Lex tensed, worried the black bear might attack her. Most distrusted vampires at best and openly despised and hunted them at worst.

"I'm not going to attack anyone," Imani assured him. "I'm well fed, and my instincts are under control."

Pike waved a hand in the air. "I'm not worried about that. But it's already one in the morning. You only have another five hours before sunrise." He looked over to Mac. "You need to be careful! Even light through a window without the right treatment could be deadly for her."

He was concerned about Imani? Blinking in surprise, Lex realized this black bear was probably one of the most kind and genuine people he'd ever met.

Mac's expression was fond as he responded to Pike's comment. "I have an alarm set on my phone, and I've given us plenty of time to get her home safely."

Pike looked relieved and swept his gaze over the three of them. "Good, good. Are you here to dance? We've got a fucking brilliant DJ tonight. She's a fox shifter that goes by Red Sandz."

Imani's face lit up. "Red Sandz? I love her."

"Who doesn't? She's the best!" Pike declared with equal excitement while he unclipped the plastic chain and urged them inside. "Go on in. Enjoy yourselves."

Lex was quick to pull out some of the cash he'd stuffed in his pocket to pay for cover charges, but Pike put his hands behind his back and shook his head.

"Nope. This is my mating gift to you guys. You get in free any night I'm here," he promised. "Besides, I'd do anything for the man that rescued my little sister."

Lex caught the flash of annoyance on Mac's face before the sloth bear smoothed out his expression. Mac opened his mouth to say something but some of the humans in line started getting rowdy at the three of them being allowed to cut the line. With an unwavering smile, Pike addressed the humans and smoothed ruffled feathers by chatting with them and promising they'd be let in soon.

The guy was so damn genuine and nice it was hard to stay angry at him.

"You saved his sister?" Imani asked as they made their way deeper into the club. The music was loud enough that he wouldn't have been able to hear her if he wasn't a shifter.

Mac frowned. "It's complicated, but the short version is that Pike has a twin sister who's a piece of shit. I swear he got all the kindness and Lucy got all the selfishness. She went missing last year and Pike was out of his mind with worry. I found her and talked her into going home, and she made up this whole big thing that I'd rescued her from an abusive boyfriend so she wouldn't sound like the loser she is. I tried to set him straight, but he wouldn't listen to me."

"Poor Pike," Imani murmured. "I can understand wanting to think the best of your family despite the evidence."

Lex had strong opinions about what family was for and using each other wasn't one of them. The thought of helping Pike out by making his sister permanently disappear crossed his mind, but he dismissed it. If Mac or Imani ever found out, they might get upset, and he'd hate it if his mates were mad at him.

They'd forgiven him for his past. It would be for the best to limit his murdering from now on.

Dismissing Pike's problems from his mind, Lex focused on tonight's goal—Imani getting to dance and enjoy herself. Why else would he be standing in this loud, dark, crowded place, potentially full of hidden dangers masked by magic spells and powerfully spelled perfumes?

"We need to buy true sight charms," he muttered.

Mac frowned down at him in confusion. "What?"

They'd stopped at the entry from the bar area to the dance floor. Imani was moving her hips to the music's strong beat, focused on the mass of writhing bodies. Mac leaned his head into Lex, his expression confused.

Pointing to the crowded dance floor, Lex repeated his words. "We need to buy true sight charms. Any one of those people could be a powerful predator, and we might not know if they have magic strong enough to cover it up."

With an amused expression, Mac gave Lex a quick kiss on the cheek. "It's unlikely anyone here will cause a ruckus. And no creature strong enough to overpower the two of us will be able to hide, no matter what spell they buy."

Lex grunted, acknowledging Mac's point. Before he could say anything more, Imani grabbed his hand, then Mac's.

"Come on!" Imani shouted, tugging at both of them. Lex looked up to see panic on Mac's face. It was clear the big shifter was terrified of going out on the dance floor.

Hiding his smirk, Lex pulled Imani up short. "We should leave Mac here."

Imani turned to meet Mac's gaze. "You don't dance, baby?"

"I could try," he offered, his body language screaming with discomfort.

Imani let go of his hand and reached up to cup his cheek. "Aww, sweetie, you can wait here. Maybe grab you and Lex a beer or two?" she cast a heated glance at Lex. "I plan to work you hard, white boy. You ready for it?"

"Bring it," Lex answered, letting his smirk show. Imani laughed and Mac looked both surprised and pleased. With a relieved smile, Mac headed to the bar. Lex walked Imani into the crowd of dancers, pushing gently to get them in a good spot where she'd have some room to move and could see the DJ.

Turning to face her, he put a hand on her hip and leaned in close, brushed his lips across hers, then started moving.

Mac

Mac made his way to the bar and bought two beers. If Lex didn't make it back in time to drink his before it got warm, Mac would simply consume it and buy another one. With his size and shifter metabolism, it would take half a keg before he would feel the effects of even a really strong beer.

Putting the beer to his mouth, he turned around and surveyed the dancers. He barely managed not to do a spit take when he spotted Lex and Imani. His female mate was gorgeous as she moved with sexual grace. That wasn't a surprise at all. What shocked him was the sight of Lex moving with equal grace as his body flowed in the small space he'd created for the two of them to dance.

"Damn, your mates are good," Pike murmured as he set down a crate of bottles on the bar next to where Mac was leaning. Straightening away from the bar, Mac smiled at Pike.

"I knew Imani could dance, but I would've never guessed Lex could also," he admitted. "I thought you were stationed at the front door?"

"Toby took over for the rest of the night. He likes to flirt," Pike explained with a grin. Then he nodded his head at the dancers as he emptied the crate into a spot under the counter. The bar was long and almost everyone was crowded near the other end where the hot bartenders were pouring shots and shouting friendly insults at the patrons. "You should be out there with them."

Mac shook his head. "I was built for strength, not beauty. If I went out there, lives might be lost."

Pike laughed. "Yeah, I'm not one to dance either." Pulling out a bottle of cheap beer, Pike opened it with his bare hand and took a long draw. That's when Mac noticed how worn out the black bear looked. He'd lost some weight and there were dark circles under his eyes.

"What's going on with you?" Mac asked.

Pike shrugged and set the mostly empty beer down and pulled a deep breath. "I'm good, mostly. Money is a little tight, you know? But nothing a few extra shifts won't help."

Judging by the slump of Pike's shoulders, that last part was a complete lie. "Do you need a loan?"

Pike grinned and shook his head. "Naw, I'm good. But thanks. But, um, could I ask you some questions about being mated to a vampire?"

That wasn't a request Mac was expecting. "Our relationship is really new, but I'll tell you what I can."

After a brief hesitation, Pike asked his first question. "You and the other guy are her flock, right?"

"Yes. Lex and I have been friends for years. Then we met Imani at the same time and when we touched her, it was like bang." Mac slapped the counter with the last word. "The connection was so powerful it scared Imani. We worked it all out though."

"Obviously," Pike commented. "Does she drink from you guys? I was told vampires can't drink from their flock, that it hurts them to take blood from someone they're bound to. The guy who told me was an old school druid, so I'm thinking he might've been wrong."

Mac scowled. He wasn't fond of the Foundation Druids and their archaic outlooks. "They can drink from their flock; it doesn't hurt them. Most vampires probably don't because their flock is human. Imani takes from Lex and I all the time. She's so much healthier because of it."

Pike's brows furrowed. "And it doesn't hurt you guys?"

"Feels amazing," Mac admitted, and knew he probably had a dopey expression on his face, but even the thought of Imani sinking her fangs into him made the crotch of his pants get tight.

Pike's eyebrows rose before he laughed and slapped Mac on the back. "Nice!"

Their proximity allowed Mac to focus. He was able to pick up an unfamiliar scent of something powerful clinging to Pike. It was faint and masked by a mixture of the humans, shifters, pixies, and fae Pike interacted with during his shift. But it was there and distinctive.

Mac took an educated guess. "Did you meet a vampire you're interested in?"

The black bear shifter had never been good at hiding his emotions. The guy was simply too open and friendly. Even knowing that, Mac was unprepared for the sudden change in Pike's behavior.

The black bear dropped his gaze to the counter and stared at his hands with an incredibly sad expression. "Something like that."

Feeling horrible for whatever was causing Pike's hangdog expression, Mac turned to fully face him. "Do you want to talk about it? I might not have any advice, but I can listen."

Pike let out a long, heartfelt sigh. "I don't feel comfortable telling anyone about what's going on. It's kinda dangerous and if the wrong people found out, someone I love could get hurt."

That wasn't what Mac was expecting at all. What had Pike gotten himself mixed up in? "Sounds complicated. I'm not into gossiping. Whatever you tell me won't get passed on."

Raising his face to meet Mac's gaze, Pike gave a little shake of his head. "Thanks for the offer, but this can't get out. You'd feel bad keeping secrets from your mates, even if it didn't involve them. I can't risk it getting past your mates to others who might take advantage or see a threat. But I've got your number. I might call you, you know, to ask more questions."

Pike's explanation was too vague and unsettling to do anything but increase Mac's concern. The black bear's attempt at a half smile did nothing to alleviate his worry.

"Are you in danger?" The question came out far harsher than Mac meant, his unease deepening his already low voice.

"No danger," Pike assured him, the half-smile tipping up into a real show of mild mirth. "At least not in the way you think."

Mac leaned in a little closer. "There's a lot of ways to be used or abused. I don't want any of them happening to you."

Pike's kind features softened to an expression of happiness. "Thanks, man. It's good to have friends."

Mac couldn't make Pike confide in him, but he could make sure the guy knew he had options. "Call anytime, day or night."

"I will," Pike agreed, then focused on something over Mac's shoulder. "Damn, your mates are hot!"

Mac swung around in time to see Lex pick Imani up and swing her around, then slide her down his front while both of them stared intently into each other's eyes. It was almost enough to push Mac out onto the dance floor himself.

Not to dance, though. He wanted to drag his mates off and find a dark place to ravage them both. If they kept doing moves like that, it was going to take a lot of restraint to leave them alone to dance.

He downed the second beer in one long pull, then tossed the bottle to Pike. "I'm going to need more of that. Probably a lot more."

Pike

Mac's mates were gorgeous. Even as Pike admired them, he thought of his own sexy trouble, probably lurking out back in the dark area behind the club. The connection between them was weak, but he wasn't picking up any worry or anxiety yet. That meant he had time to grab another couple of boxes for the bartenders before taking out the trash. It wasn't his favorite job at the club, but because his own personal shadow would be able to set eye on him while he slung bags into the dumpster, he always volunteered for the task.

"Oh my god, stop it already!"

The angry feminine voice drew Pike's attention. He found the woman immediately. She was a tiny thing with long, purple highlighted black hair flowing around her shoulders. Pike recognized the guy who had her backed up against a wall. Steve was a wolf shifter and unlike most wolf shifters, he'd gotten himself kicked out of two different packs for reasons no one would talk about.

To Pike's dismay, this was Steve's favorite club right now. Without fail, he was here every Friday night. The guy would hit on anything with a pulse and wasn't always good at backing off when he got a negative. Now was a perfect example. Steve had the woman boxed in with one hand resting on the wall next to her head and the other on the wall near her hip.

Guilt made his shoulders tense up. Pike was usually better at keeping an eye on Steve when he was in the club. It was Pike's fault that the little human was being harassed. Rounding the end of the bar, Pike focused on the couple. He could hear what Steve was saying despite the loud music and the distance separating them.

"Aww, but don't you want some love too? You're standing here all alone and shit. Looks like you might be lonely. I don't mind taking the ugly friend for a fun ride."

Outrage built with every word. Others might think Pike was oblivious and maybe a little innocent. It was true he'd grown up sheltered by a loving bear family, but no one could remain unaware while working these jobs. He heard guys negging girls all the time or harassing them when their charm didn't work. He'd seen every one of the latest ploys the dude-bros were teaching their followers.

Pike hated it and always confronted these men the moment he could, even though the manager frowned on it. If the guys were buying drinks, the manager didn't care if they got a little aggressive with the women. It drove Pike crazy, but he couldn't afford to lose this job by arguing with Stan about sleazy customers.

The best were nights like this one, when Stan was busy in his office and Pike got to throw out all the guys he wanted to. Tonight, he didn't plan to be gentle.

"I said back off," the woman snarled. Pike admired the aggressive tone of her voice. She wasn't intimidated by Steve, even though he was a foot taller and almost twice as broad as her. Pike loved this woman's fearlessness!

Steve moved the hand resting on the wall next to her head lower to touch her hair. Pike's earlier outrage vanished, replaced by a seething anger he'd rarely ever experienced.

How dare Steve touch this woman?

The presence he always felt in the back of his head perked up and pressed concern at him. Breathing hard, he ignored the inquisitive feeling and focused on getting across the bar area as fast as he could. Other shifters saw his face and moved, but most of the humans remained unaware. He was forced to skirt around several groups and momentarily lost sight of Steve and the woman.

When he could see them again, he was brought up short. Steve was curled up in a fetal position on the dirty floor at the woman's feet. She looked flushed and annoyed, but also triumphant.

Oh, his little female had moves!

Wait, "his little female?" Why was he thinking like that? No, she wasn't his. He didn't need any more complications in his life.

Pretty. Fierce. Ours.

Confused, he stood there and tried to separate his own impulses from what was coming from the presence. It didn't help that his inner bear was urging him to sniff the woman all over and take her out to forage for berries. Shifter instincts could be really distracting sometimes.

Shaking himself out of his thoughts, he resumed his journey. When he got there, the woman was leaning over Steve, her straight purple and black hair obscuring her face.

"No means no, asshole," the woman said.

"I think you broke my dick, you crazy bitch," Steve moaned. Pike accidentally stepped on Steve's leg, making the wolf shifter yelp and uncurl as he tried to crawl away. "What the fuck, Pike? Get off!"

"Oops, sorry about that." Grinding his heel in before lifting it off Steve, he addressed the woman. "Are you okay?"

"Is *she* okay?" Steve screeched. "I'm the one on the floor with a busted dick."

"I'm sure you deserved it," Pike shot back, never taking his eyes off the woman. He needed her to look up. He was suddenly desperate to see her eyes.

Look at me, he silently begged.

With her hands still on her hips, she straightened and swung her luxurious thick hair over her shoulder, meeting his gaze defiantly. "He touched me first. I told him to back off and he wouldn't. This isn't assault. It's self-defense."

Pike was dumbstruck. She was gorgeous. Easily the most beautiful woman he'd ever seen. Her scent confirmed she was human, but her delicate facial features and high sharp cheekbones made him think of pixies. Her skin was almost as pale as Mac's mate Lex, creating a strong contrast with her raven and dark-purple hair. All of that was stunning, but it was her eyes that captured him. He'd never seen dark-gray eyes ringed with black before. They were magnificent.

"You're so pretty," he mumbled out before his stunned brain came back online. Her expression turned salty as he winced at his own stupidity. "I mean, um, I'm sure Steve deserved what you did."

"Pretty?" Steve laughed from his position on the floor. "You think this stick-figure bitch is pretty? You're an idiot! I didn't know you went for women with no hips, ass, or—"

A foot on his chest kept Steve from being able to finish that sentence. The wolf shifter grabbed Pike's ankle and tried to move his foot off, but Pike put more weight down and Steve started struggling to breathe.

Pike ducked his head a little to get her attention. "Ignore him. I'll toss him into the dumpster out back in a minute. My name's Pike."

The woman's expression turned amused. "Dumpster? Solid plan, I approve. I'm Cora."

Then she did something miraculous; she held out her hand. He was quick to reach out and grasp her delicate hand in his. His world changed the moment they touched. There was perfect agreement between himself, the presence in his head, and his bear.

Cora was theirs.

He must have held onto her hand a moment too long for civilized society because she tugged at it. He reluctantly let go and racked his brain to keep the conversation going without coming off as a creep or idiot.

"I've never seen you here before," he started. "I work here nights from Tuesday to Friday. I know I'd remember someone like you."

Tucking her hands behind her back, she gave a little shake of her head. "Yeah, this is my first time. I came with some friends. I'm not usually into clubbing, but it's Julie's birthday, and all she wanted was for all of us to come out with her."

"Where are they?" he asked, risking a quick glance around before returning his gaze to Cora.

"Somewhere on the dance floor," she answered with a tired sigh. She brought one hand forward to tap the purse at her hip secured by a sturdy strap running across her chest. "I'm the designated driver and the one holding everyone's ID, cards, and lipstick. I think there's even a pair of ballet slippers in here. It feels like I'm the adult version of a camp counselor or something."

She tried to smile past her discomfort with the situation. Irritation at her friends hit him hard. How could they abandon her like that? No one should have to be in charge of a group of adults and left behind while everyone else had fun. They were using her, plain and simple.

"Do you want to spend the evening with me? I'd like to buy you a drink." The moment the words were out, he wanted to smack himself. He probably sounded like Steve.

She raised an eyebrow. "Aren't you working?"

"Oh, yeah," he agreed, then reached down to pick Steve up with one hand and hauled him over his shoulder. "I'm on trash duty. Don't go anywhere. I'll be right back."

With that, he hustled out the back door to literally toss Steve in a half full dumpster. Hearing the wolf shifter land in the sinking trash and start cussing was immensely satisfying. He felt the presence in the alley, but he knew better than to search the shadows for a figure.

"Try not to kill him," he called out before heading back into the bar. He heard the swoosh of wings, Steve's cut-off cry of surprise, then nothing.

Steve was taken care of; it was time to find his little mate.

Cora

After Pike disappeared carrying Broken-Dick guy, Cora leaned back against a nearby wall and let out a long sigh. This wasn't the first time she'd been called the "ugly" girl. The idiot she'd put on the floor had thought she should be an easy conquest, and it was satisfying to prove him wrong. Still, it was disheartening how often men thought like him.

She wasn't under any illusions about herself. At five foot nothing and skinny as a rail, she didn't have the curvy body guys seemed to like. Normally Cora didn't think about her body much, outside of when something hurt. Unfortunately, going out with Julie and her party group had been a reminder at how bad she was at "girling." Not only were these women all gorgeous, but they also knew how to dress.

That thought made Cora look down at her blouse. It was her favorite color, royal blue, and while the shimmery fabric of her top sparkled even in the dim light of the bar area, it was nothing compared to the tight dresses and matching shoes the other women were wearing.

Peering at the dancers, Cora admitted to herself she needed to let go of her jealousy. She refused to wear one of those bras that squished a girl's boobs together to give them cleavage or don a skintight dress with a plunging neckline. She would end up spending the evening uncomfortable and miserably self-conscious. She needed to be content with what she had.

The bonus to her current outfit of nice jeans and sturdy shoes was the ability to break a guy's dick when he got obnoxious. It was a tradeoff she was more than willing to make.

Then there was Pike.

He'd looked at her with genuine interest. She hadn't seen any hint of the manipulation she'd dealt with when guys thought they could talk the mousy girl into bed. Unlike the movies would have everyone believe, she didn't suffer from low self-esteem, only a little doubt from time to time.

"You're still here!" Pike's excited declaration brought her out of her thoughts to focus back on the large, eager man looming over her. He must have realized what he was doing the moment she looked up because he took a hasty step back with an apologetic look. "Sorry about that, I'm used to getting close so hum—uh, people can hear me over the music."

He was so cute and sincere she found herself giving him
a reassuring smile. "I get it. No worries. Thanks for giving me
space though."

"Can I get you that drink?" he asked, gesturing with his
thumb over his shoulder to the bar.

"Yeah, sure," she agreed. He turned and created a path to
the less crowded end of the bar. Instead of getting one of the
bartender's attention, he simply reached over and plucked a few
beers out from a hidden fridge.

"This okay?" he asked, holding up the bottles in one
hand by the necks.

They were IPAs from a local micro-brewery and
normally she'd happily accept, especially in a club made hot by
so many bodies moving around. Common sense won though.
She was a lightweight and did most of her drinking at home
where she could enjoy her easy buzz off one bottle of a tasty
beer without worry.

Her unease at drinking in public was why she often
ended up being the only sober one in the group, and, by default,
ended up in charge of a bunch of raucous drunk women.

"How about something without alcohol?" she countered.

Pike didn't miss a beat. With an easy smile he leaned
back over, rummaged around, and brought out two old-fashioned
glass bottles of Coke. Holding them up, he gave her a triumphant
smile.

"I bring these in myself," he explained. "They're the
ones made down in Mexico with cane sugar instead of the high
fructose corn syrup. I swear they taste better."

Intrigued, she accepted one of the bottles. It felt ice cold
in her hand and smaller than she expected. "Thanks."

"Here." he handed her something else, and it took her a
moment to realize it was a bottle opener. "I thought you'd like to
do it yourself, just to be extra safe."

A little confused, she opened the bottle and handed him
back the opener and cap so he could open his and toss both caps
behind the bar. "Safe?"

"Yeah, because I hear hum–, I mean, women get
drugged all the time," he answered, flushing from
embarrassment. This was the second time he'd fumbled for

words. How curious. Maybe English was his second language. She couldn't hear an accent, but she was bad at stuff like that.

One thing was for sure, Pike was a sweetheart. A giant, six-foot-ten-inch, brawny, mahogany haired, tan skinned, hazel-eyed sweety.

"Are you sure you're real?" The words were out of her mouth before she realized she was speaking. Now it was her turn to blush, and unfortunately when she got embarrassed, it showed really well on her pale skin.

"Um, yes?" Pike answered, confused. "We're not in the Matrix."

"You seem so nice, it caught me off guard," she explained, then took a drink of the Coke. "Oh wow, that does taste better!"

"It totally does," he agreed cheerfully, bouncing on his toes a little in happiness. "I really like sugary things, so I have to be careful because I could drink a case of these things if I'm not paying attention."

Why did she have the sudden urge to buy this sweet man a truckload of these drinks? "I wouldn't worry, you're so big I'm sure the extra calories won't hurt you."

"Oh, that's not the issue," he assured her with a boyish grin. "I can get a little hyper. Last time I had too much sugar, I started to rearrange furniture at three in the morning. My downstairs neighbors weren't amused."

Cora snorted out a laugh and started to ask him about where he lived when a familiar face appeared past his left shoulder. "Imani?" she gasped.

Imani was flanked by two men, both of them large and muscled, and one of them even taller than Pike. Both of them looked intimidating, but the one without hair looked like he'd killed in the past and had no qualms about doing it again. She'd seen that same expression from her brother after he'd gotten back from his last tour. It made unease compete with shock at the sight of Imani after all this time.

Imani looked as surprised as she was. "Cora?"

"Imani!" Cora cried out and launched herself. She wrapped her arms around the taller woman in a tight hug. "Fuck,

I thought you'd been kidnapped, and some guy was starving you in a pit so he could skin you later."

There was a beat of silence before Imani hugged her back and let out a soft chuckle. "You watch too many horror movies."

"But you disappeared without any warning," Cora pointed out. "No one knew what happened to you. I went to your place, and everything was still there. I stayed there, waiting for you to come back. After a week, I got really worried and went to the police and filed a missing person report."

"You went to the police?" Imani asked.

Cora felt close to tears as she let go of Imani so she could step back. "I went to them, not that it did much good. Your car was found parked near the club, and someone said they saw you leaving, but then nothing. I kept bugging the detectives, but they started ignoring me. When I realized they weren't going to do anything, I hired a private investigator. She did some digging but said you must have moved without telling me. She suggested you were hiding from an abusive boyfriend or something. I knew that wasn't it, but I kept hitting dead ends."

Imani looked stunned. "You did all that?"

Frowning, Cora wiped an errant tear away. "Of course I did all that! What else would I do? Your mom is gone, and the rest of your family is back east. You didn't have a wife or husband. If I hadn't looked, who would have? I was sure I'd never see you again. What happened, Imani? Why did you disappear?"

Imani shook her head, her long magenta braids flowing around her shoulders. "Life was rough there for a little while, but it's better now."

Hearing that made her anger flair. Cora popped her hands on her hips and scowled. "You were in trouble so bad you had to hide from everything? Why the fuck didn't you call me? What the hell, Imani!"

"I didn't want to cause—"

Cora didn't let Imani finish. "No! I don't care if it was a stalker, or you were wanted by the FBI. You should've called me." One of the guys with Imani moved a little to block someone from crowding them and Cora got suspicious.

She grabbed Imani's shoulder and tugged the taller woman a few steps away. Cora ignored the way both guys frowned. It was harder to dismiss the shorter pale guy growling and moving threateningly.

Cora squared her shoulders. Fuck it, she didn't care how much bigger he was than her, she'd take him down without hesitation.

Imani held up a finger. "It's fine," she told the guys, who both obediently stayed where they were as Cora dragged her a few more steps away.

Whispering so the men couldn't hear her, Cora spoke quickly. "Are these guys holding you against your will? I've got pepper spray and a collapsing baton in my purse. Which one do you want? The guy behind me is named Pike. He might step in and help if we have to fight them off. Don't be afraid. We can take them."

Imani was biting her lip when she pulled away and Cora knew the woman was trying not to laugh. "These guys are the reason I'm not in a rough spot anymore." She pointed to the smaller of the two. "That's Lex, and the one trying not to giggle is Mac."

With the volume of the music and how quietly she'd spoken, there was no way Lex and Mac could've heard what she'd said, yet she got the distinct impression they were amused by her.

"Hello, I'm Cora. If you hurt Imani, I'll find some way to kill you," she stated loudly with her signature bluntness. Instead of looking scandalized, angry, or annoyed, both men burst out laughing. It wasn't a reaction she was used to, but she wasn't surprised. People always underestimated her, but that only made it easier for her to fuck them up when they weren't looking.

"I wouldn't be laughing too much," Imani announced dryly. "Cora is an electrician. She could probably rig something up to make it look like you'd died of an accident." That statement sobered the men up.

"I'd never do anything to intentionally hurt Imani," Mac told her with a hand over his heart.

"Same," the other guy grumbled. "And I'd never let anyone hurt her or take her from me."

Cora found herself transfixed by Lex's gaze. The guy had the brightest yellow eyes she'd ever seen. They had to be contacts. Human eyes didn't come in that color, did they? Suddenly she felt threatened, as if someone was brandishing a gun or knife, except no one had moved.

"Stop it, Lex," Pike rumbled, coming up behind her. He didn't touch her, but he was so close she could feel his warmth. Lex raised his gaze to Pike and the threatening feeling vanished. That was fucking weird!

"Sorry," Lex mumbled, then pushed up against Imani and wrapped his arms around her waist. She leaned back against him and relaxed. Whatever was going on, it was obviously consensual and loving.

"So, Lex is what, your boyfriend?" Cora asked, looking over to Mac. "Are you Lex's brother or friend?"

Mac grinned and moved behind the couple. Pressing his chest against Lex's back, he wrapped his arms around both Lex and Imani. "Not the brother."

If these two guys were comfortable enough to share Imani and embrace each other in public, they were a lot less likely to be assholes. Feeling more reassured, Cora chuckled and met Imani's gaze. "Lucky bitch."

"You have no idea," Imani agreed with a satisfied grin. Cora was still upset that Imani hadn't reached out to her, but at least her friend was alive and well.

"I want your number," Cora demanded. "And we're going to text, and call, and meet up again. And when you're ready, you're gonna tell me about what happened, got it?"

Cora could've sworn she saw some kind of dark, pearlescent liquid fall from Imani's eye, but the woman wiped it away before she could be sure. It must have been a tear that got saturated by some sparkly black eyeshadow or something.

"Yes," Imani agreed, pulling out a phone. "I'd love that."

Mac

Mac was really enjoying the evening routine they'd developed. It started with feeding Imani the moment she woke up. It wasn't that she was always famished, rather he and Lex couldn't wait for Imani to sink her fangs into them, so they'd practically be hovering over her as the sun set.

Needless to say, the feeding usually led to sex. Really spectacular sex. It was to no one's surprise that after such great sex, all three of them needed showers, which sometimes caused more sex. Turns out Lex was a fan of shower sex.

Then it was dinner time for him and Lex. After all that, they migrated to the living room for cuddling and digestion. Right now, he was stretched out on the couch with a bunch of pillows pushed against one arm so he could sit reclined with Imani laying on him and petting his chest.

"You're so soft," she murmured. "Like a plushy."

Mac chuckled. "Good thing you like it because ain't no way I'm getting waxed."

From his spot on the floor next to the couch, Lex snickered. "No one has that much wax."

"Whatever, you bald bastard," Mac shot back. "Do you even remember what it was like to have hair? Or was that too long ago?"

"We can't all be covered in fur while in our human form," Lex teased. "You should probably be studied."

Fighting a smile, Mac growled half-heartedly "Shut up, baldy."

Lex flashed him a grin before tucking a handgun away and clicking open a long hard case. He pulled out a rifle with the most sophisticated sight Mac had ever seen. "Sounds like I hit a nerve, Ignatius."

A true growl escaped Mac at the sound of his hated first name. "If I hear that word out of your mouth again, you'll be wearing a ball gag for a month."

"Why are you so upset at the sound of your legal name? Ign—"

"Be nice you two," Imani admonished, interrupting Lex.

"Yes, ma'am," Lex murmured without looking up. He'd pushed the coffee table out of the way and had all the guns he'd packed in his truck spread out on a sheet. He was going through each one, inspecting, cleaning, and then putting it away in one of the many specialty-made hard cases he used for traveling.

Mac had one leg off the couch and his foot resting on the floor. Lex was leaning back against his leg instead of the couch. The chimera had a hard time when he wasn't in physical contact with one of them.

Lex would get better about being able to step away from them as time passed, but for now, he didn't handle separation well. It made Mac consider their future.

Traveling for assignments was obviously out of the question now. Even being out of sight from either of them for too long made Mac's instincts go haywire. Being without them for days at a time would be impossible. They were going to have to figure out some new career where they could all work together or from home or something.

Imani's phone chimed several times in a row. Without her having to ask, Lex plucked it from the coffee table and handed it to her. All his movements were done without looking away from the gun in his left hand.

"Thanks, baby," she murmured. Lex didn't look up when he grunted, but Mac saw the small, pleased smile on the chimera's face.

Mac grunted as Imani wiggled around until she was lying on her back with her head propped up a little on his pec.

He loved that she'd remained draped on top of him while checking her texts and that Lex was using his leg as a backrest. The casual intimacy was everything he'd always dreamed of and never expected to have.

"Who's blowing up your phone?" Mac asked.

"Cora," Imani murmured. The two of them had been texting regularly since Friday, and it made Mac happy to see Imani getting to interact with such an important part of her old life.

"She's an interesting one," Mac commented.

Lex snorted. "You mean violent. She threatened to use pepper spray and other weapons on us."

"And sic Pike on us," Mac added.

"She would've done it too," Imani assured them. "She was the oldest girl in a family with six brothers and no mother. I know they loved her, but it was a rough throw-you-in-the-lake-to teach-you-to-swim kind of love. It made her tough and fierce. I've seen her go toe-to-toe with general contractors, and those guys can be intimidating."

"You mentioned she's an electrician, is that how you two met? She did work for you or something?"

"Not me personally, but I made sure the construction company I worked for hired her all the time," Imani explained. She paused for a moment, then sighed. "I really fucking loved that job. I was the office manager and sometimes a project manager. I often knew more about most of our projects than the people running them, and I made friends with all the subcontractors we dealt with. I was so damn indispensable that when I came in dressed really nice one day, the owner gave me a pay raise."

Mac didn't follow that logic at all. "Why?"

"He thought I was interviewing with other companies," she explained. "After the first week, I didn't bother dressing up for work. Everyone wore casual clothing there. Then a year goes by. I hadn't done laundry in a while so I dust off my business casual to wear that day. George saw me and freaked out, called me into his office and offered me a nice bump in my salary."

"I wouldn't have made the connection," Mac commented.

"It took me a few days, then I figured it out," Imani admitted. "After that, I made sure to dress really nice for a week every year. It helped that a couple of his competitors tried to hire me away a few times."

Mac could easily visualize her bossing around burly crew leaders. "I have no trouble seeing you as indispensable. Why'd you always hire Cora?"

"Besides the fact that she's good at what she does," Imani said as she typed on her phone. "She was also willing to go against a project manager or foreman if they were trying to cut corners on safety or build quality."

"I can't imagine she'd ever back down from a challenge," Lex commented without looking up.

"I don't think she ever has," Imani agreed. "And it's gotten her into trouble a time or two."

"Trouble?" Mac asked, feeling worried for Imani's small friend.

Imani stopped texting and looked up at him. "She's had her tires slashed and her van tagged a few times by guys who didn't like that a woman called them out. There was one job site where I was so worried that I paid one of the guys extra to hang out with her all day and make sure no one harassed her."

Mac's eyebrows went up. "I bet she hated that."

Imani grimaced. "She didn't know. I told her he was a friend of mine, and I didn't have a specific job for him. Then I asked her to let him hang out and watch her work to see if maybe he'd like to go into her field. She agreed because once you're her friend, she rarely says no. I felt a little guilty for fibbing, but it was for a good cause."

"I bet she doesn't have many friends," Lex commented.

Imani returned her attention to her phone, read something, then started texting again. "You'd be right about that."

"What are you and Cora chatting about now?" Mac asked as Imani's phone buzzed with more texts.

"She bought a fixer upper, and we've been talking about carpenters. But now she's asking if I'd like to meet her at a club this Saturday." When she named the place, Mac didn't recognize it.

"Never heard of it," Mac confessed. "But I've only recently realized I like going out to dance clubs."

"And I recently realized giant plushies are sexy," Imani countered. "This relationship has broadened both our horizons!"

"You two are weird," Lex said over his shoulder, making them both laugh.

Imani's phone rapidly buzzed half a dozen times in a row. Mac watched Imani's expression turn amused as she read the texts. "Ah, now I see why she's picked this club. Pike works there on Saturday and Sundays."

"Does she date guys?" Mac asked. "He's really sweet. I'd hate to see him get his heart broken if she's not into masculine-presenting people or Pike specifically. It wouldn't take much on her part to make him think she's interested. If anyone is going to fall deeply and irrevocably in love quickly without much encouragement, it's Pike."

"Damn, that sounded like some seriously enlightened and emotionally aware shit," Lex tossed over his shoulder.

"We can't all be like you," Mac volleyed back, then tried to make his voice sound as gravely and serious as Lex. "I see mate. Want mate. Must have mate. I've licked mate. Mate is now mine."

When Lex went still and silent, Mac worried he'd gone too far with the teasing. Then both Lex and Imani burst out laughing, allowing him to relax and join in the laughter.

Once the laughter had died down, Imani rolled on her side and propped herself up on one arm to better meet his gaze. "I wouldn't worry about Pike. Cora texted that she's going even if I don't want to meet her there. That's some serious interest because she's not fond of the club scene. She likes low-key neighborhood bars better. She's also suffering from outfit crises, which means she wants to look nice for him. Considering how unconcerned she normally is about clothes, that's almost a declaration of love."

"Does she know?" Lex asked, making both Mac and Imani stare at him in confusion.

"Know?" Mac repeated.

"Bear shifter," Lex elaborated.

Imani sucked in a breath. "Ah shit, she doesn't. She's human and has no idea about any of us."

"Don't worry, love," Mac soothed her. "If it turns into more than a few dates, Pike will explain things. All of us end up revealing ourselves to a human at least once in our lifetime."

"I wish I could be in the room when that goes down," Imani commented. "I really can't tell you how Cora will react."

"Look at it this way," Lex chimed in, "if Pike breaks the news to her, then it'll be easy for you to tell her about being a vampire with a flock of shifters."

"There's that," she agreed. "Now I'm really hoping the two fall madly in love and Pike paves the way. I'd really like to tell Cora everything."

Before Mac could comment that they could break the news to Cora instead of waiting for Pike, his phone started to ring. Again, Lex was quick to grab it, but this time he tossed it to Mac instead of handing it over. Mac easily caught it in the air and answered without looking at the caller ID; he was too distracted by Imani wiggling around on top of him again.

"Mac here," he grunted into the phone.

"I've got a job for you," Ted said. "A local wolf pack had a member go AWOL instead of facing pack justice. They've been looking for him for days and are ready to get help. It's easy money. The pack is willing to pay big bucks to find this guy quick. There's a bonus if you can get him tonight. You're the first one I thought of for this."

"I'm sure," Mac drawled, amused by Ted. "After talking to Uri, Mark, and Jenna."

"I haven't talked to Mark yet," Ted answered with a self-deprecating chuckle. The pixie pawn shop owner wasn't a bad guy, but he was always looking for opportunities to make money, some more legal than others. Subcontracting a collection was something Ted did all the time.

"I guess you get to call Mark because I'm not taking jobs anymore," Mac told him. "In fact, I'm—"

Imani grabbed the phone from him and started talking to Ted. "Hello?"

Mac could clearly hear Ted's confused answer. "Who's this?"

"I'm Mac's boss. If you want to hire him, you've got to go through me," Imani declared without hesitation, making Lex look over with raised eyebrows. Mac gave him a little shrug. He didn't know what their vampire was up to either.

"Boss? Huh, okay then. Here's the deets," Ted said, switching gears quickly to try to turn Mac's *no* into Imani's *yes*. After he'd given a more elaborate explanation to Imani, listed the wolf shifter's crimes, which include at least one sexual assault, Imani was nodding her head. She asked a few surprisingly insightful questions, including if the guy had guns and was known to be more violent than the average wolf shifter.

"Okay, this sounds like something well within Mac's skill set. Now let's negotiate the price," she said.

When Ted named a figure, she immediately rejected it. "I know you're taking a cut. Now tell me the full price the wolves are willing to pay, and I'll let you keep five percent of it."

"Five percent?" Ted objected. "That's not worth my time."

"Five percent is a hell of a lot for doing nothing but calling around," Imani argued. They went back and forth for a while before settling on a price almost double what Ted had originally quoted him. After Imani accepted the job on his behalf, she ended the call and handed him the phone. Mac didn't say anything as he took the phone back because he was too busy gaping at her.

"Looks like we're going to be busy tonight," she declared gleefully as she wiggled off him and stood up to stretch. "What's appropriate attire for hunting down a slimeball wolf shifter?"

Imani

"I still don't see why we had to take this job," Lex argued as Mac pulled his vehicle to the curb several houses down from their intended target. "I've got plenty of money saved up so none of us have to work for a while. We could be home, snuggling and shit."

Imani stifled a laugh at Lex's grumbling. "Because your money won't last forever, and I want a new career. I can't go back to construction or most jobs that require daytime hours. But what you guys do might be a fit for me. For us. We could open a whole operation. Finding this Steve guy seems like a way for me to see what it's all about."

"It's low risk," Mac pointed out, backing her up. "And Imani got more money out of Ted than I thought possible."

She gave Mac an approving smile. "That's right, low risk, especially because there's three of us and only one of him."

"Two of us," Mac argued, making her approving smile disappear. "You're staying here."

"The hell I am," she argued. "I need to be there to see how this works. Don't worry, I know better than to get in the way."

Lex shook his head. "You need training. Even then, I'm not sure we can risk it until you're older and stronger. Right now, a shifter could rip you apart."

As much as she hated being reminded that she was close to helpless in the preternatural world, she had to concede his point. The last thing she wanted to do was be a distraction and put the guys in danger.

"I'll stay behind," she agreed. Then tacked on, "This time."

Lex made a grumpy sound at the *this time*. Ignoring the chimera, she turned her attention to Mac. "I still don't understand how we ended up here. No one mentioned this place, and Steve's sister didn't give us this guy's name as one of his non-pack friends. Where did this address come from and why are you so sure he's here?"

"Process of elimination," Mac explained. "Guys like Steve aren't smart, and they don't tend to have a lot of friends because they make enemies fast. After talking to the list of acquaintances we got from Steve's sister, I got another list of people they'd heard Steve talking about. When I called those people, only two of them weren't looking for Steve because he owed them money."

"I'm following your logic," Imani agreed, then shook her head. "But why did you pick the Jim guy to visit instead of the other one? Was it a flip of the coin?"

"Jim was chatty," Mac proclaimed, as if that explained everything.

"So?"

"People who aren't good at it talk more when they lie," Lex explained without looking away from the broken down, blocky, two-story house. "As if adding extra words and details will make the lie more credible."

"And he was way too friendly," Mac added. "Everyone else I talked to was at least a little annoyed at having some stranger calling them out of the blue. Jim wanted to talk to me about the weather and his bad back."

Imani felt doubtful. "It doesn't seem like much to go on. He could be the type of person who just likes to talk to everyone."

"In that case, we'll move to the next one on the list. Besides, all I need is for Jim to open the door." Mac tapped his nose. "It was obvious from our conversation that Jim is human, so if I don't smell any shifter when he opens the front door, then I know we're in the wrong place.

"Is this how it always is?" Imani asked, feeling mildly let down. "When are you going to bust in some guy's front door, hold him against the wall with the front of his shirt, and demand he tell you the truth?"

Mac barked out a laugh. "Someone watches too many shows."

Lex didn't laugh, but Imani could feel the amusement radiating off him. "We've busted down doors in the past. It's usually better to do it this way first." Then he met Mac's eyes. "You take the front door. I'll go around back."

Both men nodded and started getting out of the car when Imani grabbed Lex by the sleeve. "What do you mean you're going around the back?"

"If Steve is there, he'll run," Mac explained for Lex. "I'm going to flush him out for Lex to chase down."

That made sense, but Imani's protective instincts were starting to kick up. Faced with the potential for real danger, she was suddenly scared for her flock. "Right, okay, sure. Be careful, okay? Don't get yourselves hurt or, um, no sex for two days."

Both men's jaws dropped at her threat. "Not a scratch," Mac vowed.

"I won't even let him hurt my feelings," Lex added, then he smirked. "Besides, no one throws sticks, stones, or words when they're dead." Imani didn't have a chance to respond before he slammed the door shut and disappeared into the evening shadows.

Mac gave her one last reassuring smile before closing his own door and strolling down the sidewalk to Jim's house. Although she knew he was carrying several guns, they were artfully hidden by his large button-up shirt and general bulk of his body. Because he was sneaking around the house, Lex hadn't bothered with subtle and even had a rifle slung across his back.

When she couldn't see Mac anymore, she gave up on ignoring her instincts and got out of the car. There was no way she could stay inside and wait peacefully. She was going to need to at least pace a little.

The last thing she wanted to do was cause a distraction and potentially put Mac or Lex in danger, so she crossed the street, then walked the few houses down until she could fully see Jim's house. The front door was wide open, and a friendly looking man was talking animatedly to Mac.

Leaning against a tree, she watched Jim invite Mac inside. She couldn't hear everything, but she caught enough to know Jim wanted to show Mac that Steve wasn't in the house. No sooner had the front door closed than Imani saw a head and shoulders pop out of a second-story window.

This was one of the typical San Diego country areas where old giant properties had been divided then subdivided again over the years, creating densely populated neighborhoods. Instead of another house next to Jim, there was a long, two-story apartment building filling the property from edge to edge. The apartment building and Jim's house were so close that Mac might have had a hard time walking between the two of them.

As she watched, the head disappeared back into the building, then two feet appeared. The figure fully emerged from the window and positioned himself with a foot on each building. It reminded her of how rock climbers travel up and down narrow crevasse. Using both hands and feet, he started sliding down. In only seconds, he'd be on the ground and gone.

This had to be Steve. Lex and Mac weren't anywhere to be seen. Calling them would take too long and force her to take her eyes off the escaping wolf shifter.

Imani didn't think; she acted. Uncaring that she was running far faster than a human could naturally move, she sprinted across the road. She was only a few yards away when Steve landed on the ground. Using her momentum, she lowered her shoulder and tackled him. They went down in a tangle of limbs, the wolf shifter crying out in surprise.

The momentum rolled them up against the side of the apartment building with Steve taking the brunt of the impact. It was dumb luck that she ended up on top. She was a little disoriented and couldn't get her limbs situated fast enough. Steve was able to pull his legs in, planted his feet in her belly, and kicked out hard. He sent her flying, but her vampire instincts helped her land on her feet about two yards away.

"What the fuck, man?" Steve hissed at her, scrambling to his feet. "Get the fuck away from me. I've already been bitten once this week. I'm not gonna be your midnight meal too."

Imani wrinkled her nose as she stalked toward the wolf shifter. "Eww, I wouldn't put my fang in you even if you were the last living thing on earth."

Steve didn't respond; he was too busy throwing a punch at her. She might not be as trained as Mac and Lex, but Imani was familiar with the basics of brawling. Working at Pounders had made her even better. She ducked his clumsy haymaker and delivered a solid blow to his belly. Steve folded like a lawn chair and fell back on his ass.

She fought the desire to shout out a loud whoop of triumph. This man was a fully grown wolf shifter, and she'd managed to take him down. She couldn't wait for Lex and Mac to see that she was stronger than they'd thought.

Standing tall, she put her hands on her hips and gloated. "Shut up and stay down," she ordered. "Good dog."

Breathing heavily, Steve glared up at her. He opened his mouth to say something, but no sound came out. He tried to get up, but it was as if his limbs weren't working properly. His brows knitted with fear as a half-sob of fear came out of him.

"What's wrong with you?" she asked. She hadn't hit him nearly hard enough to get this reaction. It wasn't until he looked up at her and she felt the magic bouncing between them that she realized what was going on.

"I used thrall!" she breathed out, excited. "My stay command had power to it!"

Steve's expression went from scared to shocked as his eyes went wide and he focused on something behind her.

Alarmed, she turned her head in time to see a man with a gun pointed right at her head. In a split second, she took in his sneering face and the telltale star with a line through it tattooed on the side of his neck. The man was a professional vampire hunter.

The rounds in his gun would be silver and imbued with magic that would kill a vampire far older than her. She didn't stand a chance.

"Lucky me," he mocked.

Time slowed down. She saw his finger tightening on the trigger even as she started moving her body to the side.

She wasn't going to make it.

Then there was a strange popping sound and the guy's head exploded, showering her with blood, bone, and brains. The vampire hunter's sudden and gory end made her stagger and fall to her knees in shocked surprise.

The man's headless body thumped to the ground in front of her, blood pouring from the open neck and pooling on the hard-baked Southern California ground. She couldn't take her eyes off the body. The man had almost killed her and by extension her death would've been the end of Mac and Lex. Now that they shared souls, none of them would survive if one of them died.

There was some scuffling behind her, but she couldn't look away from the corpse. Couldn't take her eyes off her first true brush with death since being turned and the man who nearly cut her flock's lives short. One reckless act almost lost them everything.

Strong arms grabbed her and picked her up, crushing her against a muscled chest. Closing her eyes, she went boneless in Lex's arms.

"Is she hurt?" Mac asked. She could sense him standing nearby.

"No," Lex answered. "I think she's in shock. She's shaking."

She was? How strange, she couldn't feel it.

Lex's voice turned to an angry growl. "Is the wolf still alive?"

"Yeah," Mac said, sounding regretful.

"He doesn't have to be," Lex responded. "We can bury him in the same shallow grave as this fucker."

She felt strangely disconnected, as if everything happening to her was something being done to someone on a show she was watching. Her flock was with her, but they sounded like they were talking from far away. Lex was a solid physical presence, holding her and rocking slightly, but it wasn't really registering.

It was only midnight, barely midday by vampire standards, but she was suddenly lethargic. She couldn't have moved even if she wanted to.

"It's okay," Lex whispered in her ear. "I've got you."

Trusting Lex, Imani let her body fall into a vampire sleep and went limp.

Lex

For as long as he lived, Lex would never get the image of the tooth-puller poised and ready to fire out of his mind. He'd heard the scuffle and burst out from behind the house in time to see Imani with a gun to her head. The sounds of Mac breaking things as he rushed out of the house told him neither of them would make it to Imani in time.

In one fluid motion, Lex had dropped to one knee and swung his rifle from his back. He'd taken it as a back-up, thinking there might be a slight chance he'd need to take Steve down from a distance with a bullet to the thigh. There hadn't been an expectation that he'd need it to save Imani's life.

As he pressed the stock of the weapon tight against his shoulder and put the man's head in his sights, he'd seen the tattoo. It was the mark of a vampire hunter, more commonly called tooth-pullers. No matter what title you used, it all meant the same thing: death to vampires.

Years of training kept him from breathing erratically or jerking the trigger. There wouldn't be a second chance for him to fire if he missed. His aim had been quick but accurate. The muffled sound of the suppressed rifle firing and the kick against this shoulder barely registered. The hunter's head disappeared in a puff of red.

With the threat gone, the need to hold Imani was overwhelming. From one breath to the next, he was on his feet running, the rifle once again slung across his back. The elapsed time from when he came around the house and saw Imani with a gun to her head, destroying the hunter, and then being able to pick her up was barely a minute. It was sixty seconds that had lasted an eternity.

"What happened? Why did she pass out like that?" Mac asked, dropping to his knees next to Lex. He had Steve slung over his broad shoulder and his sudden movement made the wolf shifter moan in pain. Both of them ignored him.

"She needs a reset," Lex answered, trying to keep his voice calm even as the leftover effects of fear and adrenaline were coursing through him.

"What the fuck do you mean 'reset'?" Mac snarled.

Lex didn't take his tone personally. "I've been talking with Tobias about young vampires. He said this happens sometimes."

Mac's tone gentled. "You mean she's not hurt?"

"No," Lex assured him. "She'll be fine in a little while."

Lex registered the sound of curious people coming out of their homes to investigate the ruckus they'd caused. Steve had stopped moaning and was now trying to bargain with them, drawing people's attention toward their hidden spot.

"You got a hide charm on you?" Lex asked, nodding toward the tooth-puller's body. "We need to make sure no one sees the corpse until we can get it cleaned up."

Mac nodded and dug into his pocket. Pulling out the disk of wood, he activated the charm then dropped it onto the headless body. The body rippled like a heat mirage in the desert. Then it looked like a mound of dirt, matching the earth under the body. The illusion wouldn't last long, but all they required was a few hours.

"We need to get out of here," Lex said as he stood up, holding Imani's limp body securely in his arms. "We can come back to dispose of the tooth-puller after everything dies down."

Pulling Steve off his shoulder, Mac thumped the shifter on to the ground, stunning the wolf immobile. Unbuttoning his large overshirt, Mac stripped out of it, leaving himself in a black t-shirt. Mac draped the large article of clothing over Lex's back, helping to hide the rifle.

"That's better," he grunted as he hauled Steve to his feet. The wolf had gotten his breath back and pulled fruitlessly against Mac's hold.

"Come on man, I've got money," Steve protested, his greasy brown hair no longer held by the baseball cap he'd been wearing. "You can have all of it. Just let me go and pretend you didn't find me. I'll leave tonight. I've got friends up in Santa Barbara. I'll go stay with them."

"You don't have friends anywhere," Mac countered. "Your buddy Jim isn't even coming out here to find out what happened to you."

"Don't be like that," Steve whined. "I got friends. A shit ton of friends. Just not here. The packs around here are too uptight. I really didn't do anything. I swear I didn't."

"Tell that to your alpha," Mac countered as they stepped out of the shadows. "You're facing pack justice."

Steve started thrashing violently, causing several people to point and whisper at them. A few even held up their phones to record. Through their link, Lex could feel Mac getting irritated but was also unsure what to do about Steve's antics. The last thing they wanted was the human authorities being called. Then Lex got an idea.

"Your drunk ass is going home to your wife," Lex announced nice and loud. "I can't believe you. Two kids and a baby on the way? How could you do this to Cindy?"

"Who the fuck is Cindy?" Steve shouted.

"You're so damn drunk you forgot you're married!" Mac said with exaggerated astonishment, picking up on Lex's ploy. "I didn't think anyone could get that wasted."

Lex heard tittering and bits of conversation from the crowd. They believed the lie, and a few were wondering if Imani was passed out from drinking or drugs. He didn't care what they thought as long as no one tried to take her from him.

Ignoring the wolf's cursing and struggling, Mac strode past Lex and opened the back door of his SUV to shove Steve in. Unlike Lex's new and shiny truck they'd been driving around, this vehicle had been modified to carry unwilling passengers with bars over the inside of the windows, bars across the back window, and a heavy-duty grate between the backseat and the front.

It was the type of setup where Mac didn't worry about restraining Steve after he was in the vehicle. Given time, the

wolf shifter could get free, but where was he going to go with
Mac and Lex right there?

Lex waited for Mac to open the passenger door so he
could climb in. He ignored the rifle digging into his back as he
settled into the passenger seat, Imani cradled in his arms. He
hoped she wouldn't be out for much longer.

Mac hurried around to the driver's side, jumped in, and
made quick work of getting them out of there. As he drove, he
called Ted and arranged for a wraith to dispose of the body.

"How much is that going to cost us?" Lex asked,
curious. If it wasn't too expensive, he might use a wraith next
time he had to get rid of a corpse. Having a creature eat the
entire thing sounded much cleaner than anything he'd done in
the past. "Or is Ted paying for it?"

"Wraiths do it for free," Mac explained. "I'll bet you
Ted's got a list of wraiths who pay him for locations on
unmonitored, above-ground, freshly-dead bodies."

"Let. Me. Out!" Steve screamed from the back seat. He
violently pounded on the bars separating the front from the back.
"Whatever Trish said is a lie. I never touched her."

Lex looked over his shoulder. Steve flinched away and
pressed himself against the seat back. "Chimera eyes! Shit, don't
eat me!"

"As if," Lex muttered.

"No really, you've got to believe me," Steve pushed. "I
didn't do anything wrong."

"Be quiet or I'll let Lex loose on you," Mac grumbled.

Steve opened his mouth, closed it, then huddled against
the door farthest away from Lex. Satisfied the wolf shifter was
obeying Mac's order, Lex turned his attention back to Imani.

"Tell me about this reset thing," Mac demanded as he
sailed through a yellow light.

"It's only happened to me a few times," Imani answered,
opening her eyes and sitting up. "Young vampires can get
overwhelmed, and I guess the best way to describe it is like
fainting. My mind shuts off for a little while. I'm back now."

She tried to move off Lex's lap to take the spot on the
bench seat between the two of them, but Lex wasn't having it.

He tightened his arms and snuggled her close to his chest. "How do you feel now?"

"Stupid," she admitted, huffing out a breath.

"You're not stupid, love," Mac argued.

"I bet Lex thinks differently," Imani countered, her voice full of self-recrimination.

Lex didn't need to see the look Mac gave him; he already knew the assignment. "Not stupid, impetuous."

Imani's expression went from guilty to amused. "Aren't they related?"

Lex shook his head. "What happened was a direct result of Mac and I being stupid."

"How do you figure that?" Mac asked, clearly affronted.

"Did we really think Imani was going to stay back?" Lex asked, looking over at Mac.

The bear shifter met his gaze briefly, then set his eyes on the road ahead. "Put like that, we do sound like the stupid ones."

"And you make me sound like a child," Imani added, brows furrowed. "I don't like it."

Lex sighed and tried to explain. "Asking you to stay behind was asking you to go against your nature."

"My nature is to be childish and stupid?" Imani shot back. Because he could still feel self-disgust coming from her through their link, Lex wasn't upset at her sharp tone.

"Your nature is to care for us," Lex answered. "We're your flock, and you're our mate. Would we let you go off to a potentially dangerous situation alone? Never."

"But it wasn't even that dangerous," Imani argued. "I acted like an idiot and almost got myself killed."

Lex made a negative sound. "You acted like a partner to Mac and I. Someone who wants to be a part of our lives and world. It's reasonable and healthy for relationships like ours."

Both Imani and Mac stared at him with almost identical looks of surprise. Feeling uncomfortable, he scowled. "What?"

"That was enlightened," Imani murmured.

"Like it could've been out of one of those books people read to help them be effective communicators with their lovers," Mac added. "My mom reads them all the time."

"It's nothing special, just common sense," Lex argued. "Telling Imani to stay behind is like asking either one of us not to shift. We could do it for a while, but it would be uncomfortable, and we'd be fighting our instincts the entire time."

"I'm not arguing with you," Mac answered quickly. "I think you got everything right. We were asking Imani to do something we couldn't have done if the situation was reversed. It wasn't fair."

"I still think I could've been smarter about it," Imani chimed in. "But you make a good point. I'm not one to stand on the sideline."

"That leaves us with the question of where should we go from here?" Mac asked. "I mean, do we scrap this type of work and figure something else out? Become real estate agents or something?"

"I have no idea," Lex answered honestly.

Imani

"Now pull this one," Lex demanded as he held up a gun in a holster. This was the sixth time she'd done this, and he still hadn't explained why he kept asking her to take guns out of holsters, then putting them back in.

They were both sitting on the same side of the kitchen table facing each other while Mac sat on the opposite side munching popcorn.

"Are you ever going to explain what we're doing?" Imani asked as she wrapped her fingers around the small black gun and tugged it free of the holster, careful to keep the muzzle pointed straight down as Lex had demonstrated.

"Yes," Lex answered. "Now put it back."

She slid the gun back into the holster, and Lex nodded and set that one aside to grab another one. They did the same thing again. Then again. After she'd pulled every gun he and Mac owned from holsters, Lex finally nodded his head and set the last one down.

"I think we should go with the Heckler and Koch VP9SK for you," he announced.

Mac made an inquisitive sound. "Was that what all this was about, picking a gun for Imani?"

She looked over at the sloth bear. "You didn't know what we were doing either?"

"I had a guess but wasn't sure. I thought Lex would want you to fire them first," Mac commented, then shoved a handful of popcorn into his mouth. She'd cooked and fed them both multiple burgers, country fried potatoes, and a giant salad yet here was Mac still eating.

Shifters were never full!

"I want her to learn with something that's going to fit her hand," Lex explained as he started putting everything away. "She drew the VP9SK more smoothly than any of the others. After she's proficient with this one, she can use a wider variety during practice. For now, I want her only using a single gun until practice turns into instinct."

Everything Lex was saying made sense and gave her hope for their future working together. "If you're going to teach me to shoot, does that mean I get go on an assignment or job again?"

"Maybe," Lex grunted.

She was surprised at the answer; she'd expected an outright no. A glance over at Mac revealed that he was just as startled by Lex's one-word reply. "If I'm not going out with you guys, then why are you determined to teach me this stuff?" she asked.

Lex set down everything in his hands and turned his body so he was fully facing her again. His expression was intense but loving. "Our world is dangerous."

Imani scoffed. "Tell me something I don't know."

"Yes, you're aware of the dangers and did a good job of staying alive before you met us," Lex acknowledged. "But you're in danger even with us to help protect you. A tooth-puller could still get to you."

She blinked, startled by his worry. "That's unlikely. Most tooth-pullers are human, and they wouldn't want to go up against either one of you. Besides, you have to admit that yesterday was an anomaly. We couldn't have known Jim's neighbor was a tooth-puller."

Mac joined the conversation. "I think Lex has a point. We might be powerful shifters, especially with him being a chimera, but even the two of us can be put out of commission.

No one's invulnerable. There are spells or charms out there that could knock us out. Or at least knock us on our asses."

"If a tooth-puller thinks he can get enough money by selling your body parts, it would be worth it for him to buy that magic," Lex continued. "There'll even be times when we'll have to be separated. We need to know you've got the equipment and skills to protect yourself."

"I want to be able to protect myself better," she agreed. "But I want to go out on jobs with you guys too. I know I fucked up yesterday, but my thrall worked on Steve. It worked! Do you know what that means? I'm strong enough to control a wolf shifter. This is huge. There are so many ways I could help you guys. Interviewing people, getting people to give up without fighting or running. I could make it all easier."

"We can talk about it later," Lex responded, reaching out to take her hands in his. "After you're trained."

His willingness made her grin. "Great! Let's get to the learning!"

"Wait, hold up." Mac said, thumping his mostly empty bowl of popcorn onto the table. "She almost gets killed and you're seriously thinking of taking her back into a dangerous situation?"

"Only the moderately dangerous situations," he responded. "Like you pointed out in the car, we need to do something. I can support us for a while without working, but in a few years, we're going to need to figure something out. If I sell my house and we're careful with money that could buy us another year. After that, we'll need income."

"That should be my job," Imani griped. "Everyone must think I'm a failure."

Vampires were usually at least a hundred years old by the time they found their flock. This gave the vampires time to accumulate both wealth and power. It was the vampire's job to provide for and protect their flock. Right now, she couldn't even buy them a candy bar. Well, maybe a candy bar, but definitely not a meal at even a moderately priced restaurant.

"Fuck that noise," Mac growled out. "Every vampire and flock are their own special world. We get to decide what we want to do. I'd like to see someone try to judge us."

"I'll kill them," Lex announced quietly, his eyes going dead. "If anyone even looks at either of you wrong, I wouldn't hesitate to end their life."

"That's sweet," Imani murmured, using his grip on her hands to pull him close. "Murdery and violent, but sweet. Now that I feel safe and loved, you can put dark Lex away and let happy Lex back out."

Lex blinked several times. "You think that's sweet?"

"Hell, yes, I do," Imani answered with a grin. "Anyone could buy a girl a box of chocolates, but a willingness to commit first-degree murder is a whole new level of love."

"I'd kill for you too!" Mac interjected.

Imani swung her gaze over to him and smiled. "Aw, thanks baby. I love you too."

Lex chuckled. "I didn't think I'd ever say this, but we might be the perfect amount of weird for each other."

"And that's really the most important aspect of any relationship," Imani concluded. "Complementary weirdnesses. Look at Briar, Memphis, and Tobias. She is the punk version of Cora at her most aggressive, Memphis is a big, scruffy-looking, biker dude, and Tobias is the quintessential vampire: old, wealthy, and stylish. But they all work."

"Does that mean you're not going to be so hard on yourself because you're not rich?" Mac asked.

Imani took a deep breath and looked back at Lex. "It's instinct, you know? Still, I'll try."

"Good," Lex grunted, looking satisfied. "Now we need to go out and practice actually firing."

Sitting up straighter, Imani grinned. "I get to fire the pew-pews!"

"Not if you keep calling them that," Mac laughed. "You should put on some comfortable clothing and heavy jeans. We're going to be driving way the hell out into the desert where it's legal to fire off guns. It's rocky out there with a lot of nasty cacti just waiting to slap you on the leg."

Imani gave Lex's hands one last squeeze before letting go and jumping up. She couldn't wait to learn this new skill. A skill that would potentially help keep her flock safe and might even bring in some money. Plus, handling guns wasn't something she'd ever done before. Tonight was going to be exciting!

Lex

"Lex!" Imani whined. "This is the millionth time I've drawn this stupid gun. When do I get to fire it? I didn't think learning how to handle a gun would be this boring!"

It was a fight, but Lex managed to keep from smiling at Imani's dramatic tone. They'd only been at it for an hour, but it was obvious Imani had a very different idea of how this evening was going to progress. Unlike how it was portrayed in movies and shows, learning how to handle a gun included things like being able to pull it from a holster and aiming down the sight quickly but smoothly.

So far, he'd had her practice drawing her weapon while standing in the traditional blade stance, then kneeling on one leg, and now she was running a few yards, stopping, and drawing.

The area Mac had brought them to was perfect. San Diego was a large, sprawling city, but within an hour or two of driving, it was easy to be out in the middle of nowhere with nothing but scrub brush and rattlesnakes for company.

There was nothing but dark secluded desert for miles with rocky outcroppings on three sides, perfect for setting up targets. The lack of light didn't bother any of them, as they could see almost as well in the dark as they could during the day.

Unfortunately, he'd only ever trained one other person before, so he was unprepared for Imani's reaction to the monotony of practice.

Holstering the weapon at her side, Imani crossed her arms and cocked a hip. "This all seems a little excessive. Am I even going to get to fire at a target tonight?"

Stepping close to Imani, Lex gave her a soft kiss on the cheek. "I promise, this is important. And yes, I do plan to have you fire."

"*Perfect* practice makes perfect," Mac commented from the tailgate of Lex's truck. "You're not doing anything he hasn't made me do."

Imani stepped away from Lex to look over at Mac. "He trained you?"

"Yes," Lex answered.

At the same time, Mac spoke. "He polished my skill set."

Lex raised an eyebrow at Mac. "Polished?"

"Okay, maybe you did more than polish," Mac amended reluctantly. "But I had some skills. I wasn't totally clueless."

"True," Lex agreed. "You knew how to dress yourself before we met." There was a beat of silence before Mac barked out a laugh and Imani chuckled.

"Ouch," Mac said with a shake of his head. "Fine, you might not be too far off. It's easy to think you're more badass than everyone else when you're a sloth bear shifter and mostly hanging out with humans. After the first time we worked together, Lex pulled me aside and taught me a few things."

"I get it. Lex has skills. But when do I actually get to fire?" Imani pressed.

"Show me you can do a steady draw after a short sprint and we'll start target practice," Lex offered. He would've liked to have done another few types of drills first, but he also wanted to make Imani happy. If he had his way, they'd come out every night for a week practicing these drills before Imani got to fire, but he knew better than to bother suggesting it.

"Steady draw, you got it," Imani agreed and hurried back to the starting spot. She rushed through the first three and Lex stopped her.

"Doing it wrong doesn't count," he grumbled. "Your draw is sloppy, and I can see your finger pressing too early."

"Fine, fine," Imani agreed with a stifled groan. She repeated the drill four more times, getting it perfect on the last two. Her natural grace and vampire speed combined with her intelligence made her a fast learner.

Lex stepped up behind her. "That looked good. Now we're going to fire, starting with you standing in one place. Take your time and focus on being smooth," he instructed and handed her a loaded magazine. He watched with approval as she easily slapped it home and slid the weapon back in the holster as he trained her to do. Later, they'd work on pulling from a hidden holster, but that was more advanced.

For the next few hours, they put holes in paper targets and shot at empty cans. Lex was impressed at how quickly Imani was improving, but he could tell she wasn't happy with her progress.

"This is way harder than all those action movies have led me to believe," Imani grumbled as she switched out a loaded magazine for her empty one. When they'd moved to the firing portion of the lesson, Mac took up position next to Lex. The sloth bear kept the spare magazines loaded and ready to hand to Imani.

"Isn't everything?" Mac pointed out. "I know it's frustrating because it seems like it should be easy, but firing a handgun accurately at any distance takes more skill than most realize. Be patient with yourself. It's going to take more than one session to learn all this."

Imani nodded and started again. By the time he called for a break, Lex was proud to note Imani's groupings were more uniform and consistent. Although she wasn't saying anything, Lex could tell she was getting mentally fatigued. He'd given her a lot to take in, and this might be a good stopping point. She was skilled enough not to hurt herself or them accidentally and maybe even hit a target who wasn't moving. It was a solid start.

Lex was downing a bottle of water while they all leaned against his truck when the sloth bear spoke up.

"You know, you're really good at this, Lex," he commented.

Lex swallowed the last of the water and tossed the bottle back into the small cooler. "What? Drinking?"

Mac rolled his eyes. "Not drinking. I meant teaching. I hadn't thought about it before, but you break things down and explain them really well.

Ducking his head down, Lex felt himself blushing from the compliment. "Anybody can do it."

"Mac's right," Imani argued. "Teaching isn't easy. I'd occasionally have to teach project managers how to use software for the jobsite, and I hated it. I'd forget to explain an early step because I thought it was obvious and then they'd get confused, and I couldn't figure out why. When you teach, it's like you have all the steps planned out and organized, like professional teachers with lesson plans and a syllabus."

Mac's face lit up. "That's it!"

Imani tilted her head. "What?"

Mac pointed at Lex. "What we should do as a new career. We should train people."

Lex felt lost. "Train people?"

"Yeah! We have all our contacts. We can offer training for newbies they're adding to their company or refresher courses for guys who haven't been out in the field for a while. And we could do special classes for humans who want to do that weekend warrior shit."

"I don't know," Lex hedged. This plan seemed to hinge on him being able to teach people he wouldn't have a deep emotional connection with. Could he be patient with anyone besides Mac or Imani?

"No, yeah, this is a brilliant idea!" Imani enthused. "We could start small, just one or two guys at a time. Bring them out here and run them through everything you did with me. Maybe we could see how some other schools or training facilities do it. The insurance is going to be a bitch, but I can handle that for us. I wonder if we could get Tobias to invest? We need a name, something catchy like Sure Shot."

"Wasn't that a song?" Lex asked, hoping to change the subject.

"What about the Ammunition Academy?" Mac suggested. His expression was as excited as Imani's. "Or In Site, you know, playing off the sights of a gun?"

"You guys can't be serious," Lex moaned. "I can't do that. Teaching you and Imani is one thing, but a bunch of strangers? No!"

"I'll be teaching with you," Mac assured him. "And I'm good at dealing with people. If anyone's being annoying or stupid, I'll be there to run interference for you. Think of it as a different kind of op. And bonus, we all get to stay together. We could even buy one of those nice campers for when we're out here during the day. That way Imani can be close but safe from the sun."

Lex frowned, thinking of how complicated the whole idea could get. "It'll take a lot of planning."

"My job," Imani said, pointing to herself. "I'd love to throw myself into a big project. And I know all about starting up an LLC. I helped Cora get hers up and running when she decided she didn't want to keep working for her dad. And I know about website designing, email services, tax EIN, and when to hand those tasks to more skilled people."

"None of that is happening tonight," Lex pointed out, desperate for this conversation to be over. "Let's get some more practice in before we have to head back."

"Sure thing," Imani agreed. "We can talk about it on the drive home, where you can't get away from us!"

Mac laughed as Lex dropped his head into his hands. His female mate wasn't one to let something go once she got started. It looked like he might need to prepare himself for becoming an instructor.

Mac

Lex had Imani practice for another forty minutes before calling it a night even though they had another hour before they needed to leave. Mac approved. Over practicing in a single session could be as detrimental as not practicing enough. Imani was starting to get sloppy and making mistakes. That wasn't a good way to learn a difficult new skill.

After they'd stowed everything, Mac noticed Lex hadn't moved to get into the backseat. He was leaning against the side of the vehicle, looking up at the night sky. Without looking over, he spoke. "We could stay here for another hour and still have plenty of time to get home before sunrise."

Imani cast Mac a confused look before looking at Lex. "Stay here?"

"Yeah, stay here," Lex repeated. "Where there's no one around to see us."

At first, Mac thought Lex was asking if they could have sex, but then it hit him. Neither of them had shifted in the last few weeks. That was a long time to go without slipping into their fur.

Even as he thought it, his inner beast pressed magic against his skin, eager to be let loose.

"You want to shift?" Imani guessed, her eyes moving back and forth between the two of them. "I can feel the eagerness in both your beasts. They want to stretch out, run, and…" her voice trailed off as her eyes became unfocused. Mac could tell she was concentrating on the link between them, trying to understand the animals they shared a body with.

"Imani?" Mac asked after she'd been silent for several minutes.

"Play," she breathed out, a wide smile forming on her face as her gaze landed on him. "They want to play." Stepping up, she reached out and placed a hand on each of their chests. "Let them out, my flock. Enjoy time in your fur."

Mac couldn't be sure if those words had magic attached to them or their beasts had simply been waiting for her to give permission. Either way, he felt his sloth bear push hard for release.

"Fuck, wait for me to strip," he hissed, struggling to get out of clothes that were becoming more restricting by the second. He could hear Lex cursing as he raced to undress before his chimera ripped through his outfit.

No sooner had Mac pulled free of his jeans than his bear took over, ripping his boxers apart during the shift. At least that was the only thing he lost; he'd managed to get out of the rest of his clothing in time.

Stretching his front paws high in the air, Mac let out a bellow. He pulled in a deep breath of the warm, desert night air and a rich mixture of scents filled his nose. His ears twitched as he caught all the faint sounds he couldn't hear in his human body. Sensory data flooded his bear brain, forming a clear picture of the world around him.

A lizard nestled among a group of rocks, taking advantage of the radiant warmth left over from the heat of the day. The small troop of coyotes was not far off, probably waiting for them to leave and hoping they'd leave something tasty behind. Rodents, most likely squirrels, hiding among the caucus behind him. The owl flying overhead, waiting for his group to flush out small game.

What would appear to be a nearly barren wasteland to the average human was alive for him.

Then he noticed the woodlouse infesting a small pile of wood near an old makeshift fire pit. Someone must've left the unused wood behind after a campout. They weren't as good as some nice juicy grubs, but they were still fun to crunch.

Excited to share the treat with his mate, he dropped to all fours and lumbered over to Imani. She'd stepped back to give them room to shift and now watched him approach with an encouraging smile.

"You're so damn adorable as a bear," she praised as he drew close. "I never understood the whole teddy bear thing when I was a kid, but I get it now. All I want to do is wrap my arms around you and cuddle!"

Her words filled both his human and animal side with delight. As much as he wanted to let her cuddle him, the woodlice were waiting for them. Moving his body to her side, he nudged her with his head. She responded by turning around to face him and scratching behind his ears.

Oh shit, that felt amazing! For the first time in his entire life, he wished he was one of the cat shifters simply so he could purr. Damn, no wonder dogs and cats constantly pestered humans for pets. This was nirvana!

"I think your eyes just rolled back in your head," Imani laughed. "I didn't know bears could do that."

Mac shifted his head a little to encourage Imani's hand to a slightly different spot. That was when Lex decided he wanted attention. The chimera put a shoulder into Mac and shoved him away from Imani. Lex's placement was so skillful that after he'd gotten Mac out of the way, his head occupied the spot under Imani's hand.

Falling back on his bear butt with a grunt, Mac huffed as he watched Lex get petted. Unlike his bear form, Lex could purr and was doing it loudly. Mac would be jealous if he wasn't so happy seeing both his mates enjoying the moment.

"I think I'm seeing a glimpse into our future," Imani teased as she held out her free hand to Mac. Falling forward onto his belly, Mac slid his head under her hand and gave a deep bear sigh when she started scratching him again.

When he was in his bear form, Mac had a very poor sense of time passing. Imani could've been standing there scratching their heads for a few minutes or hours. One thing was certain, when she stopped, it was too soon.

"That's enough of that," Imani said, withdrawing her hands. Lex stopped purring and butted her hand with his head before stepping away. From his spot on the ground, he idly watched Lex stretch like a cat, his deadly segmented tail held rigidly out straight and claws digging into the desiccated desert earth.

Then he remembered the woodlice! Scrambling to his feet, he went back to nudging Imani in the direction of the scrap lumber.

"You want to show me something?" Imani asked, probably picking up a vague intention from their link. It would be interesting to see how refined their link became as Imani developed her vampire powers. She was advancing so fast; she might even be able to talk to them through their shared souls in the future. Not many vampires and flocks could do that, but he wouldn't be surprised if Imani managed it.

"Do you want me to start a fire?" she asked once they were standing in front of the wood pile and firepit. He reached out a paw, easily flipping a few of the pieces over. Woodlice covered the ground under them, rolled up in their little shells and fast asleep for the night.

It was hard, but he managed to pinch one between two claws and held it up to her. She leaned over and took a closer look.

"That's a pill bug," she commented, obviously confused. "Why are you showing me where the roly-polies live?"

She obviously didn't understand. He carefully dropped the woodlouse in his mouth and crunched. Oh, nice! These guys were surprisingly plump for woodlice. Imani really needed to try one.

He patted the ground next to the slowly waking woodlice while looking at her. When she didn't move to grab one and pop it in her mouth, he tried to pick one up between his claws again. He must have gotten lucky the first time because he couldn't manage to repeat it and kept dropping them.

This wasn't going to work. He was going to have to show Imani how to root for herself. Leaning over, he snuffled through the dirt, ate a few, then looked up at her and patted the ground again.

"Yeah, no," Imani said with a laugh and shake of her head. "I'm not eating roly-polies. I'm a vampire, baby. I can't eat those. Not that I would've been tempted when I was human, but it's sweet that you want to share."

Mac's bear brain took a solid minute to understand what Imani was telling him. Then his bear side felt bad because his poor mate couldn't enjoy the tasty morsels with him. Lex had followed and quietly watched everything.

While Mac was struggling to understand Imani's refusal, Lex leaned his lion face close to the little crawlies and took a sniff. Mac got a sense of curiosity from Lex as he licked one up with his rough tongue. He spit it out a split second later with a soft yowl of disapproval.

Imani burst out laughing at Lex's antics, but Mac was upset. Now both his mates had rejected his offering. Grumpy and hurt, he tried to walk away, but Lex was fast. The chimera jumped in front of him with one leap, putting them face to face.

For a brief moment, Mac's sloth bear temper rose, and he was about to take a swipe at Lex. Before he could become violent, Lex's giant cat tongue unrolled from his mouth and swiped a long trail diagonally across Mac's face, getting his snout and one ear. Then he made a chirping sound and bounded away.

He looked over at Imani, hoping she'd help him understand what the chimera had done. She met his gaze and grinned. "I think you're it."

It? Mac's bear was slow to understand what Imani was saying. Then it registered, and he gave a little roar and sprinted over to where Lex was standing, his chimera lion face full of anticipation. He didn't try to evade so Mac barreled into him, sending them both tumbling.

"Hey, don't hurt each other!" Imani shouted, but Mac didn't pay any attention to her.

When they stopped moving, Lex was on the bottom. Mac was on top not because of any skill or planning but because Lex made sure they landed that way.

Knowing his time was limited, Mac was quick to get even with the chimera. He didn't have the same long rough tongue, but he did have a massive jaw, so he opened it up and put most of Lex's head in his mouth.

Imani gasped, and he felt concern coming from her, but before she could even utter a word, he lifted his mouth away from Lex's now sopping head and jumped off the chimera. Face wrinkled in disgust, Lex batted at his face with a paw, trying to get all the saliva off.

"What–oh, eww!" Imani exclaimed, coming to a stop next to them and seeing the state of Lex.

When Lex's narrowed eyes trained on Mac, the sloth bear belatedly realized he should be running. Turning on his heels, he sprinted into the desert, joyful to hear Lex's footsteps behind him and Imani's laughter floating in the still night air.

He didn't think he'd ever had such a perfect night of childlike fun, not even when he'd been a child. Now he was determined there were going to be many more carefree nights to come.

Imani

Imani frowned as they neared the entrance to Club Prism "I don't see her."

"Maybe she's already inside," Mac suggested as they bypassed everyone waiting in a long line to get in and headed straight for the guy working security. Pike had promised he'd put them on the guest list and instructed them to talk to Don, who was working security at the door.

"She'd text me, right?" She glanced down at her phone again but still no new text from Cora. The last text from her diminutive friend was hours ago when they'd been planning the evening. Imani had texted her three times in the last ten minutes and hadn't gotten a reply. That wasn't like Cora. The woman was compulsive about responding to text messages and DMs.

Lex pulled in a deep breath through his nose as they came to a stop at the barrier to the entrance with a human male standing guard. "She was here."

Imani leaned in close. "You can smell her?"

"She wears a distinct scent," Lex explained. "I noticed it the first time we met her. She's been through here within the last twenty minutes."

"She must have forgotten her phone at home," Imani decided. "That's the only reason I can think of that she's not responding."

While Imani and Lex were talking, Mac greeted Don and gave their names. The human was quick to smile and welcome them in, snapping at the people at the front of the line who complained.

Once inside, they found the place wasn't as crowded as Imani expected. Club Prism manager must be deliberately keeping the inside numbers low. The dance music had a great beat, and the DJ was dancing behind his soundboard. Brightly colored lights created pools of color on the dancefloor and strobes randomly illuminated people and places. Then the square panels under everyone's feet lit up, creating patterns to match the music.

"Damn!" Imani exclaimed, excited to join everyone dancing. She started for the dance floor then stopped abruptly and turned to survey the rest of the place. She needed to find Cora before she lost herself to the beat.

Not that she was worried about Cora's safety, but rather that she didn't want the tiny woman wreaking any havoc while unsupervised. She looked at Lex with a questioning expression. "Can you smell her?"

He nodded his head to the left. "That way, I think. It's hard to tell."

"What's that way?" Mac asked, taking position at her back as Lex led the way.

"Cora, hopefully," Imani answered.

Lex stopped at a spot near a metal truss tower holding up a bunch of lights and pointed. "I think I've found out why Cora didn't answer you."

"What the hell?" Imani exclaimed, completely unprepared for the sight that met her eyes. Never in her wildest dreams did she think she'd see Cora with her arms and legs wrapped around Pike's upper body like a baby monkey, kissing the guy like she wanted to pull his lungs out with her tongue.

"Pike looks like he's having fun," Mac snickered. Pike was leaning against a wall and supporting Cora's small body with one arm under her butt and another arm wrapped around her waist. He was holding her high enough on his chest that they could clearly see the giant bulge in the crotch of his jeans that continued down his right leg.

Imani blinked. Damn, Pike was packing a cannon!

"Cora might be his mate," Lex commented, drawing Imani against his chest. "His beast was probably pushing him to touch her. It's hard to ignore that instinct and behave, even when we're dealing with humans who don't know anything."

"I'm sure that however this situation happened," Mac said, waving his hand to encompass the passionately kissing couple, "Cora started it. There's no way Pike would do anything pushy. The guy doesn't have it in him. I bet she climbed him like a tree."

"Can humans feel a mate pull?" Lex asked.

"They must," Imani answered, "because that's the most un-Cora thing I've ever seen her do."

As if she could sense they were talking about her, Cora broke off the kiss and looked around. When she spotted the three of them staring, her pale skin turned tomato red, and she hastily let go of Pike and tried to wiggle out of his hold.

Dazed, Pike tightened his grip for a brief moment as he blinked and tried to figure out what was going on. Imani had nothing but sympathy for the guy. If the way his pants were filled out was any indication, most of the blood in his body was pooled just below his belt buckle.

"What—" he started, then saw them. Sheepishly, he lowered Cora to the ground, then tugged his shirt out from his pants in an attempt to cover up his arousal.

Once she was standing, Cora was quick to straighten her clothes then gave Imani an embarrassed grin. "You're here."

"Yup," Imani drawled. "Did you get lonely waiting for us?"

Cora rolled her eyes at the teasing. Then she stepped close to Imani and spoke softly, well, as softly as she could in the loud club. "Pike's hot. I'm definitely going to fuck him, but I might try dating him too."

Imani could see Pike's face over Cora's head. The bear shifter's expression went from excited to enamored as Cora spoke. "I'm 100% sure Pike would like both those plans."

Nodding her head as if making a decision, Cora waved Pike over. "Pike isn't working right now, so we can all hang out together," she offered.

The bear shifter ambled over with a big, friendly grin. "Heya. I have to help with closing, but I've got the next few hours free."

As they stood next to each other, Imani watched Cora's hand twitch as if she was fighting the urge to touch Pike. These two needed to find a quiet corner together, not hang out with her, Lex, and Mac.

"I was really hoping to dance," Imani told her, looking over at the dance floor with an exaggerated expression of longing. "And Mac promised he would give it a try this time."

"I did?" Mac yelped, taken by surprise. "How high was I when I agreed to that?"

Lex snorted. "Postcoital high."

Mac gave him a sloppy happy grin. "Yeah, probably. That's the best high."

Cora ignored their sexual banter and kept her focus on Imani. "I'm not really into dancing."

"I know that." Imani assured her. "Pike can keep you company while we have some fun. When he has to go to work, you and I can hang out and talk."

Cora nodded, her hand twitching again. This time, she shoved it in the pocket of her jeans. "Good. Yes. Like." She shook her head, sending her black and purple hair flying. "Let me try that again. That's a good idea. We'll find each other later."

Working hard to keep her face straight, Imani turned to Mac. "Okay, big guy, let's see your moves."

Mac looked close to panicking. "I have none. No moves. Zero abilities. Four left paws."

"Paw?" Cora repeated as they moved away.

"Aw, shit," Mac muttered.

"I wouldn't worry," Imani consoled him. "With what Pike's packing in his pants, he's going to need to confess he's a shifter or claim to be a porn star if they ever have sex."

As if summoned by his name, Pike appeared next to Lex. For a guy who was almost as big as Mac, Pike could be quick and quiet when he wanted to be. They all stopped to look at him. Cora had stayed back, checking her phone and wincing. She was probably finally seeing the texts from Imani.

"Uh, Mac?"

Mac was quick to apologize. "Hey, I'm sorry about the four left paws comment."

Pike's lips quirked. "Yeah, no worries. But remember what you asked about? It's all arranged. All you gotta do is punch in 2727."

"Nice!" Mac exclaimed and held up his fist for Pike to bump. "Thanks, I owe you."

"Naw, we're even," Pike assured them, then looked at her and Lex in turn, his eyes twinkling. "You guys have fun!" Then he was striding back to Cora.

"What was that all about?" Imani asked.

"Nothing," Mac answered, then exchanged a conspiratorial look with Lex.

"What are you two plotting?" Imani pressed.

Mac's grin could only be described as shit-eating. "You'll find out."

When she looked at Lex, he only shrugged and tried to hide his smile.

"Fine," she huffed, pretending annoyance. "But this better not be some kind of practical joke. I don't like those."

"I'll make a note of that for future reference," Mac murmured and tugged her close. They were on the edge of the dance floor. Instead of moving with the energetic beat pumping out of the speakers, he started swaying slowly to music only he could hear.

She let him lead. "This is very Fonzi of you."

Mac's brows scrunched. "Fonzi?"

Lex looked equally puzzled. "Are you calling him the guy from that old Happy Days show?"

"Yeah," Imani answered Lex. "I dated a guy who loved that show and made me watch all of them. The thing I noticed was no matter what kind of music was playing, the Fonzi character was always doing a slow dance, like our boy here."

"Fonzi had it right, slow dancing is always the best," Mac agreed. Then looked mildly apprehensive. "You're not really going to make me dance like you guys, right? I'll look like I'm a zombie having a seizure."

Imani could feel his distress through their link and was quick to soothe him. "No, baby. We don't have to do anything else but this."

"Yeah, this is nice," Lex agreed, snuggling to them and making it a three-way slow dance.

When Lex put his lips to hers, she didn't hesitate to accept the kiss. One of Mac's hands slid down her back and grabbed a palm full of her ass and squeezed.

"Fuck, this is lush," he whispered.

She sighed into Lex's mouth, loving the feel of Mac's giant hand basically covering one of her butt cheeks. Arousal from both of them pulsed through the link, sending her lust skyrocketing.

With her men huddled close to her, other people couldn't see them copping feels as they took turns kissing. She heard a few humans commenting about how sexy the three of them looked, but no one tried to bother them.

It wasn't until Mac drew away that she realized he'd been gradually slow dancing them to a specific spot. She followed his gaze to find an Employees Only door behind her.

"What do you think you're doing?" she asked as Lex turned the knob and swung it open.

Mac answered for him. "We've got a little surprise for you."

They guided her into the poorly lit corridor that looked like it ran the entire length of the building. Not far down the corridor, Mac opened another door, revealing a set of stairs. Imani's high heels clicked loudly on the battered wooden steps as they climbed.

"I didn't think this place had a second story," she commented.

"It doesn't really, just one room," Mac answered as they got to the door at the top. He tapped the code into the keypad, and the door swung open. Mac stepped inside and swung his arms out with a flourish. "For you!"

Inside was a rectangular room with a wall of windows opposite of the door. There was one other door that was wide open and looked to be a bathroom. There wasn't much furniture inside, only a short couch and a couple of chairs sitting around a small table. The real star of the room was the bank of windows.

Striding over to the glass, Imani found she could see almost the entire club. Muffled music filled her ears as Lex and Mac took up positions on either side of her.

"This is our room until closing," Mac announced, his voice prideful.

"But why?" Imani asked. "I mean, it's nice to see everything, but—" a thought hit her, causing her to wince. "Is this so you can dance without anyone seeing you? Baby, I'm sorry if you're that embarrassed. You don't have to come out on the dance floor again."

Mac looked confused for a second before he flushed and shook his head. "No, love. It's not about that. This room is about us having some fun."

"Fun?" she repeated, confused. They'd been having fun downstairs. Why come all the way up here where the music was muted?

"This kind of fun," Lex growled and tugged up the tight hem of her dress. Imani gasped as he traced a hand over her lace panties.

"Just think about it," Mac murmured, putting his lips to her ear. "All those people down there, drinking and dancing. None of them are aware of the three of us up here, fucking. You can moan or scream all you want, and they won't hear you over the music."

"Oh." Imani couldn't think of anything else to say. The moment Lex had pulled at her dress, she'd gone from interested to aroused in nothing flat.

"Maybe you could try taking both our cocks at the same time," Mac continued. "Like we talked about the other day. Think about it. The two of us filling both your holes."

As Mac spoke, Lex dropped to his knees and nuzzled her mons. "Please," he begged.

She widened her stance without thought. Taking the invitation, he licked across the crotch of her panties and moaned. That's when she realized she'd managed to soak her panties. They hadn't even touched her yet, and she was this damn turned on. Considering that, there was really only one answer she could give.

"Yes."

Mac

The elastic nature of Imani's dress made it easy for Mac to slide the straps down her arms and over her breasts. The matching bra was more lace than anything else, revealing as much as it hid. He wanted to rip it off her but knew better than to destroy it.

"Oh!" Imani exclaimed. Dropping his gaze, Mac saw Lex had pushed her panties to the side and gotten access to her sex. He was eating her out like a starving man faced with a feast. As much as Mac wanted to put his lips on Imani's sweet wet pussy too, he never wanted to deprive Lex. It wasn't only that the chimera found the act sexually arousing, but Lex's submissive nature made it a form of worship.

Imani's tight dress was now bunched around her waist. Wanting to get it out of the way, Mac grabbed it and pulled up. Imani put her arms up and let Mac pull the dress off over her head. Tossing it onto the nearby table, he returned to the problem of Imani's bra.

"Let me—oh! Yes, there!" Imani tried to reach for her bra, but Lex's talented mouth made it a challenge. She swayed a little, and Mac wrapped his arms around her waist to support her.

"I… I think I'm close," Imani stuttered, her entire body shuddering.

"Let go," Mac whispered in her ear. "I've got you."

"So fast," she gasped.

He knew what she meant. She'd confessed a few nights ago that she'd never come as fast or as powerfully as she did with them. Part of it had to be the strength of their link. Everyone felt each other's arousal. Their growing lust rippled back and forth, creating a positive feedback loop that made him pull in a sharp breath of air.

Right now, he could feel her pleasure building through their link, making his dick hard enough to pound nails.

"Off, please," Lex moaned. Mac looked down to see him tugging at the top of Imani's panties.

Wordlessly, Imani nodded her head and Lex hooked a finger into the top and dragged them down her legs. With his arm around her waist, Mac effortlessly picked her up a few inches so Lex could pull the underwear all the way off. Before he set her back down, Lex had his mouth back in place.

Imani threw back her head and moaned. With only one hand, Mac tried to unhook the clasp at the front of the bra. At least he thought that was a clasp. Even if it was, he couldn't figure out how to open it. Giving up, he slid his fingers under the bottom of the garment and popped it off over her breasts. It's wasn't a perfect solution, but it was better than trying to touch her through the lacy, but rigid cloth.

With his free hand, he palmed one of her breasts, kneading the soft flesh gently. She gasped and tilted her head to look up at him.

"You're the most beautiful woman I've ever known," he whispered to her before covering her mouth with his.

The pulsing music from downstairs got noticeably louder as the lights flashing through the long windows turned from blue to green on the beat.

Imani started to breathe heavily, her body tense. He broke off the kiss and moved his head to the side, baring his neck.

"Please," he begged.

With a sharp inhale, Imani opened her eyes. Her pupils were blown and full of need. Pulling back her lips, she struck. There was no pain as her fangs sunk into his flesh, only a wave of desire. She pulled at his throat, swallowing down his blood and pulsing pleasure through their link.

Mac wasn't sure he'd be able to keep from coming in his pants. He'd never been one to shoot before he was ready, and he'd never had a hands-free orgasm. Forget that they'd had sex earlier when Imani had first woken up; this felt like they hadn't touched each other in days. Imani and Lex made him feel like a teenager again.

"Oh, love, yes!" he breathed. "Take from me."

Imani moaned against his throat, the vibration along with her bite making gooseflesh rise on his neck and shoulders. A delicious shiver ran down his spine, and he let his eyes fall closed. Who knew heaven was in the observation room of a dance club?

When Imani's body started to quake, she withdrew her fangs from his neck. He knew she hadn't drunk her fill but was concerned about hurting him. No matter how many times he and Lex told her the bites felt good, she still worried. She swiped her tongue over the marks, cleaning off the blood. He knew from experience the wounds would close quickly because of his rapid shifter healing and his powerful link with Imani.

He often wished they wouldn't heal. The feel of those small punctures on his neck felt important. Imani's mark on his body.

Did anyone ever get vampire marks tattooed on their body? He'd have to look into it.

Imani's soft cry pulled him from the aftereffects of her bite. She was shivering violently in his arms; her legs no longer holding her up. Pleasure crashed through their link, making Lex moan into her pussy. Mac groaned and dropped his head to her shoulder, kissing her hot skin.

With her head thrown back, Imani screamed as she came. Bright blue light illuminated her face, making her fangs glisten. The orgasm rolled through her, then crashed into him and Lex. It was a close thing, but he held on. He could hear Lex groaning but didn't smell the distinct scent of Lex's cum, so he assumed the chimera managed to restrain himself as well.

That was good because Mac had a plan and no interest in discarding it.

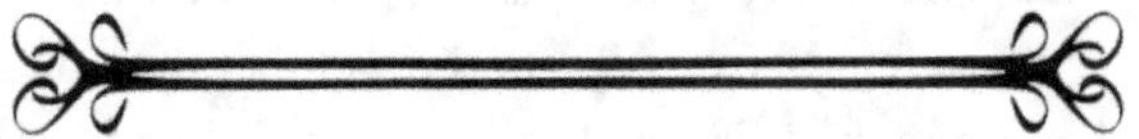

Lex

Lex almost came in his pants. Only the thought of disappointing Mac kept him from succumbing to the intense pleasure flooding him from his link with Imani. When Imani pushed his head, he sat back. Shifting only his tongue, he licked his face clean of Imani's juices, reveling in the taste of her.

Imani watched him with heavy-lidded eyes. Mac was holding her up as she panted, her body mostly limp. Her look of interest made him want to do it again even though he'd gotten everything with the first swipe.

"I didn't know you could do that with your tongue," she said. "It gives me ideas, Lexie."

He loved the nickname she'd given him. The way she pronounced it always made him feel special and loved. Right now, her voice was throaty and full of sin and sex, making the name sound sensual and sexy.

"Anything you want," he promised without hesitation, his dick throbbing in his pants.

"Don't I know it," Imani purred.

"Get up, Lex," Mac ordered. "You're wearing way too many clothes, my man."

Happy to obey Mac, Lex scrambled to his feet and stripped. Mac continued to hold Imani as Lex disrobed. Once he was naked, he stood before them, eyes down and waiting for his next order. His pulsing cock was jutting straight out, thick and needy with a drop of pre-cum beading at his slit.

"God, you're a handsome boy," Imani murmured, reaching out to draw him close with a hand around his neck. Guided by her, he stumbled half a step forward and brought his lips to hers.

As they kissed, she wrapped her legs around him, her hot wet pussy pressing against his abs. Then her arms went around his neck and Mac stepped back. He could hear the sound of clothing rustling. It wasn't long before Mac was pressed against

Imani's back and gently guiding Lex's face away, ending the kiss.

"Can you get this off, love?" he asked Imani, tugging at her bra.

With a grumpy sound, she let go of Lex and tackled the garment. She cursed under her breath, struggling with the front clasp. Lex took the opportunity to lick over a beaded nipple. Imani sucked in a breath, gave up on the bra and arched up for more.

"No, bad Lex," Mac admonished, lifting Lex's face with his hand under the chin. Gazing up into Mac's gentle expression, Lex whimpered. "Shhh, love. I'm not upset. But you need to be good for me. Don't distract Imani."

Thankfully all three of them were deliciously naked.

"Now we're all going to have some fun," Mac announced, letting go of Lex and holding up a single use packet of lube with his other hand. Ripping it open, he squirted some out on his fingers, then dropped them down. Lex felt Imani tense, then suck in a breath.

"I'm going to take my time opening you up," Mac murmured, kissing the side of her face. When I'm done, you'll be ready to take my fat dick. Don't worry, love. I'll make it good for you."

Imani dropped her head forward, arms and legs tightening around Lex. Looking around the room, he found a mirror hanging off a nearby wall, giving him a good view of what Mac was doing.

As he'd done with Lex, Mac was gently sliding a single finger in, working lube into Imani's back hole. He could feel phantom fingers doing the same to him. It felt so real he had to be experiencing what Imani felt through their link.

Imani's eyes were closed, and she was moaning and whimpering as Mac focused on sliding in a second finger. There was no discomfort coming from her, only new sensations.

The beat of the music changed to a slow thrumming and the lighting became darker with purple and deep bluish-green hues. The beat seemed to reach the slow build as Mac worked to make Imani comfortable taking three fingers, then four.

"Sweet baby Jesus, fuck me already!" she shouted after Mac had sunk four fingers in past the second knuckle. Her outburst made Mac chuckle and Lex grin. He knew exactly how she felt; Mac was good at this type of torture.

"Patience, love," he murmured, withdrawing his fingers and making Imani whimper.

Lex wasn't sure what he was doing when Mac crouched down until he felt the bear shifter's hand on his throbbing cock. Lex hissed out a breath as Mac stroked him a few times, then guided him to Imani's pussy. With one hand on Lex and the other on Imani, he pushed them together like a porn puppeteer.

"Oh, yes, there," Imani moaned as Lex slid inside her. He wanted to moan also but all his focus was on not giving into the impulse to pump himself inside her hot, wet sheath.

"Good boy," Mac praised after Lex was fully inside Imani. "Stay there."

"Please," Lex begged. It was the only word he could get out, but Mac seemed to understand.

"Soon," Mac promised, then took his position at Imani's back. Looking over at the mirror, Lex watched Mac ease into Imani's back hole with slow, gentle care. Imani was mumbling incoherent words as he filled her. Nothing but pleasure radiated through their link. Lex felt his jaw lock from tension as he kept himself from moving. Even when Imani undulated between them, desperately trying to move on and off their dicks for more sensation, he kept still.

"Not yet," Mac gritted through clenched teeth, testament to the strain he was under. He held her hips steady as he finished sliding inside of her. Even when he was fully inside her, he didn't let her move. Instead, he took his time sliding out, sweat dripping down his face.

"Mac!" Imani whined. Lex was with her; he wanted to whine and beg too but wanting to be good kept him from voicing any pleas. Still, he couldn't help the whimper that bubbled up his throat.

Mac made a sound, drawing Lex's eyes to his. "I'm going to hold her hips, you hold her waist so we can keep her still while we fuck her. Got me?"

Finally—*finally!* Lex nodded with an eager huff. "Yes, yes, please!"

Imani started to say something, but her words were lost in a moan as both of them started moving. The first few strokes were awkward and didn't feel right, but they were quick to find a rhythm.

The music in the club changed again, this time rolling into a frantic fast beat. The lights got bright, filling their small room with gold and soft orange. The timing was so perfect that if Lex didn't know better, he'd think Mac had cued the DJ. The new tempo built, urging them to a faster cadence. They pulsed in and out of her, all three of them moaning and panting.

Words fell from Imani's mouth, a jumbled mixture of encouragement and cursing. Sweat stung Lex's eyes as he worked hard to hold back his looming orgasm.

This was torture.

This was heaven.

Lex watched Imani's face as her pleasure built. Her fangs were out and there was a slight gash in her lip where she'd accidently cut herself. He licked across her lips, tasting her blood in his mouth and getting her attention.

Desperate for her bite, he leaned his head to the side. "Take," he begged. "Take me inside you."

She blinked at him, as if she didn't understand right away. Then her focus snapped to his neck. Putting her mouth over his pulse point, she licked a few times. Lex whimpered at the feeling of her tongue on his skin. Then she bit and all three of them exploded.

Mac roared as he came. Lex couldn't make a sound, but he was sure his heart was about to beat out of his chest. And Imani sounded a deep moan that vibrated through her body. Mac and Lex kept pulsing in her body while Imani drank from him. Their pleasure crashed back and forth between them through their link.

Lex wasn't sure how long they stood there but the music suddenly cut off and all the lights came up. They could hear the DJ thanking everyone for coming and encouraging them to come back the following night.

High in their dark perch, the three of them grinned sloppily at each other.

"Best night clubbing ever," Imani declared. "Let's do it again tomorrow."

Mac

Due to the club closing soon, they didn't bother with much more than a quick clean up in the bathroom attached to the observation room. Lex looked wrung out and was moving sluggishly. Imani was a little dazed and pulsing content happiness through their links. He ended up being the one to help them wash up in the sink and put their clothes back on.

Both Lex's brain and body were moving slowly. The chimera paused to stare out the big windows at the bright and almost empty dancefloor below. At first Mac thought Lex saw something significant or suspicious. Then he noticed the childlike grin on the chimera's face. The boy was high on pleasure-endorphins and full of the emotions Imani was broadcasting.

Leaning over, Mac growled in his ear. "Do I need to carry you?"

Far from looking affronted, Lex turned his gaze up and nodded like a child. "Please."

Imani stopped in the open doorway of the suite and turned around. "Me too."

Affection for his sex-drunk mates filled him as Mac put an arm under Lex's ass and picked him up, settling the shifter on his left hip. Lex wrapped his arms around Mac's neck like a child and snuggled into the hold.

"Now me," Imani demanded.

Mac obligingly bent his knees to do the same with her that he'd done with Lex and soon he had a mate resting on each hip, both snuggled against him. Imani was tiny compared to him, but Lex was a little more substantial. Thankfully, Mac's seven foot plus frame along with his shifter strength allowed him to carry his precious burdens safely downstairs without any problem.

"This is nice," Imani murmured, and Lex made a sleepy sound of agreement. Who would have thought his fierce chimera mate and his dynamic vampire mate could turn into such cuddly kittens? The future would probably be full of such moments, but that didn't keep him from treasuring this one.

He nudged open the door at the bottom of the stairs with his back and stepped into the active main level. Even with the music off, the place was loud, and people talked, laughed, and walked with heavy tread as they found friends and made their way outside.

Pike was right near the door, dragging a struggling human toward the front of the club. The guy was obviously drunk and cursing profusely. Easily holding the much smaller and weaker male, Pike looked over at Mac with a wide smile.

"I was about to go up and check in on you guys," he explained. "You know, because it's getting late. But this guy didn't like being cut off so I had to take him outside first."

"No worries," Mac answered as Pike looked over at the vampire and chimera in his arms. He thought Lex was nearly asleep and Imani was humming to herself, almost as if she was intoxicated. Considering how much she'd drunk from both of them, she might very well be a little blood-drunk. "We're heading home now. Where's Cora?"

Pike's face transformed from happy to besotted. "She had to use the bathroom, so I let her into the employee one. We were going to hit that all-night donut shop after I'm done helping with closing." A rare frown marred Pike's face as he pulled the still struggling guy completely off his feet. Dangling about a foot in the air and being strangled by his own shirt, the guy started gasping and flailing. "I'd be finished sooner if it wasn't for guys like this one. Come on, I'll walk you out."

Mac nodded, but they only made it a few steps before the crowd stopped them. There were many people bottlenecked at the front trying to exit. Judging by how slow everyone was moving it was going to be a while before they made it outside.

"I'm not sure I have the patience for this," Mac muttered. Pike cast him a sympathetic look.

"Here, follow me." Changing direction, Pike led Mac to a side exit door and pushed up the one-way security latch and held the door open to make it easier for Mac to carry his mates.

"If you parked in the lot behind the building, you can follow the alley back there," Pike said, pointing. "Unfortunately, I've got to take this guy to the front, it's the rules if we're escorting an unruly customer out. It'll take me a while. But my Cora is really fond of your Imani, so I'm sure we'll be hanging out again real soon."

There was no mistaking the way Pike was talking about Cora. He already thought of the human as his. "Congratulations on finding your mate."

Pike ducked his head, smiling. "Thanks. I hope she accepts me."

The human was turning blue from not being able to breathe well. Mac nodded at the guy. "You better go deal with that."

With a roll of his eyes, Pike stepped back and dropped the guy to his feet. The door swung shut, audibly latching. Mac turned, but before he could take a step, the door opened again. Thinking Pike had forgotten to tell him something, Mac turned with a smile on his face.

The unfamiliar human faces that greeted him filled him with an unexpected dread. The feeling must have made it through their link because both Imani and Lex stiffened in his arms and roused themselves to straighten up. He felt shock, distress, and rage coming from Imani at the sight of these humans.

Lex was wide awake now and pushed himself out of Mac's hold. Letting go of Lex so the Chimera could drop to his feet, Mac kept his eyes on the humans while he eased Imani to the ground.

"I thought that might be you," the woman said. She was a small, delicate looking human that reminded Mac of a porcelain figurine. With black hair, a heart-shaped face, and slim figure, she appeared to be a beautiful and ordinary human, but the eyes gave her away. They were hard and cold. They were the eyes of a killer with no conscience.

The man next to her stared at them with an expression of cool calculation. "You were right. And now we have her again. There'll be no leaving us this time."

With her back ramrod straight and her expression tight, Imani addressed the humans. "Simon, Opal, I'd hoped never to see either of you again."

Next to him, Lex hissed out a breath. "These are the ones who hurt her."

Mac had already guessed that and was fighting the urge to hurt these two. Normally, he'd be quick to exact revenge, but these humans were a powerful vampire's flock. Doing anything to a vampire's flock was risking the vampire's reprisal. That reprisal could mean their death.

Opal turned her gaze to Lex and answered in a voice that belonged more to a child than a fully grown woman. "We never hurt our pets. We trained her, like you're supposed to do. It wasn't our fault she was so stubborn."

Simon's gaze never wavered from Imani. "It turns out that your stubbornness was probably the best part of you. No one has held up like you did. Our other toys keep breaking."

Imani shuddered. "Both of you are sick."

Opal ignored her. "And Vincent hasn't been able to make us another vampire pet. That's why we kept begging him to bring you back."

"Never," Imani spit out, backing up a step. Mac was quick to push her behind him and Lex moved to stand at his shoulder.

Opal's mouth tightened into a petulant frown as she looked up at Mac. "Imani wasn't made for you. Vincent made her for us. Give her back."

"She's not a fucking toy or pet," Lex growled. Mac could feel the power radiating off the chimera. Lex was getting ready to fight.

"They're Vincent's flock," Mac hissed to him. "We can't kill them."

"Correction," Lex answered. "We can't kill them and leave Vincent alive. As long as we get rid of all three, there's no problem."

Simon's features twisted into a grimace. "As if you could hurt Vincent. He's over six hundred years old, and we've been with him for five hundred. Do you really think after all that time it'll be you who ends him? Don't be naïve."

"No one's invincible," Mac answered.

Simon ignored his comment, focusing on Imani behind him. "Come along, Imani. We have your room all ready. It's been over a month since Vincent agreed to bring you back to us. You shouldn't have run away like you did."

"That was very naughty," Opal said in a sing-song voice, then went back to her high-pitched, little girl voice. "We might have to punish you for a while before we let you have a room or bed. Do you remember the doghouse? The chains are all still there. Wouldn't that be a fun punishment?"

Simon turned his head to look down at Opal, his expression delighted. "And my whip," he added. "We could use my whip on her until she's tame again."

A combination of rage and horror washed over Mac. Rage that these two wanted to take and hurt his mate, but also horror at all the things Imani must have endured. These two were sick and twisted.

Mac edged them back. Despite how badly he wanted to break both these humans in half, it was more important that they get Imani away. His head filled with plans. They'd seek out Tobias's help, then flee to Oregon. Vincent wouldn't invade Tobias's space without exhausting diplomatic relations. While Vincent wasted his time bargaining with Tobias, they would see about getting to Bend. Vincent wouldn't know to look for them there and they'd have Lex's family to help guard. Even an ancient and powerful vampire would think twice about tangling with an entire family of chimera.

The first step to all of it was getting out of this alley.

Simon's eyes narrowed. "Where do you think you're going?"

"Away from you, you sick fuck," Lex growled.

"How dare you speak to him like that!" Opal exclaimed, losing her childlike voice for a moment. "You're nothing! I'm going to have Vincent drink you dry."

Stepping forward, Simon tried to reach around Lex to grab Imani. Although he was flock, making him faster and stronger than the average human, he was still human and didn't hold a candle to Lex's abilities. Before Mac could blink, Lex had a hold of Simon's hand and twisted it. Everyone heard the snap and there was a brief moment of stunned silence, then all hell broke loose.

Simon dropped to his knees, crying out and cradling his broken wrist. Opal screeched something unintelligible and pulled an item from her purse. Mac only had a second to recognize the crackling-clicking of a taser before it was jabbed into his side.

It didn't incapacitate him, but it hurt like hell, and he reacted instinctively. With a roar of pain, he swiped at her. She went flying with a cry of surprise and bounced off a nearby wall, landing hard on the dirty alley ground.

Simon spewed out a string of words that Mac knew had to be curses but couldn't figure out what language. Russian maybe? Not that any of that mattered when Simon tried to punch him, cradling the broken wrist to his chest. Mac easily blocked the blow and pushed Simon away. The human lost his balance and sprawled on the ground next to Opal.

Opal was sitting up and glaring at them. Her face was flushed, and tears were streaming down her cheeks. She looked very much like the child she pretended to be. Ignoring Mac and Lex, Opal focused on the small sliver of Imani she could see between them.

"Imani, come here and help me up!" Opal demanded. "Right now, or I'll let Simon use his whip, even though it makes a mess."

"Never again," Imani vowed behind him. He could feel a combination of fear and determination coming from her through their link.

"We need to leave now," Lex urged them.

"Agreed," Mac answered, already in motion. "I'll get Imani. You cover our backs."

"What—" Imani started to ask but was cut off when he snatched her up. Holding her securely against his chest, he turned to sprint to the truck.

They didn't even make it three strides before he heard the whoosh of feathers and a figure appeared in front of him. A split second later, he hit a powerful wall of magic that sent him hurtling back. Curling his body around Imani, he took the brunt of the landing. It hurt and his back would be one massive bruise for a while, but nothing was broken.

Uncurling, he scrambled to his feet, unsurprised to find his legs were a little shaky. Imani was quick to stand up next to him. Lex had been sent tumbling as well but managed to twist in the air like a cat and land on his feet. He pulled a gun out of nowhere and aimed it at the vampire blocking their escape.

"How dare you—"

The vampire didn't get a chance to finish his diatribe. Mac watched Lex put the vampire's face in his sights and pull the trigger without hesitation.

Lex

Lex didn't have to think twice about pulling his weapon and firing on the vampire. A lifetime of training had created this moment. Hours upon hours of drills. Countless assignments where one potential outcome was death. He'd thought he was well prepared. Ready to face any challenge in defense of his mates, only to watch his perfectly aimed round do nothing.

A fissure of magic flared inches in front of Vincent's face. Then the bullet pinged into the brick wall of the next building, sending red shards flying. Beyond the magic barrier that protected him, Vincent gloated.

"Do you really think I've gotten this old by being negligent of my own safety? I might have been born in an age before gunpowder, but I've never been one of those vampires who refused to change with the times." Holding up his wrist, he pulled back his jacket sleeve to show a silver armband etched with witches' marks. "I paid a small fortune for this, but it's come in handy many times over the years."

Realizing his pistol wouldn't work on Vincent, Lex ducked back. He planned to grab Opal or Simon and use them as a hostage. Vincent must have guessed what he was doing because there was the sound of wings again and then the vampire was standing in front of his flock. By now, the two had gotten to their feet. Vincent took in his humans; their clothing was dirty and torn in a few places and Simon's wrist was bent at an odd angle.

"What have my sweetlings gotten into?" he asked in a voice that didn't fit the tension in the alley.

"We found our most favorite toy, but she doesn't want to come home with us," Opal claimed as she hurried up to Vincent. He held up an arm so she could wrap her arms around his waist and snuggle into his side. "Those animals hurt me and Simon. Make them pay."

"I will," Vincent murmured as he rubbed a hand down her back. He opened his other arm, inviting Simon to snuggle into his other side. With an expression of relief, Simon did just that. "What were you two thinking, confronting these dirty animals without me? Where are your guards? You should've had them deal with the shifters."

"They left," Opal pouted.

"Left?" Vincent questioned.

"We found someone inside we thought would make a good toy and tried to put the drugs Simon gets in her drink. They make people compliant, and she was such a pretty specimen. Before she took a drink, one of the men you hired took the drink away then said he quit and not to even call the office for a refund. He stormed out and took the other two with him."

"He was very rude," Simon added. "We hadn't even done anything yet. Those gargoyles have no concept of fun."

"Stone Protection has an excellent reputation, but I didn't think they'd interfere if you wanted to play with a human," Vincent said with an apologetic expression. "I'm sorry you didn't get to collect anyone new; however, we have Imani back so both of you can forgive me."

When Opal looked up at Vincent, the smile she had on her face was disturbing. While they'd been talking, Lex had been edging backwards, getting close to Mac and Imani. He wasn't sure how they were going to get away, but he felt better once he was standing close to them.

"I'm under the protection of Tobias," Imani stated boldly. She strode out in front of them, head held high. A wave of admiration hit Lex at the sight of Imani standing fierce and proud.

Imani's words had Mac speaking up. "That's right, Tobias granted Imani his protection." Mac pointed to Lex. "And his brother is in Tobias's flock. Hurting any of us will make him angry."

"Even if that was true," Vincent answered, obviously unconcerned, "Tobias is barely a few hundred years old. Let him challenge me. I'll take his life and wealth."

Fear washed over Lex, some of it was his and the rest was coming from Imani. If invoking Tobias's name didn't intimidate Vincent, there wasn't much else that would. Running wasn't an option. They were going to have to fight their way out of this. They weren't at a complete disadvantage. The spelled bracelet might stop projectiles, but as far as Lex knew, there wasn't much any spell could do to protect against a chimera's bite. If he was quick and lucky, he'd be able to take a chunk out of Vincent before the vampire retaliated and potentially separated Lex's head from his body.

Lex pulled in a deep breath. He was probably going to have to sacrifice himself to save his mates.

"Don't even think about it," Mac grumbled. Lex looked over to find Mac glaring at him. "We do this together. Live together and die together. No one's going to be the noble sacrifice."

Lex blinked a few times. Had Mac suddenly developed the ability to read minds?

Mac shook his head, a small tense smile on his mouth. "I know you, Lex. I know how you think and right now you're all about making sure Imani and I survive this. That's a hard no. We're not running unless you're with us."

Imani twined her finger with his, gripping his hand tight. "Mac's right. We're in this together, no matter the outcome."

Snapping fingers made all three of them look up to find Vincent staring impatiently at them. "Are you finished? Imani, come here, the animals can go off and find another female to enjoy."

Letting go of Imani's hand, Lex gave his beast up to his body. It was now or never. With a roar, he attacked.

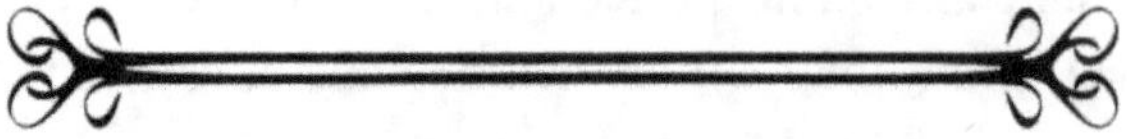

Cora

Cora pushed open the side door to the club, hoping to catch Imani. The bartender who'd seen Pike lead them this way said it had happened a while ago. Imani and the boys were probably already long gone, but a girl had to try.

The sight that met her eyes after she'd gotten the door open made her stumble and fall into the alley. There was a fight going on, but it wasn't between some drunken patrons. This was a battle of titans! There was a bear and something else that looked like a combination of lion, bear and… was that a segmented tail with a scorpion stinger at the end?

Stunned into immobility, she pressed her hands to her cheeks. There was no way she'd been drugged. All she'd had to drink was one of Pike's Cokes sealed in a bottle. And no one drugged someone with acid these days, it was all about being roofied. But here she was, having an epic fantasy of a hallucination where a bear, a made-up creature, and Imani were all battling some guy with glowing red eyes.

Wait, Imani's eyes were glowing red too. This was a weird trip. Didn't most people see green fairies, talking bushes, and colorful lights?

Then the guy with the glowing red eyes backhanded Imani, sending her hard into a wall. That pulled Cora out of her stunned stupor.

Imaginary or not, no one treated one of Cora's friends like that. Digging the pepper spray out of her bag, she ran to the red-eye guy. His back was to her as he held off both the bear and the lion-creature. Weird blue sparks were flashing in the air around them, reminding her of magic battles in manga.

"Hey, asshole!" Cora shouted once she was right behind him. The guy turned his head, snarling at her. Woah, what the fuck was up with those teeth? He looked like he had fangs!

Ignoring every part of her primitive brain screaming for her to run, Cora emptied the canister and covered the guy's face in pepper gel. He froze for a split second, his expression hilariously confused. Then he roared in pain, let go of the two animals, and rubbed his eyes furiously.

"What did you do to Vincent?" a male voice shouted. Before she could turn to look, someone tackled her. She landed on her back with a slim guy on top of her. He reminded her of a young Jude Law, but without the kind eyes. This guy's face was twisted in anger and his eyes looked cold and ruthless. "How dare you hurt him!"

He pulled back a fist to punch her, but she was already in action. She couldn't get a knee up to bury in his crotch, so she jabbed the guy in the throat with her small hand. She might have used a little too much force because she heard a crunch and the man's face went from enraged to open-mouthed fear. His eyes bulged, and he gripped his throat, trying to pull in some air.

"I hope I didn't kill you," she muttered as she wiggled out from under him. "It would be just my luck that I killed a real person while on a bad trip."

She heard the cracking of a taser a moment before she felt it touch her shoulder. Then she was on the ground stiff and unable to move. The person holding the taser followed her down to keep the connection. Familiar with the effects of tasers, she didn't try to fight it. Beyond her, the sounds of battle suddenly stopped, and everything went quiet. Eerily quiet. Was this the end of the trip? Was she about to wake up?

The taser stopped and her body went limp. Damn, that had sucked.

"Very well done, Opal," a voice said. Cora blinked until her vision cleared. Red-eye man was leaning over her. The whites of his eyes were bloodshot to match the red iris and pupils, with tears streaming down his face. Except, they couldn't be tears. They looked black and sparkled in the harsh artificial light of the alley.

Yup, she must still be tripping balls.

"She's aggressive," the guy she punched commented as he got to his feet. He sounded horse and held his hand to his throat, but was breathing fine. Huh, she'd been sure that punch had killed him. She'd have to try harder next time. "And surprisingly strong for a human her size."

Human? What was he then? An alien from the planet Asshole?

Opal looked past the red-eyed man. "What happened to the animals? Did you kill them?"

"I put them in thrall," red eye said. "After this one hurt my eyes, fighting them was no longer entertaining."

The man she'd punched licked his lips, as if faced with something tantalizing. "I should slit their throats while they're helpless. We could watch their blood drain into the gutter."

Cora wanted to say something about them being psychopaths but thought better of it. If she got lucky, they'd forget about her, and she could strike without warning. She still had her purse slung across her body. She didn't have her taser tonight, but there was a telescoping baton in there.

"Leave them alone, Simon," red eye ordered, his expression amused. "I'm hoping they'll come after Imani, and I'll get to play with them again. It's been a long time since I've had any challenge and both of them were surprisingly strong for shifters."

Simon's smile was anticipatory as he pointed at her. "Then I want to take this one home too."

Cora struggled to sit up and wrestled open her purse at the same time. No way was she letting them take her to a secondary location. "Fuck off."

Red eye looked resigned. "You do like to break the strong ones, don't you? Very well. I suppose I owe you a new toy for all this drama." He crouched down in front of her. Cora opened her mouth to cuss at him and raised her hand gripping the baton. This time, she wouldn't show mercy. They were getting blows to the throat that would *absolutely* kill instead of *maybe* kill.

Her gaze met red eye. Her hand froze in midair, and she couldn't form a sound.

"Hello, human," red-eye murmured. "You're going to sleep now."

What if this is real? was the last thing she thought before everything when dark.

Imani

The moment Imani could throw off Vincent's thrall, she started struggling with the bonds holding her. Opal had put silver shackles on her, sighing with happiness when they clicked closed. Imani wanted to scream in pain as they burnt her skin but under thrall, she couldn't even whimper.

Vincent had dumped her and Cora in the basement of the house. It was nothing but cinder block walls and a concrete floor with fluorescent lights hanging from the ceiling. The only thing Vincent had added was a heavy-duty metal door at the top of the stairs and bolts in the wall to restrain someone.

Judging by the way Simon had been whining about his broken wrist, they wouldn't be back in the basement for a while. If she could get free of the silver restraints, she might be able to get her and Cora out of the basement. She wouldn't be able to leave the house since dawn was fast approaching, but Cora could make a run for it.

Guilt washed over her. Poor Cora, she didn't deserve to be dragged into this. Really, no one deserved the attention of Vincent and his demented flock.

"Imani?" Cora's soft, questioning voice had her rolling over. The small woman was lying on her side facing Imani, blinking rapidly and looking dazed.

It was a struggle, but Imani managed to sit up. "Are you hurt?"

Cora didn't answer right away. She closed her eyes and Imani thought she might have fallen back to sleep. Then she spoke without opening them back up.

"I didn't get drugged, did I?" she asked, her voice strangely calm. "That bear and weird lion creature were Lex and Mac. The guy with the glowing red eyes and long teeth is a vampire. The blue stuff I saw was magic. It was all real. And now we're prisoners of a vampire."

"I'm afraid so," Imani answered, there was no point in sugarcoating their situation.

"Is he going to eat us?" she asked. "Like in the movies?"

Shouldn't Cora be acting more scared? Maybe she was in shock. Imani tried to remember how she'd reacted when she first woke up, strapped to a table with Vincent looming over her. "He might drink your blood, but he's not going to cook and eat you like Hannibal Lecter. He might try to turn you into a vampire too."

"Too?" Cora finally lifted her lids. Intense dark gray eyes rimmed in black focused on Imani. "Are you like him?"

Bracing for Cora's disgust, Imani nodded her head. "He turned me two years ago. That's why I disappeared."

Cora didn't react. "Did you want it?"

"Hell no," Imani spit out. "Vampires can do this thing called thrall. It takes away your will and makes you do whatever they order. One minute I was at the club dancing. Then the next thing I knew, I was here."

"Okay, then I'm going to kill him," Cora said in the same tone she might use to decide she was ordering pizza for dinner. It made Imani smile despite the situation.

"I'll help," she offered.

"Why do I smell something burning?" Cora asked, struggling to sit up and wincing once she'd finally managed it. "Damn, my head hurts."

Imani grimaced. "I think you're smelling me."

Cora jerked and fumbled around until she was on her knees. With surprising speed, she knee walked the few yards between them. "What's on fire. Is it your clothing? Let me see," she demanded.

She tried for a little humor as she showed Cora the silver manacles securing her wrists behind her back. "I'm not on fire, just smoldering a little."

"What the fuck!" Cora cried. In her haste to get to Imani, she flopped over, hitting the concrete floor hard on her side. "Goddamn it!"

"Easy," Imani tried to caution as Cora rolled back onto her knees. "Eventually Simon and Opal are going to come down here and start hurting us, we don't need to do it for them."

"Those silver chains are already hurting you," Cora countered, knee walking more carefully this time. Once she was behind Imani, she moved until her bound hands were next to Imani's.

Remaining still, Imani craned her neck to look over her shoulder but couldn't see anything. "What are you doing?"

"Helping," Cora gritted out. Imani heard the distinct sound of fabric ripping then Cora's small hands shoving smooth silky fabric between the skin of her wrists and the silver cuffs. Relief was immediate.

"Try not to move," Cora warned. "I couldn't see what I was doing so my sleeve probably isn't tucked very well. Is it helping or should I try to put my fingers between you and the cuffs? They don't feel hot to me."

"The fabric is perfect, it doesn't hurt anymore," Imani assured her. Moving carefully, she turned and leaned against the wall. Cora did the same thing and soon the women were sitting shoulder to shoulder.

Letting her head fall back against the wall, Cora closed her eyes. "All of it really happened. I'm not tripping or in a dream."

Imani wasn't fooled by Cora's calm tone. The small woman was at her most dangerous when she spoke in such a monotone, emotionless voice. Her friend was putting everything together. Processing the nightmarish events of the evening, and soon she'd realize this was all Imani's fault.

Imani turned her head to look at Cora. She waited until the other woman opened her eyes, but Cora refused to look anywhere but straight ahead. Unable to take the silence any longer, Imani started talking.

"I'm a vampire. The guy with red eyes is Vincent, my maker and an evil son of a bitch. The two people with him are Opal and Simon. They're his flock."

Cora's expression didn't change. "If he's the reason you disappeared, did Lex and Mac rescue you?"

"Vincent let me leave," Imani explained. "It's complicated, but most vampires don't like having other vampires hanging around them when they have a flock."

"But Opal and Simon seem close to him."

"They aren't vampires, they're human. Or I guess you could call them human-plus because they get a little extra strength and speed by sharing their soul with a vampire. Lex and Mac are my flock."

"And they love you," Cora murmured with a hint of envy in her voice. "They were ready to die protecting you. And you fought like the badass bitch I know you are to save them."

"You jumped in too," Imani reminded her. "That was brave. I'll never forget the sight of Vincent getting pepper sprayed. That was brilliant."

Cora finally slid her eyes over to look at Imani, a grin flashing across her face. "Best part of the evening," she declared, then winced a little as she shifted. "Do vampires kill their victims like in the Blade movies?"

"They don't have to," Imani answered. "But some do."

"Great," Cora said, voice dripping with sarcasm. "This was always a lifelong goal, to be dinner for a red-eyed, fanged-face asshole."

Imani snorted. "Considering how sadistic Simon and Opal are, a quick death by Vincent might be preferable."

Cora sounded a mock cheer. "Way to make everything better. I feel positively buoyant!"

The situation couldn't get much worse, and yet Cora managed to make her laugh. "There's hope, though. I can feel my link to Lex and Mac. It's stretched thin, but they're still alive. They'll come for us."

"That's exactly what I'm hoping for," Vincent said, emerging from the shadows with Opal and Simon on either side of him. "This is going to be the most fun I've had in decades."

Lex

"Mac? Wake up for me, please. Come on." Pike's pleading voice roused Lex enough to fight the strange sleep holding him hostage. The fear in Pike's voice and the sound of his mate's name helped push Lex into opening his eyes.

It took an enormous amount of effort to get his lids lifted, then it took a minute for his eyes to pull everything into focus. When he saw the alley around him illuminated by soft pre-dawn light, it confused him. They'd been in the club. Why was he laying in an alley, beat to hell, with Pike talking to Mac?

Sitting up caused a dizzy spell that made his stomach heave. Fighting against the need to be sick, he forced himself to his feet. He was as wobbly as a newborn foal and probably would have crashed back down to the ground if Pike hadn't rushed to his side.

"Woah, let me help." Pike slipped an arm around him and led him over to where Mac was sitting up, blinking and looking confused.

"What—" his question was cut off by a violent bout of coughing.

Pike helped Lex sink to his knees next to Mac. His mate's face was battered and bruised with several spots where the skin was split and was now scabbed over. They were both naked, so Lex could see all the injuries healing on Mac's body.

"You're hurt." Lex reached out and took hold of Mac's arm to examine a bloody wound on his forearm.

"You're not looking Instagram ready either," Mac quipped, coughing a few more times before pulling in a ragged breath. "What happened?"

Lex shook his head, memories fuzzy. "We needed to get Imani home. It was… *dawn!*"

The significance of the light finally hit Lex and he looked widely around, expecting to see a hurt and unconscious Imani laying in the alley. They needed to get her to shelter before sunlight flooded the area. The bar was right there, they'd have to…

"Where is she?" Mac's frantic question echoed what Lex was thinking. Mac grabbed Pike's arm. "Did you see anything?"

He shook his head, worry making his movements jerky. "I gave up looking for Cora and was going to head home. I came out here and found you guys. What happened? Who attacked you?"

Lex rubbed his head, wishing it didn't hurt so much. Why couldn't he remember? Had they failed Imani, and she'd been forced to leave them and seek shelter from the deadly sun in some random place?

"Vincent."

The single hissed word made Lex drop his hands and meet Mac's eyes. "What?"

"Vincent was here," Mac answered. "Him and his flock. And Cora."

Pike jerked. "Cora? She was here?" His voice gained volume and panic as he spoke.

Memories of the fight with Vincent and then being overwhelmed by the vampire's magic hit Lex like a blow. "He has her."

"Them," Mac corrected. "I think he took Cora too."

Pike grabbed Mac and Lex under an arm and lifted both of them to their feet. "We have to get them."

Between sheer determination and Pike's steadying hand, Lex managed to stay upright. Mac didn't look much better than him as he staggered like a man on a rough boat ride.

"We'll get them back," Lex promised Pike. "Take us to Mac's place first. We need supplies. And give me your phone. We're going to need help."

Pike started dragging the two of them down the alley. "This way."

He unceremoniously shoved them in his ancient Cadillac covered in rust spots, then jumped into the driver's seat. A plume of gray smoke coughed out the exhaust pipe as Pike started up the ailing vehicle.

"Where?" he barked out the question while backing the land yacht out of the parking spot. Mac rattled off his address, then closed his eyes while Pike drove. Lex spent the ride planning.

This was the most important mission he'd ever had, and more than his life was riding on their success.

Mac

"I said no," Lex growled into the phone as Mac carefully packed the last of the weapons he and Lex had assembled. Leaning a hip on the kitchen counter, he unabashedly eavesdropped on Lex's conversation with his brother Memphis.

"You can't do this alone," Memphis argued.

"I won't be alone," Lex responded, his voice gruff. He was still too pale for Mac's comfort, but neither one of them had fully recovered from the fight with Vincent and then being put under thrall. They'd be as good as new with a couple of hearty meals and a good night's sleep, but there was no time for that. "I'll have Mac with me."

"That's good, but you're going to need more than Mac. You need all the help we can put together. Wait until tonight," Memphis suggested. "Then both Tobias and I can come help. Even if this Vincent is as powerful as you say, he wouldn't be able to stand against all of us at once."

"We can't wait until tonight," Lex responded, voice steely. "We need to strike while we have the sunlight. And I'm not willing to leave Imani there a second longer than I have to."

"Fuck, fine," Memphis roared into the phone. "Give me forty minutes, and I'll be at Mac's place."

"No."

Mac blinked, surprised by Lex's refusal. He tilted his head questioningly at Lex. His mate's unreadable eyes slid away.

"No?" Memphis repeated, outraged. "Lex, don't be an idiot. You need my help. I might not be a secretive, weapon collecting bastard like you, but I still know how to fight."

"That's not it," Lex responded. "I can't lose you too. If this goes badly, Imani, Mac, and I are all dead. If one of us doesn't make it, we all don't make it. We're flock, Memphis. You know what that means."

"Yeah, I know," Memphis answered, voice heavy.

"I can't die knowing I took you with me. Tobias *might* survive losing you, but Briar wouldn't. Think about that, Memphis," Lex urged. "You have a duty to care for your mates. Don't let your loyalty to me fuck that up."

There was a long silence and Mac was sure he could feel Memphis's inner turmoil coming through the phone. "You're a good brother, Lex."

"I know."

Mac barked out a laugh at Lex's bland voice and snarky answer. The chimera didn't smile, but Mac saw his eyes twinkle with humor for a second before he was all business again.

"I need all the information Briar can get me. And I sent you an email about what I want if the worst happens."

"You're not going to die. You're so damn tough that the reaper wouldn't dare go near you," Memphis argued, his tone desperate for reassurance.

Lex didn't give him any. "I want us all to rest together, you know, in the chimera way. You have to promise me you'll make that happen."

The line went quiet before Memphis finally gave a subdued answer. "I promise. But try to keep me from having to fulfill that request."

"I plan to," Lex agreed, then hung up the phone.

"I'm coming with you," Pike spoke up, reminding Mac he was in the room. How had he forgotten the bear shifter was there with them?

"I don't think that's a good idea," Mac responded.

Pike looked affronted. "I'm strong! And I can fight."

"Bar brawls," Lex responded, his tone straightforward but not harsh. "Have you ever fired a gun?"

The shifter's determination didn't waver. "No, but how hard could it be?"

Mac winced, expecting Lex to lay into the man, but the chimera only shook his head. "Have you ever killed someone?"

Pike's expression went from confident to appalled. "No, of course not!"

Lex gave a short, sharp nod. "See, that's the reason you can't go."

"I can't help because I'm not a murderer?" Pike objected.

"You can't go because we're going up against murderers," Lex answered. "You know how in the movies they're always saying not to kill someone because then you're just as bad as they are?" Pike nodded. "That's bullshit. The simple truth of the matter is if you don't kill them, they'll kill you. That's what we're up against here, Pike. Vincent isn't like Imani or Tobias. He's a cold-blooded murderer. Old school psychopath. We aren't people to him, we are things. Sources of amusement. Our pain is his pleasure and when he's finished with us, our death is nothing more than an inconvenience because he has to call someone to dispose of our bodies."

Pike's expression grew more horrified the longer Lex spoke, and he flinched away a little when the chimera stepped closer to him. "You're exaggerating."

"You know I'm not," Lex answered.

"I'll do anything to get Cora and Imani back," Pike repeated, stubbornly.

"But could you kill him if given the chance? No warning or offering to let him surrender. You'd need to execute him without hesitation. Could you do that?"

"Y-yes?" Pike's faltering question/answer was confirmation that the black bear shifter would balk when it came time to be merciless.

Lex's eyes flashed bright gold before mellowing to a molten amber. "Don't lie to yourself, Pike."

Pike looked broken. "He's got Cora."

"And we're going to do our best to get her back," Lex answered. "We won't leave her behind."

"She's my mate." Unshed tears gathered in Pike's eyes. "I haven't even gotten to give her a Pairing Gift yet or shown her my bear." He started rubbing his chest over his heart. "But I can already feel her here. I've barely known her, but I can't live without her."

"You can come, but you've got to stay in the truck," Mac offered.

Lex turned angry eyes on him. "Mac!"

Mac met his gaze unflinchingly. "He waits in the truck, Lex. And when it's all over, he'll be there to drive us home. We might be hurt and will need the assistance. Especially if we have to wrap Imani up to keep her safe from the sun. And he'll be there for *other* things."

Lex glared at him for a moment until he realized what Mac meant by other things—like contacting Memphis to tell him they hadn't made it.

"Fine," Lex spit out and went back to preparing his weapons.

Pike looked both relieved and apprehensive. "What can I do?"

"Right now, nothing," Mac answered, watching Lex pull on a familiar bulletproof vest and strap it tightly to his body. There were witches' markings painted on the front and back of the vest and when Lex pulled a long sleeve shirt on over it, the vest seemed to disappear.

"Put yours on too," Lex insisted as he checked all the magazines, then slipped them into slots on his tactical belt. "Wear anything and everything you've got. Put a fucking sports cup on if you own one."

That last comment shocked a sharp laugh out of Mac. "Yes sir," he answered. "I'll thrown on a condom for good measure."

This time Lex laughed, then sobered and looked up to meet Mac's gaze. "I don't regret a moment with you and Imani. Even now, I don't regret us."

Mac grabbed him by the back of the head and pulled him close for a rough kiss. Lex melted against him with a sigh. When he pulled away, he waited until Lex opened his eyes. "You and Imani are my everything. Alive or dead, now or forever. Got me?"

"Yeah," Lex whispered. "Same."

That single word sounded like a vow to Mac, so he repeated it. "Same."

Imani

As the day had progressed, Imani fought the need to sleep with everything she had. She knew Mac and Lex were coming. They'd want to try to get her and Cora out during daylight hours, while Vincent was either asleep or weakened. It was up to her to stay alert and be ready to help when they arrived.

She wished she could warn them. But Lex was clever about these things, he probably already knew Vincent was expecting him. Right?

"Imani?"

Shifting a little, Imani looked at Cora. "Yeah?"

"Shouldn't you be unconscious or something?" Cora asked. "I thought vampire's sleep during the day."

"I should be," Imani agreed. "Normally I wouldn't be able to fight the sun, but I've gotten a lot stronger lately." As if her body wanted to betray her, she felt her eyelids dip. Her vision blurred as she forced them open again.

"You've got the exact same look on your face as I did when I took that seven am art history class. That is to say sleeping with your eyes open." Cora's dry humor helped Imani blink her eyes into focus.

"I'm close to it," Imani admitted. She banged her head against the wall behind her a few times.

"What the hell? Don't do that!" Cora protested. "Keep talking to me, don't give yourself brain damage."

Imani tried to laugh but didn't have it in her. "How's your business doing?"

"We're going to talk shop? Okay, I can do that. I hired two new guys earlier this month. One I'm probably going to fire soon because he's already fucked up a job, and the other is young but surprisingly even tempered. I'm letting him apprentice with me."

Imani pretended to look shocked. "You got an apprentice?"

"Yeah, yeah, shut up," Cora muttered. "He was being bullied by this complete asshat,
Grant Dryden. I was working the same job and I couldn't take it anymore after the third day so I told the kid he could apprentice with me. Poor guy didn't even hesitate."

"What did you do to Grant?" Imani asked.

Cora looked insulted. Or tried to anyway. "What makes you think I did anything?"

"Because I know you," Imani quipped. "You're a vindictive bitch. Now spill, what'd you do?"

"I might have rerouted some of his wiring, so he had to go into a crawl space to fix it," she answered without meeting Imani's gaze. "And I might have made sure the crawl space was full of spiders."

The mental picture made Imani cackle with real humor. "I bet he screamed like a little kid!"

"Totally screamed," Cora confirmed with a fond smile. "He jetted out of the crawlspace and stripped out of his clothes in front of the whole crew. Everyone got to see his *I love dick* tattoo."

Imani was incredulous. "Wait, he had an *I love dick* tattoo?"

"Well, no. But whoever did the coverup of the name that was originally there did a shit job. The tattooer was trying to make it look like a gun, but it ended up looking like a penis with a single ball. I yelled out 'look who loves dick' and after that, everyone at the jobsite started calling him Dick instead of Grant."

"I'm glad you're on my side," Imani said after she'd stopped laughing.

Cora nodded, then looked oddly reluctant. "Speaking of being on your side, I've got a question."

"I don't have any tattoos," Imani said before Cora could ask anything.

Cora chuckled and shook her head. "It's a question about food."

Where had that come from? "Food? Do you have low blood sugar or something?"

Cora sucked in a breath and pushed out her words in a rush. "Do-you-need-blood?"

Imani thought about Cora's question before answering honestly. "I'm hungry, but my need isn't so bad that I'll attack you. I've always had good control."

"That's not what I was asking. If you had some blood, could you break out of those chains? Would it help?"

Understanding dawned. "No, probably not. I'm not old enough yet to break silver bonds. You'd have to have some powerful magic for your blood to give me that kind of boost."

Cora's shoulder sagged a little. "Damn, I was hoping to sacrifice a pint and get out of here."

An explosion shook the building around them, sending a few things on a faraway shelf crashing to the floor.

Cora startled, looking around wildly as another explosion shook the room. "What was that?"

Hope blossomed in Imani's chest. "Our rescue."

Cora

To her shock, a hole the size of a basketball opened in the wall across from them. Then there was a whoosh of air and the entire wall caved in, spilling cinderblocks, dirt, and Mac onto the floor. Muted daylight filtered in, and Cora realized they were close to sunset. By the way Imani hissed and squinted, it was enough to still hurt her though.

"How…" Cora started to ask, then remembered where she was. Now was not the time for questions, now was the time for action!

"Over here," she called out as Mac laboriously got to his feet, looking a little dazed. What had the guy done to make the hole? It wasn't the explosion; no sound had accompanied his entry.

"Damn, that spell was potent," Mac muttered as he stumbled over to them. Dropping to his knees, he grabbed Imani and hugged her to his chest. "I was so scared I'd never see you again."

His action caused the fabric Cora had shoved around the silver bands to come loose, making Imani to whimper in pain. Mac must have thought she was reacting to his presence because he kept hugging her and rocking back and forth as if to soothe her like an upset child. "It's okay. We're going to get you out of here."

"She's got silver around her wrists, you idiot!" Cora hissed at him.

Mac jerked and set Imani down, then hurried to maneuver so he could see her bindings. With a grimace, he grabbed one cuff with both hands. For a moment nothing happened, then Cora heard the groan of metal and a snap. Mac did the same to the other cuff and then tossed them away once they were both broken. Imani pulled her arms forward, gasping from the pain.

"Now mine," Cora insisted, twisting around to give Mac her back. Her cuffs didn't take as much for him to break, probably because she was wearing ordinary handcuffs and not some kind of magically spelled silver manacles.

Wincing as blood flooded back into her hands and her shoulders finally got to move after being held in the same position too many hours, Cora examined the hole Mac had created.

"How are we getting Imani out of here?" she asked. "Won't she burn up if we take her outside?"

"Not if we put her in this," Mac answered, pulling something out from the backpack he'd brought in with him.

"Is that a body bag?" Imani asked, aghast.

"Kind of," Mac answered. "But it's specially designed for vampires. It's double reinforced Kevlar with sun blocking layers on the outside and inside. It's for emergency use only, but that's what this is."

"No shit," Cora muttered, pushing at Imani. "Get in your mobile coffin, girl. We need to have left before we even go there."

"That makes no sense," Imani said as she tried to move her body into the sack. Her coordination was poor, and she was blinking rapidly, as if having trouble focusing. It had to be a combination of the daylight and lack of food.

Another explosion further away made all three of them freeze for a second. "Damn, there might not be anything left standing after Lex is done," Mac muttered.

"Which means we should be hurrying, right?" Cora pointed out and tried to help Imani shove her legs into the bag.

"I hope you're not trying to leave." All three of them looked up to find Simon at the foot of the stairs. His left arm was in a cast while the right one was holding a gun on them. Before any of them could move, Simon fired. Mac grunted and fell back.

"No!" Imani screamed, staring horrified at Mac's prone form.

"Spelled, silver bullets are so expensive but effective, don't you think?" Simon drawled as he swung the gun around to point it at her and Imani. "Don't make me shoot you as well."

Cora didn't think things could get worse, but then Vincent came strolling down the stairs, dragging an unconscious and bleeding Lex behind him. Once he was standing next to Simon, he tossed Lex's limp body down next to Mac.

Cora saw Imani's eyes turn bright red as she looked up from the bodies of her flock to Vincent. "I'll kill you."

"Doubtful," Vincent said with a dismissive sniff. "The chimera isn't dead yet, so if you're a good girl, I'll let him continue to live. Now that I realize they're your flock, I'm astonished. It was a hundred years before I found my two perfect humans and yet you, a vampire of less than two years, already has a flock. It's disgusting."

"You're just a jealous asshole. Besides, Simon and Opal aren't anything to brag about. If I were you, I'd look into getting a refund or dropping them back off at the shelter you adopted them from," Cora taunted then wished she hadn't opened her damn mouth when Vincent's eyes focused on her.

"I hope you enjoyed those words because they'll be your last," Vincent declared as he moved toward her with his hand outstretched. Fuck, her and her stupid mouth had gotten her in trouble again, maybe for the last time.

"Don't touch her!"

All eyes moved to the open spot in the wall to find Pike barreling down on Vincent. The old vampire didn't bat an eye, simply reached out and swatted Pike away. The bear shifter flew across the room and landed hard against the wall. Groaning, he slid to the floor, clutching the side of his head, blood streaming from his nose and mouth.

"So many new toys!" Opal cried as she hopped down the stairs. "How will I ever pick who to play with first?"

Vincent smiled down at her. "You need to pick the ones you want the most so I can dispose of the rest. I'm uncomfortable having so many in my home at once."

Opal gave Vincent an exaggerated frown. "No, don't make me pick!"

As they argued, Cora saw Mac twitch. At least the shifter wasn't dead. Then she noticed Lex's eyes were slitted open and his hand was moving slowly to pull something from his belt. The playful argument between Opal and Vincent was distracting them, but Simon was still vigilant with his gun up and ready to fire.

"How's the wrist?" Cora asked, drawing Simon's attention to her and away from Lex.

Simon scowled at her. "Would you like to know firsthand?"

"Like you could hurt me," Cora scoffed, putting her big mouth and years of insult practice to work. "I totally kicked your ass. Your little sister had to rescue you. How's it feel to be that pathetic? Do you even have balls or did Vincent take them away? Does he keep them in a jar? Oh, is it a sample jar because I know they had to be small, right?"

Vincent and Opal stopped talking to watch Simon stalk over to her. Once he was looming over her, he shoved the gun against the side of her head. "Say one more word, human. Go ahead."

Keeping her mouth closed, Cora rolled her eyes as if Simon wasn't worth the effort. The man's face flushed with rage.

Opal giggled. "Are you sure you want to kill her outright? That seems gentle for you."

The hand holding the gun was shaking and he spit as he screamed in her face. "I'm going to cause you so much pain you'll wish you were dead."

Cora had to work to keep her fear from showing on her face. She was very close to dying right now. Holding her breath, she held his gaze and kept her expression defiantly bored. It was an expression she'd learned as a teenager when her father would go on enraged rants at her and her siblings, and it usually made him give up and walk away.

It didn't make Simon walk away, but he did pull the gun back and start to swing it at her head. Instinct took over, and she ducked and punched. She missed his crotch but landed a solid blow to the inside of his thigh. It wasn't enough to make him crumble and drop the gun, but he cried out and staggered. The scuffle gave Lex the opportunity to pull a remote out of his belt and hit the button.

A split-second later, Imani was on top of her, shielding her from the building crumbling around them.

"Cora!" Pike whimpered as everything started to collapse. Time slowed down and Cora got a last look at Pike's bloody face and Lex pulling Mac's head under his body before everything went dark.

Imani

She could hear screaming but was too busy keeping her and Cora alive to pay much attention. She'd noticed Lex moving when Cora started taunting Simon. Knowing Lex as she did, he would've had plans from A all the way to Z that covered all contingencies. Blowing up the building around them had to be a Plan Z.

It wasn't a horrible idea. Exposing Vincent to unfiltered daylight was a good way to incapacitate, if not outright kill him. They'd probably hoped to get her into the body bag beforehand so she wouldn't be affected. And they probably planned to get them all out of the basement before setting off the last charges.

Things had gone wrong, as they did, and now Imani was on all fours with a heavy load of debris piled on her back. Under her, Cora coughed. Her friend was alive, but Imani wasn't sure how much longer she could provide Cora with this small pocket of safety. She was feeling weaker by the second.

"Cora?" Pike screamed.

"Imani!" that was Lex.

She could hear the shifter moving debris. With relief, she realized they'd get to her soon.

Her arms were shaking from the effort. Maybe she should've taken Cora up on the offered blood.

"Are we still alive?" Cora whispered, then coughed again.

Imani grunted, unable to talk. If she breathed like a human or shifter, she'd probably be gasping right now.

"I can't see anything, but I can hear you," Cora said softly. Unlike her human friend, Imani could see clearly. Cora's face was covered in dirt and dust, with small cuts on her left cheek, and a split lip. All the damage looked superficial and if Imani could keep holding up the wreckage above them, Cora would survive.

"If this is it, I mean if we're going to die, I want you to know something." Her voice hitched, holding back tears. "You're as close to a sister as I've ever had. No matter what happens, I've got no regrets."

Imani's chest filled with love and affection for the small, irascible woman, but she couldn't spare anything to respond to Cora's declaration.

Then Imani heard something worrisome, the sound of wings. Vincent had long ago mastered the art of turning into a falcon with astonishing speed. It was how he made it look like he appeared and disappeared. If she was hearing the flapping of a bird, then he'd survived the building's collapse. Fear for her flock filled her along with a sense of helplessness.

"What the fuck?" Lex exclaimed loudly.

"Kimble!" Pike shouted, joy and relief in his voice. "Our third is buried here. We need to find her!"

The sound of things being moved and thrown with great speed created a cacophony of sound, drowning out Lex's questions and Pike's answers. Then the weight over her back disappeared, and she was lifted.

An unfamiliar face stared at her with a puzzled frown. "Not mine," he declared, his red eyes glowing with power. Imani stared at the vampire holding her, equally confused and alarmed. The sun had set but the remnants of the sunset light made her eyes water.

"That's Imani. She jumped on Cora to protect her," Pike called out, stumbling over as he picked his way through the rubble.

"Young," the vampire declared and set her on her feet. Then he nudged her away and repeated, "not mine."

Imani stood stunned, too shaky to walk. She watched Kimble go back to digging. He had an insane amount of strength, casually picking up lumber that would've made Mac strain, and tossing it aside as if it was no more than a bit of firewood.

He was quick to uncover Cora. He lifted her out of the rubble with gentle reverence and cradled her to his chest.

"Hi," she whispered. "Appreciate the save. Is everyone okay?"

Then she started coughing violently. The vampire's expression turned gentle as he rocked her like a baby. Pike hurried up to the couple, saying something to them in low tones. By now, Mac and Lex had reached her and were both hugging her between them.

"How are we all still alive?" she asked, feeling like she couldn't take everything in.

"Luck," Mac answered with a jagged laugh.

"Simon shot you in the heart with silver," Imani murmured, putting her hand up to feel Mac's chest. He was wearing something that had a slight dent where the bullet had impacted.

"And it hurt like hell," Mac commented. "But Lex gave me this amazing vest a few years back. It stops just about anything from penetrating, but it doesn't keep it from making you feel like you got kicked by a horse. Sorry if I scared you. The bullet still knocked me out for a minute while I remembered how to breathe."

"From now on, I want you to wear it all the time," Lex commented as he nuzzled Imani's neck. "Do you need to feed from us right now, or can we go home first?"

Imani was considering his question when debris went flying. All three of them looked up to see Vincent standing there holding Opal and Simon in his arms. They'd all been so busy looking after each other they'd forgotten about the deadly predator buried alongside them.

Opal was obviously dead and as she watched, Simon made a last gasping sound and went limp. Vincent's scream was a combination of rage and pain. Imani couldn't imagine what it would be like to lose both flock members almost at the same time. Parts of his soul died with their bodies, and the closest she could think would be to have multiple limbs ripped off.

As they all watched, Vincent gently set down his flock then stood up, glaring at the three of them. When he roared, it was loud enough to echo beyond the ruins of the house. There was no intelligence behind those eyes. No calculating mind. This vampire was nothing but rage and pain.

Lex cursed and let go of Imani, scrabbling at his belt for a weapon that wasn't there. Vincent charged at them, and Mac tried to get in front of her and Lex to take the first blow. Imani instinctively reached out to pull her flock behind her and take the brunt of Vincent's attack.

As they scrambled to protect each other, Kimble appeared in front of Vincent.

"Bad vampire," Kimble declared and casually grabbed Vincent in mid leap and held him in the air with a single outstretched arm.

To Imani, it looked like Kimble was expending the same amount of effort as an adult holding onto a struggling toddler. Despite how awesomely powerful she knew Vincent to be, he couldn't break Kimble's hold. With a shocking amount of ease, Kimble grabbed him with both hands and ripped Vincent's head from his body. Then he causally tossed both parts next to Opal and Simon.

That done, he turned and strode back to where Pike was holding Cora in almost the exact same way Kimble had been holding her earlier. His expression was excitedly happy, reminding Imani of a golden retriever she'd had growing up.

"Thanks for the save, guys, but if you could put me down, that'd be great," Cora said, tugging at Pike's arm. The bear tried to set her down, but Kimble was there, taking her from him.

"Good Pike," he declared and leaned over to give the black bear a chaste kiss on the cheek. Then he looked down at Cora. "Good human. Going home."

"Going home?' she echoed at the same time Pike frantically grabbed for Kimble's arm.

"Kimble, wait, we need—"

Pike didn't get a hold of Kimble. The vampire was already shifting into a goddamn griffin!

"I didn't think that was possible," Imani gasped.

Cora was held gently in the griffin's claws despite how much she was wiggling and trying to get free. Imani had to shield her face as Kimble's massive wings beat the air to gain altitude and then he was gone, the sounds of Cora's cursing disappearing into the night.

"What the hell?" Lex choked out. She guessed he'd never seen anything like that either, and he knew several powerful vampires.

Imani looked over at Pike. "Start talking, Pike. And begin with if we need to launch a rescue operation to get Cora back."

"She's safe, I promise, but I need to go. I'll explain everything later," Pike yelled as he sprinted off. He was probably the least hurt of all of them so he was far faster than even Lex could manage at the moment. In less than a minute, she heard the sounds of a vehicle starting followed by the screech of tires.

Mac let out a heartfelt sigh, and then an exhausted chuckle. "He was our ride here."

Lex

Mac and Imani looked as stunned as he felt. "What the fuck just happened?"

"I think we got rescued," Imani said slowly. "By a vampire that can shift into a griffin. I'd heard stories of vampires being able to shift into things bigger than hawks, falcons, or ravens, but thought it was legend. He must be ancient to be able to do that."

"And he kidnapped Cora," Mac grunted and reached out to wrap an arm around Imani.

"I think she might be part of his flock," Imani murmured, snuggling into Mac's side. "It was obvious Pike and this Kimble vampire knew each other. If she's Pike's mate, then she's got to be flock. It's really common for flock to be mates or married before a vampire finds them."

"Hopefully Pike can talk some sense into Kimble before he traumatizes Cora," Mac commented, then corrected himself. "Well, traumatizes her more than what's happened already."

"Was it just me or did Kimble seem, I don't know, feral?" Lex asked as he joined his mates and wrapped his arms around them both. The relief at having them both alive and relatively unhurt was enormous. Once they were home and clean, he was going to tie both of them to the bed for at least twenty-four hours so he could get some damn rest.

Or maybe he should chain them all together and then they'd never be able to go anywhere without him.

"No, Lex," Mac murmured.

"I didn't say anything," Lex protested.

"I know that look," Mac rumbled. "You're thinking of locking us in a tower somewhere so we'll always be safe."

"I wasn't thinking that, exactly," Lex answered with a half grin. Suddenly everything hurt and he could see the tension in Mac's shoulders. Like him, the bear shifter was in pain. "I'll call Memphis. He can take us home."

"Ask them to hurry, I really want to lie down," Mac urged as Lex sent a pre-written text to Memphis then tucked his phone away.

With backup on its way, Lex helped his mates out of the rubble and settled them down in a soft bit of grass away from the giant shambles that had once been a house. Sitting between Mac and Imani, he let both of them lean on him. Although they were worse off than him, he was hurting and was as eager as they were for a shower and rest.

He sat there while the two of them dozed off, considering everything that had happened. After doing a recon of the property and mapping the house out with thermal cameras, he and Mac had figured out the best way to get Imani and Cora out. The tunneling spell he'd given Mac had worked, although it had knocked Mac around a little and probably cracked a few ribs. Simon's bullet had taken those cracked ribs and broken them, but thankfully they hadn't punctured a lung.

Honestly, luck had been with them the entire time. The charges he'd set with timers had all gone off correctly. The last one was tied to a remote switch that had been his "Hail Mary." When he'd hit the button for the last charge, set against the side of the house over the basement, he hadn't been sure if would kill them all outright.

He'd also known Pike wouldn't stay in the vehicle. That's why he'd argued so strenuously to leave the black bear behind. When Pike showed up in the basement, there'd been a slight hope he'd remembered to bring the weapon Lex had given him.

Pike being the bear he was, probably hadn't thought to grab it when he had given up on obeying Lex's order to stay put. Pike's appearance had filled Lex with hope, then horror when he realized all that was going to happen was that the black bear was going to die along with them.

Kimble showing up had been a wild card he hadn't expected. Then again, who could predict the arrival of a vampire that powerful? What gods had decided it'd be a good idea to pair the gentlest shifter Lex had ever met with a monster who couldn't string more than two words together and could literally rip another vampire in half?

"You three are a mess." Memphis's comment made Lex realize he'd shut his eyes and lost focus on the world around him.

Blinking, he regarded his brother without expression. "You should see the other guy."

Memphis's bark of laughter woke up Imani and Mac. Then he pulled out his phone and started tapping on it. "Briar's on the way up with the car. I wanted her to stay back until Tobias and I checked everything out."

A hawk flew down and when it was the right height from the ground, shifted into Tobias. The vampire looked at Lex with astonishment. "Vincent is dead. How did you manage it?"

"We didn't," Mac answered. "A vampire named Kimble did it."

"Kimble?" Tobias repeated. "I've never heard of a vampire by that name. Was that his first or last name?"

"No clue," Lex answered. "But the mother fucker grabbed Vincent in mid charge and popped his head off his body like he was opening a bottle of beer."

Memphis and Tobias both stared at him, agog. "Are you shitting me?" Memphis asked.

"It's true," Mac commented, then groaned a little. "I don't think I can get up without help."

Lex wanted to scramble to his feet and help his mate, but suddenly his entire body felt heavy and uncoordinated. Evey muscle and joint hurt and his head was throbbing. Imani was moving slow too.

A shiny black Range Rover pulled to a stop near them, and Briar got out carrying a familiar cooler. "Wow, you guys look like you went nine rounds with a tornado."

"Tornado would've been gentler," Imani quipped as Briar dropped her to knees in front of the vampire.

"Here, I've got a nice snack for you," she said, opening the cooler and offering the contents to Imani. Lex wanted to protest and make her drink from him, but practicality kept him quiet. He needed to heal before he fed her, and Mac was in the same boat. She'd need to drink bagged blood for a few days until they'd recovered a bit.

"Can you take us home?" Lex asked, looking up at Memphis.

"You should come home with us for a little while," Briar offered, ignoring the displeased sound Tobias made. "We can make sure you get some medical care and Imani gets all the blood she needs."

"No," Imani and Tobias said at the same time, making Briar roll her eyes.

"You could use your mansion in La Jolla," Tobais commented.

"Excuse me, but we don't have a mansion in La Jolla," Imani mocked in a haughty tone. "We'll have to make do with Mac's estate at the Twin Palms apartment complex."

Mac chuckled at that, then winced and gave a little moan. "No more funnies. Laughing hurts."

Tobias frowned down at Imani. "Vincent was your maker, correct?"

Lex answered for her. "What does that have to do with anything?"

Tobias made an impatient sound. "She's basically his child, so according to vampire law, she inherits all his wealth."

Lex could feel his mate's shock at Tobias's words. "You're joking."

Now the vampire looked contrite. "You didn't know. I'm sorry, I forgot what a poor mentor Vincent was. It's true, you now own everything Vincent had. When we were looking for his place of residence, Briar uncovered several very nice and expensive private homes scattered through San Diego along with many rental and industrial properties. They're all owned by a trust, but I'm sure it wouldn't take much to make you the beneficiary of the trust. We vampires have to be able to transfer wealth at a moment's notice if we need to assume new identities. It's all as simple as finding out the names of the trust's beneficiaries and creating a new identity for Imani."

Lex looked over to Imani and flashed her a grin. "Heya, sugar mama, I'm gonna start working on my Christmas list right away."

A year later - Club Gaudium

Imani

Brightly colored lights moved and flashed with the rhythm of the music, pushing the dancers below to gyrate at an even more frantic pace. Imani watched from her high perch as a man paced the edges of the dance floor, looking at women until he spotted one he liked. He advanced, but a single motion from her had several wolf shifters from Mikey's pack hustling over. She couldn't hear them but knew they were "inviting" the man to step outside. He wouldn't be allowed back in.

A satisfied smile unfurled across her face as she went back to surveying the crowd, keeping watch over her domain.

"Enjoying yourself?" Mac asked from behind her. Massive arms wrapped around her shoulders, and she leaned back against Mac's solid bulk.

"Always," she answered. The platform they stood on gave her a clear view of the club she'd painstakingly created. This place had been a labor of love and she couldn't be more proud of the accomplishment. This club was a safe haven for anyone who simply wanted to enjoy their evening.

Hiring men and women from Mikey's pack as staff had been Briar's brilliant idea. Lobos Gris members were exceptional at spotting people in distress and had a natural instinct to protect and help. When she wasn't there, someone else occupied her spot and acted as shot caller.

Mac nuzzled his face next to where her braids were coiled high on her head. "Lex just texted. The new house is done. He wants us to come over to see it. Tomorrow night we can move our stuff from my place to there."

"It's about damn time," Imani grumbled.

"Remodeling a house isn't a fast process," Mac said with a chuckle. "Getting it done in a few months is pretty quick."

"I guess," she acknowledged. The conversation reminded her about the fox shifter they'd recently hired. "Speaking of homes, did we find a place for Bree?"

"Not yet," Mac admitted. "I think we're going to need to go with your idea of buying another apartment complex. For now, she and Tanner are getting along, sharing a place."

Reaching down, she tangled her fingers with his. "I don't hate the idea of buying more property."

"We can do that, but remember, you can't save everyone," Mac murmured.

It was a statement both Mac and Lex made repeatedly. She knew they were trying to keep her from being disappointed, but it still bothered her.

"But I can save Bree," she countered. "And the next outcast coyote shifter or scared pixie or whoever comes to us in need."

Mac pulled in a deep breath and dropped the topic. He knew he wasn't going to convince her to stop. Their first and only fight they'd had as a triad had been about her accepting all the strays that showed up.

Mac and Lex worried about her safety and her emotional health. It'd only happened a few times, but occasionally one of the strays would attack Imani, hoping to cash in on her being a young vampire and easy to kill.

Imani refused to stop, and her flock had finally given up on talking her out of the goal. It hadn't escaped her notice that Lex always carried several weapons with him now and installed weapon safes at various locations. Mac was less obvious about it, but he'd started carrying at least one powerful magicked weapon whenever they left home.

"Imani?"

She and Mac turned to find Tag standing at the top of the stairs. The slim, black-eyed druid looked nervous, but that wasn't a surprise since he often looked nervous. He'd been kicked out of his conservative druid family the moment he turned eighteen. Black eyes were seen as cursed among Foundation Druids. Struggling to survive, he'd gotten a job at a poorly run club. While working, he was cornered by a couple of mountain lion shifters and brutalized. Instead of banning the shifters, the club had fired Tag.

While unemployed and healing, he'd gotten evicted from his apartment and was couch surfing with the few druids who'd allow him in their home. They refused to let him stay more than a night or two at a time, making life even harder. He'd gotten a job at Club Gaudium and come to Imani's attention when she realized he was sometimes sleeping in a nearby park.

She hadn't thought twice about offering him one of the studio apartments in the building she'd bought. He was still skittish and looking for danger in every shadow, but he was doing better.

"What's up, Tag?" Imani asked.

"Um, Kiera wants to, uh, talk to you before you leave?" He always phrased everything as a question, probably a survival technique he'd developed while growing up in a family who saw Tag as a duty instead of a child.

"No problem, I'll go talk to her now," Imani answered with a gentle smile. "Thank you for telling me. And I wanted to mention what a great job you did painting the locker room. It's perfect."

Tag flushed and looked down with a wide smile. "Thanks." Then he turned and scampered off.

Imani shook her head as she pulled her phone out of the small purse she carried around at the club. She texted Kiera and found out the club's manager wanted to increase the alcohol order for next week. She'd already given Kiera permission to make decisions regarding these types of tasks. This was the first time the wolf shifter had managed a club this large, so she was overly cautious. Imani was sure Kiera would grow more confident quickly and the club would be all the better for it.

Then she sent off another text to Kiera to send someone up to take over for her as shot caller. She'd barely put her phone away when someone else called out her name.

"Hey, Imani," Maria said as she stepped onto the elevated platform everyone referred to as the throne. The tall wolf shifter pointed to where Imani was standing. "Kiera sent me up so you can leave."

"The throne is yours," Imani answered with a sweep of her arm even as Mac pulled her away from the railing.

"Thank fuck," Mac muttered. "Let's get over to the new place before Lex decides to come looking for us."

The chimera shifter had gotten better at being away from his mates, but still struggled if the separation lasted more than four hours. His brother Kingston had come down to do the renovations on their new home and demanded Lex help him. That was probably the reason it had taken longer than Kingston's first estimate.

Both Kingston and Lex were probably relieved it was all over. Kingston could go home to Bend and Lex didn't have to be separated from Mac and Imani for more than a few hours at a time.

Mac was so eager to leave, he practically picked her up and carried her down the stairs and out of the club. Both employees and regulars called out and waved, but Mac's scowling face kept anyone from trying to engage her in a conversation. It wasn't a tactic Mac used often, but when he did, it was effective.

Imani was outright laughing by the time he opened the passenger door and urged her in. She could never have guessed her life would turn out like this, but now she couldn't imagine it any other way.

Mac

Imani's phone buzzed with incoming messages as Mac piloted the vehicle out of the club's parking lot. With so many things going on, Imani's phone was constantly demanding her attention, but this time she read the message with a broad smile instead of a slight frown of concentration.

"Cora wants to know if we can meet up tomorrow," Imani said.

"I'm glad everything worked out with her, Pike, and Kimble," Mac commented.

Imani winced. "Yeah, that was a big mess for a while. I'm surprised Pike and Kimble survived an enraged Cora."

"Kimble is an incredibly powerful vampire," Mac pointed out. "Remember what he did to Vincent."

"I still stand by my earlier statement," Imani argued with a grin. "There's an African proverb that sums up Cora. *If you think you're too small to make a difference, you haven't spent a night with a mosquito.*"

It took Mac a second, but then he laughed. "Comparing Cora to mosquito? Did you hand me blackmail material?"

Imani shook her head, disturbing the bright pink braids resting over her shoulder. Lex had been a little upset the first time he'd seen a different color making up her long braid. Chimeras didn't always handle change well. It hadn't taken long before he got used to Imani's new hair color and even suggested colors he liked.

Not only had Lex suggested the current Barbie pink, but he'd spent hours braiding the colored extensions into her hair. Unknown to either of them, the chimera had been studying haircare videos and was determined to be Imani's perfect helpmate. Mac wasn't surprised to find out Lex had bought a wig and dummy head to practiced with. Lex wasn't one to do anything in half measures. The result was a perfect head of braided hair, with a little extra encouragement and some substantial input from Imani as he worked.

He didn't stop at learning to braid, he also learned how to create all kinds of elaborate styles with the braids. He was the one who'd put Imani's braid in the intricate updo she'd worn all night. The only one of them with no hair turned out to be an excellent braider and stylist.

"Cora wouldn't care if I compared her to a mosquito," Imani responded. "The only thing she'd probably say was she

was a bigger threat, like a tarantula hawk wasp or hornet. That
girl is unabashedly aggressive."

They continued to chat about Cora as they drove. Mac
could feel tension draining from his body with every mile they
covered. As much as he loved everything Imani had built using
Vincent's money, his needs were simple. He wanted to have both
his mates close. Lex might be more vocal about hating their
separations, but Mac struggled with the exact same issue.

"You're a good mate," Imani murmured, putting a hand
on his thigh.

Mac glanced over at her. "Thanks?"

She chuckled. "I didn't notice how much tension was
coming through the link until it started to calm. You've been
doing such a good job putting up with me the last few months. I
know the club isn't your favorite thing."

He tried for diplomacy. "I don't hate it."

She gave his leg a squeeze. "Still, I think it falls closer to
the dislike side of the scale than like for you. When I outfitted
the office so you could hang out and watch TV or whatever
when you needed a break from the music and crowds, I expected
you to use it."

He gave her a flat look before concentrating on the road
again. "The best part of the club is getting to be with you." He
placed one of his hands over her hand resting on his thigh. "And
touching you."

"You love me more than that big ass, expensive TV?
That's saying something," she teased.

A touch of concern came through their link. "What's
wrong?" he asked.

She sighed and didn't speak right away. Mac let the
silence stand, giving Imani the time and space to find her words.

"The club costs a lot of money," she finally began,
staring fixedly down at their joined hands. "I could be buying
more apartment complexes and helping more people instead of
distracting myself with Gaudium."

"You could," he answered. "But the club is important
too. It gives people a safe place to experience joy. That can be
hard to find for humans and non-humans alike."

"But going out dancing isn't saving lives," Imani argued. "Now that it's up and running, I wonder if I'm being selfish."

"You don't know that it's not saving lives," Mac answered firmly. "You've set up a place for everyone. Even if it was only ever a dance club, I'd be proud, but you didn't stop there. I know you've got Marco and Eva running some kids and teen programs during the day. Gaudium isn't simply a club, it's a second home for some of those kids. A safe place to hang out after school. I heard you talking to Eva yesterday about getting food in there. I know it's not for the club scene because you already said you didn't want to figure out the food licenses. That means the only reason you'd be talking to Eva about food is because of those kids."

Imani didn't respond right away, but the link between them buzzed as she chewed on his words. He took the opportunity to add his thoughts on the topic.

"The most important thing you need to ask yourself is this—would it piss off Vincent? If the answer is yes, then we need to keep doing it."

That made Imani laugh. "You make a good point. He'd hate the thought of a club geared towards keeping 'lessers' safe. Although he might be even more upset with the self-defense and weapons training course you and Lex are putting together for the preternaturals under our care. Honestly, he'd be appalled at every single thing we're doing."

"That's your answer then," Mac concluded. "We stay on this path. Enjoy the club and help as many people as we can while we're at it."

Soft relief filtered to him through the link. "You're a wise teddy bear."

"And you're a sexy vampire," he responded with a grin as he pulled into the driveway of their new home. "That sounds like a children's book that should never be written."

Lex

Lex hurried out of the house when he heard Imani and Mac pull up. Kingston had long since left. With the work all done, he'd decided to leave that night and drive back home. Lex had tried to talk him into getting some sleep, but Kingston missed his mate and children too much to wait. It wasn't a big deal, because chimeras were a tough group that could go without sleep or rest for a surprising amount of time.

He and Kingston had finished the renovations on the two-story Spanish colonial house much earlier that evening. Instead of telling Imani and Mac it was done, he'd talked Kingston into helping him move everything from Mac's apartment into the new house.

It looked a little on the empty side with only Mac's few pieces of mismatched furniture, but that would be easy to fix in a few shopping trips. The important part was that the three of them were going to spend the rest of the night and sleep away the next day in their new home.

He was so excited; he threw open the passenger side door with a little too much enthusiasm. He ignored the way the vehicle door creaked in protest at the abuse. Reaching in, he unbuckled Imani and pulled her out. Cradling her against his chest, he kissed all over her face.

Laughing, she caught his face in her hands. "I missed you too, Lexie."

Then she claimed his mouth as thoroughly as she'd claimed his soul. It was only Mac's big arms wrapping around both of them that brought Lex back to the present.

"It's all ready!" Lex announced the moment Imani ended the kiss. "You have to see. It's perfect."

Setting Imani on her feet, he grabbed her and Mac's hands and pulled them to the wide-open front door.

He showed them the remodeled kitchen, new bathrooms, and Mac's big bed already taking up space in the main bedroom. His mates were appropriately impressed as they went from room to room. He was about to suggest they christen the house by getting naked and fucking until the sun rose when he felt a frisson of awareness.

There was someone in their new home.

"Did you feel that?" Mac asked, freezing in place. They'd just come out of the bedroom and were standing in the hall.

Lex grunted and went for his weapon only to find it missing. Fuck, he'd put it away in anticipation of having some fun with Mac and Imani. "Nothing should've gotten in here without me noticing."

"Guys?" Imani asked. "I can feel your concern, but I don't sense anything."

"There's something here with powerful magic," Mac answered.

"And it feels familiar," Lex added, trying to figure out where he'd felt this type of magic before.

"Yeah, you're right," Mac agreed.

"Maybe we should—" Imani started to say when a figure stepped out of the short stairwell that led up to the unfinished attic space. She sucked in a startled breath. "Sopek?"

"Greetings, Imani vampire," Sopek said cheerfully. He had a small stack of books in his hands and held them out with formality as he stepped forward. "These are for you."

Mac and Lex stepped in front of her, blocking Sopek from getting to Imani. The hobgoblin frowned but didn't lower the books. "You have nothing to fear. Your vampire is perfectly safe. All three of you are safe from me. I want to discuss books with Imani. Hurting any of you will keep her from doing this. Now please step aside."

Neither he nor Mac moved. All kinds of calculations were going through Lex's head, but he discarded all of them one after another.

A disappointed expression wrinkled Sopek's scrunched features. "I can see my words aren't working. It will take something more extreme to achieve what I desire."

Before Lex could get worked up over the word "extreme," Sopek closed his eyes. Power started radiating from the hobgoblin, lighting him up so brilliantly Lex had to look away.

"What's going on?" Imani asked, also shielding her eyes.

"Be at ease, I'm making everything perfect," Sopek intoned, his voice shockingly deep. His words seemed to vibrate through them as the light started emanating from his small body. The brightness filled every space, making it impossible for Lex to keep his eyes open.

He blindly reached for Mac and Imani. They all grasped each other as strong magic pressed in on them. He could feel fear coming from his mates through the link, but there was nothing he could do. His senses were blinded by the magic emanating from the hobgoblin.

Imani tried to push back with her growing powers. Lex sucked in a breath when there was relief from the relentless pressure as Imani built a small bubble of magic to shield them. It didn't last and Imani's power collapsed back down, covering them in Sopek's magic like a tidal wave.

All three of them dropped to their knees, dazed and gasping. Then, as quickly as it had built, everything disappeared. Lex blinked rapidly trying to get his vision back. He could feel Mac violently shaking his head as the two of them were sucking in air like they'd been sprinting.

"There," Sopek announced cheerfully, his voice back to normal. "Now you know the truth of my intentions."

"What did you do?" Imani croaked. Lex's vision was starting to clear, and he could see Sopek still standing there holding his little stack of books.

"I removed any impediment to our relationship," the hobgoblin answered. "Now you have no reason to fear me, and we can speak of books at any time."

Lex had to clear his throat a few times before he could manage a single word question. "Safe?"

"Look upon your auras," Sopek said as he stepped forward.

Imani was the only one could see auras so both he and Mac looked to her and waited.

After rubbing her eyes, she stared at each of them, her gaze bouncing back and forth as her expression grew more startled. "What the hell?"

Alarm shot through Lex. "What do you see?"

"You guys look the same except there's a thin layer of bright yellow overlaying your normal auras. It feels powerful as fuck." She reached out and brushed something in the air. "And it's reactive. I've never seen anything like it." Then she stared at her own hand. "And I've got it too."

Mac looked at the hobgoblin. "What did you do?"

"I've shared," Sopek said simply. "Now you are as I am. My magic can't affect you, and you can draw from the void as I do."

"The void?" Imani asked.

"It's believed by some that all magic comes from a place called the void. Some creatures like hobgoblins and Nephilim are said to draw directly from it instead of using what flows out naturally," Mac explained, his deep voice rough. "I've heard it compared to dipping a finger in to get a drop from a stream versus being able to draw out an entire bucket full."

"Your example is crude but somewhat accurate," Sopek commented. "And now you can access the void if you wish. I suggest doing so cautiously as the void is a tool that can easily destroy its user. I'm willing to trade lessons for discussions about books if you like. But the most important thing is that I'm no longer a threat. If I attempt to hurt you, it would be very easy for you to turn the void against me. We're at a stalemate. This leaves no reason for any of you to fear me."

Imani tried to stand but fell back to her knees. Lex and Mac were quick to get up on shaky legs to help her stand. Holding on to each other, the three of them stood there trying to understand the significance of what Sopek had done.

Stepping up, Sopek held out the books with a wide smile on his face. "Now take these. When you've finished, I'd like to speak about them."

Imani wordlessly took the books. Satisfied, Sopek turned and walked away. When Imani followed, he and Mac were with her. Sopek led them into the attic that had been nothing but open beams and exposed insulation yesterday. Today it was fully finished, furnished, and full of books.

As they watched, Sopek made himself comfortable in the same chair he'd had at the other house. He picked up a book and began to read, completely ignoring the three of them.

Without needing to speak, all three of them backed down the short flight of stairs and onto the second-floor hallway, shutting the attic door with a gentle click. They all stood there with equally stunned expressions on their faces, Imani clutching the books to her chest.

"Remember how we've been worried about getting attacked by more powerful creatures?" Lex asked, breaking the silence. "I don't think we need to be concerned anymore."

"Should we move?" Mac whispered.

Imani shook her head. "He'd simply find us again."

"Are you telling me we have a hobgoblin roommate?" Mac asked, his voice full of disbelief.

A giant grin unfurled across Lex's face. He was ecstatic! "Not only do we have a hobgoblin in residence, but we're part hobgoblin now. We can use void magic!"

"Let's hold off on that until we can get some instruction," Imani cautioned. "Remember the part about the void killing us by accident?"

"Details," Lex announced, then laughed at the expression on Mac and Imani's faces. He couldn't help it. As much as Sopek was a scary motherfucker, the hobgoblin had basically made them nearly invincible. Those that could see their new auras would start talking and soon no one with ill intentions would dare come anywhere near them. This was the best defense he could have ever dreamed of: a reputation that stopped attacks before they could even begin.

Feeling impossibly lighthearted, Lex wrapped his arms around his mates and led them down the hall toward the stairs. "Mates, this is the beginning of a very good eternity."

Dear Readers,

Thank you for reading *When Darkness Meets Dawn*. If you want more in the Ours Evermore series the next book is ready for pre-order: *Kidnapping Their Third*.

I hope you enjoyed *When Darkness Meets Dawn* enough to leave a review! As an indie writer without the support of a publishing company, I need all the help I can get. Your good reviews keep me writing.

If you have any questions, comments, or suggestions feel free to contact me via email: author@rk-munin.com

Visit my website for links to free novellas, social media, and upcoming books.

www.RKMunin.com

Cheers,
Rye